THE
EVERYWHEN
ANGELS

MARIE MARSHALL

First edition by P'kaboo Publishers, 2013

Cover Art: Millie Ho

ISBN 978-0-9922190-4-8

p'kaboo
publishers
www.pkaboo.net

To Angel

Who's that writing?
... John the Revelator ...
He wrote the Book of the Seven Seals

anon. American gospel song.

PART ONE

THE THIRTEENTH ANGEL

CHAPTER 1
A CURRENT OF WEIRDNESS

I think this is how it all began. Another day, same school. Another day, same walk to the bus. Another day, same bus ride. Another day, same walk the last hundred metres from the bus to the school gates. And this time, as it had been for several weeks now, another day, same game of tag with Christine Cook and the Patel sisters, and they played rough. I knew I'd have stood up to any one of them, but I didn't hang around to take all of them on; they had this way of attracting a crowd, and the crowd would join in against whoever they had a down on. Sorry – I wasn't going to play their game, and I didn't care if everyone thought I was bottling out, I preferred them under the CCTVs in the school building, where they had to mind what they did.

So, that Monday – I ran from the bus towards the side gate of the school, trying to make it look as though I was trying to catch up with a mate. I ignored the mock-friendly calls of "Hey, Angela! Hey, Poet!" from behind me, but in my hurry I took a wrong step and staggered like one of those binge-drinkers we get in town on a Saturday night, head down, making long, clumsy strides to avoid falling. My bag shot out of my grasp, and my little Book of Common Prayer with the silver angels on the cover slid out of my pocket. I bent down to pick them up and someone barged into my bum, shoving me forward towards the metal security fence which sealed off the little piece of overgrown waste ground between our school and the builder's yard.

I didn't even have time to cry out. I knew this was going to hurt, and hurt badly. Even if I managed to put my hands out to stop myself, one of them would go through the rails of the fence, pulling my blazer and shirt back and ripping at the skin on my arm. Even if I turned my face and shut my eyes, I knew my cheek would slam into that fence with all the force that my hurtling body could lend it. But I did turn it and I did shut my eyes, imagining the cuts, the bruises, the bleeding, the sprains, the broken bones, and lots of pain.

A split second before knowing that this crash must happen, I knew somehow that it hadn't. I felt nothing, and for that split second I was even convinced that I was unconscious and dreaming. Then I was convinced that I was wide awake, but rather than sprawling in pain on the pavement outside the school, I was standing about one hundred metres along the asphalt track between the side gate and the front door of the school. Alone.

Sometimes I freak myself out, because something weird happens and I take it in my stride. When I am dreaming, having a nightmare, and there is some monster round the corner, I protect myself by becoming that monster in my dream; I hang my arms out in menace, I moan and growl, I feel the need to terrify in my turn, to hunt down prey, to rip flesh and break bones. And when something weird happens while I am awake, I step back, look around, and wait for an explanation. If an explanation comes, it comes. If it doesn't, and I can't step back, look around, and wait for one, I begin to feel a pull to do as I do in my dreams, to go with the flow and become the monster. In real life that is so scary.

This time I stood there, about a hundred and fifty metres from where I thought I was, with no one around me, and everything different. All the other kids from the school were gone, all sixteen hundred-odd, and the teachers - everyone. The school appeared to be quiet and empty, and when I looked back towards the road and the houses outside, there was no sound and no movement. It was as though I had come back there at midnight, only it was daylight; and that was another weird thing – when I had dived headlong at the metal fence there had been sunshine; now there was a cold, nagging wind, grey clouds from horizon to horizon, and a feel of winter in the air. The only sound, apart from the wind in my ears, was coming from a few crows in the scraggy trees behind the main school building. It was like they were saying "We know what's going on, even if you don't". I wondered for a moment or two whether maybe I was dead, and there was no tunnel to a bright light, but instead of that my own private hell – school. The wind was certainly making my ears sting, and all I could think about as I stood there was a silly quotation about Hell being cold. Like I said, sometimes I freak myself out, and this time I said to myself, "This is totally random, scary, but it's got to be real somehow. OK, let's not just stand here."

See, it seemed to me that if I stood there and did nothing, the weirdness would overwhelm me, drown me. The only way to cope with it was to walk into it. OK there was no wardrobe, no old-fashioned lamppost, no snow, but I knew I had a choice between going insane or accepting that I was in some crazy Narnia of my own. I had stepped into a storybook, or into one of my own surreal poems. Maybe there was no monster lurking round the corner, but there was still no obvious explanation either. If I couldn't become the monster, I had to become the weirdness, swim in it, go with that flow. Maybe I would be washed up somewhere I recognised.

Going home seemed a sensible option, but as soon as the thought occurred to me, I felt like the tide of weirdness was flowing in the other direction. I wanted to go into the school, or I was being carried in that direction whether that was what I wanted or not.

I faced the big front door of the school, thrust my hands in my pockets to keep them warm, and took a couple of strides with my shoulders hunched. Then some more. They got easier as I approached the building, and my hand tightened around the little prayer-book in my pocket. I felt no surprise. That little shape in my hand seemed to belong here, and I got a kind of strength from feeling the angels pressing into my palm.

When I got to the door I half-expected it to be locked. It wasn't – it swung open easily, letting out a warm draught – and I stepped inside, stood still, and listened. I could hear the occasional muted caw from the crows outside, a slight rustle as that draught moved a piece of paper on the notice board, but nothing else. I looked to the right and the left, and as far as I could tell the school was deserted. It had that smell you get in schools after everyone has left, a smell that tells you everyone was there a short while ago, kicking up the dust, sweating, letting food smells drift out of the dining room. The smell the school cleaners leave was there, and the smell of old books and new paper, and that smell you get when a photocopier gets hot. They were all there, and all those familiar things made the school seem perfectly normal and the situation even weirder.

Suddenly, down the corridor to my right, through a couple of glass doors, I thought I saw a movement out of the corner of my eye. I turned my head and looked down that way. Nothing was moving.

"Hello?" I called out, not very loudly, and immediately wished that I hadn't. I almost felt as though I had broken something more than the silence, like a rule maybe. I wanted to turn back, go out of the front door again and run, but the moment I thought this and looked over my shoulder, I saw through the glass of the front door that the day had become darker. Or that may have been just how it looked through that type of glass – the sort with a wire mesh in it – but at any rate I could see the trees thrashing wildly, as though the wind had increased, and the crows flapping untidily in the air. Could one cry from me, and a single thought, really have conjured that?

Again I felt in my pocket. That little Book of Common Prayer was still snug in my hand, and again it felt good there, sort of right, meant to be. I felt my confidence return again, and a suggestion that the tide of weirdness was flowing down the corridor down which I thought I had seen the movement. I said "OK" under my breath, nodded as though I was trying to convince a hidden watcher and not just myself, and pushed through the double doors into the corridor.

I stopped and listened. Had I just heard a faint snatch of conversation, the scrape of a school chair on a classroom floor, a door snicking closed? It was difficult to say. What I did know was that the further I walked down that corridor, the gentler the current became which carried me along. It was just as insistent, but it seemed warmer, almost comforting by comparison with the near-panic I had felt outside. And it occurred to me that I was accepting that I could feel all this as though I had been born with this extra sense, even though discovering it was like waking up and suddenly being fluent in Japanese! Although I was walking down the corridor, looking for something, it felt more like something had been looking for me, and was pleased that it had found me.

I thought, "Maybe there really is a monster, and I am becoming it, like in my dreams," but I smiled at that thought.

I stopped at the door to a classroom. The current, faint now but still insistent, was flowing into that room. Through the glass panel I could see the back wall of the room, with maps and posters on it, and a window to the grey outside. The brief glimpse of that grey outside, like a pang, reminded me somehow that I was where I was meant to be. I thought I heard a bit of laughter from inside the room. I shifted slightly, and caught sight of part of someone's back, a shoulder in a school sweatshirt.

I hesitated for one moment longer. Monsters did not wear school sweatshirts. I took a breath, pushed the door, and stepped inside.

About a dozen faces turned to look at me – faces belonging to kids from the school.

CHAPTER 2
CROWS AND FAIRIES

Maybe this story began before that, but then how can I tell. Someone once said to me that you only have to be one tiny bit different for it to matter. I guess I must be that little bit different, although I feel pretty ordinary most of the time. OK, I write poetry. I can get up in the morning, open my curtains, look at the dawn sky and know, just by looking at it, that there is more to it than the things that make it up – and I can find words for that and put them down on a page. I made the mistake of being the youngest person ever to win the school poetry competition, and to be pleased about it. The problem was that this came just at the time when boys started to notice me and, probably more importantly, girls started to notice me too. Girls notice you if there is something that puts you just outside what they think is normal, and that matters.

One day, Christine Cook, who had ignored me completely in secondary one, said, "You're really up yourself aren't you, Poet!"

Was I? How was I to know one way or the other? No matter – that was the day she and her mates the Patels started getting at me. It wasn't bad bullying, but it was like a tap dripping. One drip was nothing, twenty drips were annoying. Days, weeks, school terms of it could drive a person crazy. I survived by being bloody awkward and toughing it out. I wasn't exactly Betty-no-mates, but I wasn't one of the cool posse either. I don't know whether I cared either way.

Maybe being different in the first place was where it all started, but then there was that little Book of Common Prayer with the sliver angel on the cover too. I remember the day that came into my life, and perhaps that was a beginning too.

I don't just write – I read. I love books, I love picking them up, opening them at any page, and seeing what it says there. The middle of stories are pure magic, with weird bits of action and conversation, names I don't recognise; the middle of any other kind of book is like a window showing a tantalising part of a view. And if what I read makes no sense at all – say if it some kind of technical manual – it is still fascinating to know that there are secrets out there, lots of things that I don't understand. That's what makes me pop into any second-hand bookshop I find. There was one very close to where I live, and I would go there once every month or so. I would browse, and the old bloke who owned the place would occasionally look at me over the top of his spectacles and smile. Sometimes I would actually buy a book and take it home, but more often than not I was happy just picking one or two from the shelves and browsing. On a rainy Saturday he was content to let me sit and read a whole book, and I would be dry and warm on his spare stool while his few customers shuffled in and out, smelling of wet anoraks.

The last time I was there was not long before that day I broke through into my weird, quiet school, and found it deserted except for twelve other kids. As I looked into their faces, the whole memory of my last visit flowed back into my mind. I felt that it connected me somehow to what was going on.

When I had opened the door, the old bloke had not been there. Instead there was a woman, maybe ten years younger in looks. As I came in, and the old-fashioned bell jangled, she turned round. She looked at me with a slight frown.

"Oh, I thought I'd locked the door," she said. "We're closed, actually."

"Sorry," I said, without moving. I could see that many of the books had been pulled from their shelves. Some were even in half-filled packing cases. My heart sank – it wasn't just a matter of being closed, it was closing down.

"I often come here," I said, feebly. "He lets me read, Mr... the man who owns the shop."

The woman looked at me again.

"Are you Angela?" she asked.

"Yes," I said, though I couldn't remember ever having mentioned my name to the man. The woman nodded.

"My brother mentioned you. Not very often, but I think he was fond of you. I warned him not to go getting too friendly with a girl in her early teens, because people would talk. He was a bit of an innocent. Look, sit down for a while – he said that's what you liked to do – help yourself to a book to read for a while, but don't get in my way. I have to pack everything up – it's being taken away on Monday."

I remember running that phrase around in my mind – a bit of an innocent – before it dawned on me what she had said.

"Miss," I said, not knowing what else to call her, "you said 'was'. You said your brother 'was' a bit of an innocent."

She stopped what she was doing, came over, and half-sat half-leant on the lip of a packing case. She looked down at me, into my face, like she was trying to work out whether I was old enough to cope with bad news.

"It was two weeks ago," she said. "A heart attack. He died in his sleep."

"I'm sorry," I said.

The woman went back to her sorting and packing. I picked up one of those coffee-table books, about astronomy, and turned the pages, looking at the inky pictures dotted with pinpricks of light. But I couldn't really settle to it. I kept thinking about the old bloke, suddenly regretting I hadn't talked to him more, hadn't got to know him. Instead of reading, I drifted, went away somewhere in my head, imagining conversations that had never happened. When I pulled myself together, the woman was perched on the packing case again.

"He left this for you," she said. "I've just remembered it. He said, 'If you see Angela, give her this – she'll know what it's for.'"

She handed me the prayer-book. I looked at it. I had no idea what it was for, but the silver angels on the front were pretty. It was very old, I could tell. The silver on the front cover, which must once have been shaped into very clear relief, was worn smooth; but I could make out the heads and tiny wings of four or five cherubs which seemed to be rising through clouds. There was a design round the edge of the cover, framing the scene as though it was a picture. I had seen photographs of this sort of thing before – art nouveau it was called – and it must have been at least a hundred years old.

"Thank you," I said. There was an awkward pause. I had wanted to ask when his funeral was, or had been, and where he was buried, though I didn't know why I wanted to know. But I said nothing. I guess I must have been a bit embarrassed. The woman broke the silence again.

"Look, I'm sorry, but I really would rather you went. I don't think I can cope with someone under my feet while I am trying to do this."

I left, of course, though later I kicked myself for not offering to help. I had missed a chance to find out a little more about the old bloke. I went past the shop three days later; it was empty, locked, a few envelopes and the local free newspaper had been pushed through the low letterbox. I couldn't even see the name on the envelopes. I never knew his name. He was simply the old bloke from the bookshop. The old bloke from the bookshop whose sister had given me the prayer-book. I only had her word that it had been his idea to give it to me.

Now it was in my pocket, as I stood there under the gaze of twelve faces.

The kids had pulled desks and chairs round, a little out of place, so that they could sit facing each other. One of them straddled a chair backwards, 'horsey' style, and one girl stood, leaning back against a desk, her head higher than anyone else's as though she was in charge.

"I'm sorry, I'm in the wrong place," I said.

"No, you're OK, Angela," said the girl who was standing, and I recognised her as Janet Mackie, from the year above mine. The rest were mostly from my year, except for a couple from the year below. One or two looked puzzled to see me, and I caught one of the younger ones counting heads; but no one seemed unfriendly, and one boy from my class, Charlie Seacole, even smiled at me. And winked.

"You wouldn't be here if you weren't supposed to be here," said Janet. "How did you get here? How did you..."

"...have your 'platform nine-and-three-quarters' moment?" said one of the boys, getting an unsubtle nudge from someone behind for having talked out of turn.

I told them about the collision with the metal fence that never happened. There were one or two looks of surprise. Someone said, "I never knew there was a way in near there!" and got a nudge in her turn.

"A way in where? To what? What is going on?" I asked.

"Angela, you're a geek. Work it out for yourself," said Janet. But I did not have a clue.

"Why doesn't someone just tell me? I mean how

weird can it be. I have just shot through a metal fence without hurting myself, found myself in my school, only it's deserted except for you guys – it is deserted isn't it? – and as I came here I felt drawn, carried along. I am not dreaming, because dreams don't feel like this. I could be hallucinating because I have bashed my head, but I don't believe that either. I even wondered outside whether I was dead, but no, I don't believe that either. There is a weird way that this all seems right, as if it makes sense but I can't see the sense it makes yet."

"Yeah, bravo Angela," said Charlie Seacole, with a chuckle that was almost a snort. I looked at him hard in case he was taking the mick, but he was still smiling.

"All right, Angela," said Janet. "Put it this way. Do you believe in fairies?"

I looked at her. Her face was serious, and at that moment the light in the room dimmed a little. It got colder, as though something was there that shouldn't be, or the chilly wind outside had broken in, and the cawing of the crows had got louder. Then there was a little, golden light flittering on a far wall, darting here and there, too quick to follow, to fleeting to make a shape. It flicked across my eyes, dazzling me for a second, and then began to dance on the ceiling, and across the maps on the far wall. It was only a tiny thing, but it seemed a little frightening, too bright in the sudden gloom.

Then I saw what it was, and I laughed.

CHAPTER 3
COUNT THE ANGELS

One stray, sharp ray of sunlight had broken the clouds outside, and had slanted like a badly-thrown javelin right through the gloom that had come upon the classroom. A boy had caught it on the face of his watch, and was making the reflection fly around the room. He laughed as I laughed, and the gloom was lifted. The room felt warm again, the lights in the ceiling cast a clear glow; all the darkness retreated outside, and the cawing grew faint. The little reflection from the watch-face softened, diminished, and rested on the lower part of a dado.

"Awwww!" I said with a grin. "Poor Tinkerbell! She's dying. But if all you boys and girls in the audience shout out that you believe in fairies, she'll come alive again. Neat trick."

Janet was smiling too, but her face grew serious again.

"Yes, that was a little trick with a little bit of reflected light," she said. "But my question was a serious one, Angela. Do you believe in fairies? Pixies and brownies, then, what about them? The little people... or do you believe in Witch Queens, giants, talking animals, fauns, Marsh-Wiggles, and a great talking Lion? Do you believe in elves, dwarves, goblins, wizards, trolls, and dragons? Do you believe in hobbits..."

"Hobbitses!" hissed the boy with the watch, and got the inevitable nudge.

"No really, do you believe in fairies? Not just the story-book Tinkerbells with butterfly wings and acorn hats, but dangerous ones who don't think like we do, but can as soon turn a room dark and curdle milk as they can leave a bag of gold outside a widow's door? How about the Banshee who wails outside the windows of houses where there is going to be a death – she's a fairy – do you believe in her? Hob-goblins, ogres and sprites? Djinns and Afreets? Ghosts, ghouls, things that go bump in the night? Believe in any of them?"

"Poltergeists maybe. Or ESP," said someone else.

"Or unicorns," chimed in Charlie Seacole. "Gryphons, chimeras, manticores, cockatrices, hippogriffs – do you believe in them? Do you believe in the Minotaur? Do you believe that monsters lurk just out of sight, just round the next corner, just inside a dream?" I wondered if he read my mind, and I tried hard not to give a shiver. I didn't want him to think he had got to me.

"How about old gods?" asked the joker with the watch. "Thor, Freya, one-eyed Odin, Loki the mischief-maker, Balder? Or Jupiter with his thunderbolts? How about Cernunnos the Horned One, or Belenos? Thoth, Ra, Hathor, Sobek, Horus, Anubis, Isis, Amun – the Gods of the Valley of the Kings?"

Another girl stood up. "Have you heard of the likes of Yog-Sothoth, Dagon, Nyarlathotep, Yuggoth? Do you believe in the ancient ones from beyond space, that can be called up by reciting spells from crumbling old books?"

"Or the one God?" said Janet. "God the Father, God the Son, God the Holy Ghost – do you believe in Him? Or Allah the merciful, the compassionate – do you believe in Him?"

Charlie spoke up again. "How about secret cults, conspiracies, the Illuminati? Do you believe the earth is hollow? Flat? Do you believe in flying saucers, Roswell, Area Fifty-One? Do you believe Ezekiel saw a space ship, or that extra-terrestrials visited the Aztecs? Or how about a secret order of telepaths, homo superior? What would you say if I told you the world was ruled by a race of four-metre-high lizards in disguise – would you believe me?"

I looked at each one of them, and at the others as they chimed in with their catalogue of legends, deities, superheroes, ghosts, ghouls, vampires, vampire-slayers, tooth-fairies, and bogey-men. "Pick one," I thought. "Add it to today, to the mix of weirdness and normality, and would it make that much difference? Add all of them in a great procession winding round and round the school – would that make much difference?" I shook my head.

"Mostly I believe what I can see and touch," I said. "Beyond that I believe in what I feel. Beyond that, I believe in... I don't know... whatever is possible. Whatever is possible might exist somewhere, and we don't really know what is possible, despite the rules we make up for ourselves."

"And beyond that?" asked Janet.

I thought for a few moments.

"Angels," I said. A sigh ran through the room, as though everyone had let out a deep breath. "I believe in angels."

"Ah, angels," said Janet. "Show us, then."

All that time my hand had been in my pocket. Now I brought it out. For some reason my heart was pounding as I gripped the little prayer-book. I placed it slowly on a desk in front of me. For a moment I covered it with my hand, as though to uncover it would be like revealing something deep and important about myself. This felt like a big step. I took my hand away and looked up. Janet was fishing a silver chain out from under her school blouse; dangling from it was a little figure, upright, wings outspread, one hand lifted as though to bless. Others were uncovering something or fetching things out of a bag or a pocket – a charm on a bracelet, a pendant, a key-ring with a hologram, a brooch, a picture one a trading card; one boy was even rolling his sleeve up to show a small henna tattoo on his upper arm. Angels. Twelve of them, and mine. Showing each one seemed to make us equals.

"Who are you people?" I asked. It seemed like a silly question on one level. I mean, they were kids from my school. But then this was my school, only it was changed, empty, with a kind of current running through it which had pulled me along, and with an empty, stormy, crow-haunted world outside, and although the fairy thing had been a trick, somehow I felt that the darkness and the shaft of sunlight had happened because of them. And, freakier, it had been dispelled by me... by me figuring it out. There was something going on, something these kids were part of, and it seemed as though I was part of it too. I got excited at that thought.

I looked at them, looked around at their faces, wondering if one of them was going to answer. But the weirdness in the place was beginning to change again. There was a dimming of the light again, but not like when the boy had done the fairy trick. That had been kind of grey, black in corners, chilly. This was as though the air itself had become brown, filtering light through it like an amber bead. If anything, it grew warmer; the air got thicker, and I felt that if I had to move through it I would have to swim rather than walk. The current I had felt as I came towards the room seemed to be flowing in to us, into us, whirling like water going down a plug-hole... only it was building up rather than running away. All twelve were looking at each other, some of them seemed a little nervous, others seemed excited. Janet looked over at me and signalled me to sit down with them. Whatever was happening to them, was happening to me too. I was part of it.

I began to see things. I knew somehow that we all began to see the same things. Sometimes It was like a hologram in the middle of the amber light, sometimes it seemed that we were right in the middle of it ourselves, sometimes it seemed to be happening in our heads, and sometimes all three at once. A vision was capturing us, imposing itself on our minds.

"It's a 'Rising'!" I heard one of the younger kids exclaim.

Whatever it was, from the swirling, amber current, a scene began to solidify, and to play over and over again. A woman of maybe thirty-five, walking down a busy street. I didn't know her, I had never seen her before, but the more the scene replayed itself, the longer this vision... this Rising... lasted, the more familiar with her I became, until I seemed to know everything there was to know her. How tall she was compared to me, the way her hair swung, her figure from the front, the side, the length of her stride, the distinctive green of her jacket. There was something else: the more I looked her, the more I saw her confident, relaxed face, the more I knew she was in great danger. The thought filled my mind that it was important to save her from the danger, more important than simply saving a life. It was her life, there was something special, or there was going to be. I became agitated, shifting in my seat. I longed to call out to her, to warn her... but about what? And how could I?

The vision and the amber light began to fade and disperse, and the ordinary light of the room came back. I looked around. The other twelve were starting to get up, and to leave the room. I felt a touch on my shoulder.

"Come on, Angela." It was Charlie Seacole.

"Ok, but where?"

"Janet will know. She will have seen," said Charlie. "Come on!"

The Everywhen Angels

CHAPTER 4
SOME BIG WAR

"We are the Guardian Angels," said Charlie, as we all walked purposefully out of the classroom and towards the main door of the school. "That's what we're called. That's what we know ourselves as. Not like those American guys with red berets, though. We really are... like... real angels."

"Uh huh."

Questions immediately came to my mind – who calls us that, how do we know we're called that, why am I thinking 'we' now? But Charlie went on talking, as we filed out of the school, and made our way down the drive, to a mad chorus of cawing from the crows. The current I had felt when I came in was easier to walk against. It may even have been flowing back on itself, or our joint purpose – saving the woman somehow – was working to cancel it out.

"Angela, there's a war going on. I don't mean over in Iraq or Afghanistan or somewhere. I mean a secret war. No it's not even like that, it's not terrorist cells or anything. I don't want to sound weird, but it's kind of like it's supposed to be in the last book of the Bible – Revelation. It's the last war there is ever going to be, and it's a big one. There is going to be one last great battle. For all I know that's going on right now, or what we're doing is like whaddya-callems... skirmishes... like two chess players arguing over who's going to be black or white, or kids picking sides for a football. No it's more than that. The fight has started, but it's like the two sides are circling each other, looking for an opening, a way in, and advantage. It's big, Angela. Forget politics, and religion, forget whatsit... economics.... This is between Good and Evil. Good so good and Evil so evil that you can hardly get your head round it. And we're part of it."

"Which side are we on?" I asked. Charlie looked shocked.

"We're the good guys, of course," he said. "Do you need to ask?"

"So if we're the good guys, who are the bad guys?"

Charlie shrugged.

"Are there actually any bad guys?" I asked.

"Oh yes, there are bad guys."

"Who are they?"

Charlie shrugged again. Either he didn't know or he didn't want to say. I tried a different question.

"If this is war, like you say, do people get killed?"

He shot me a look and walked on for half a minute without replying. Then, "Yes, people get... dealt with." I could tell he was going stonewall me all the way. I wasn't going to get anywhere, so I changed the subject again.

"How do you know all this?"

"Well Janet told me when I first came. I don't know when it started. None of the kids who were here when I first came could remember it starting, just each of them came and found the rest of the guardian angels already here. It's always been people around our age. And there has always been around twelve of us, usually twelve, sometimes we go for a while with eleven. Thirteen is rare – you came as quite a surprise to us, and by a new way in. There are twelve ways in, or there were that we knew of. Yours is a new one on us." Charlie looked at me and grinned. "You must be special, Angela."

"You picked a fine moment to hit on me," I said. He had a cute grin, but I wasn't going to let him see that I had noticed. "So what do we do, what do Guardian Angels do?"

"We protect people. We save them."

"What people?"

"People we are shown. People we see in the Risings. They're important. We don't know how important they are, or how they are important. I get the feeling that they're like... well chess pieces again. They all have to be somewhere on the board. They're being moved into position. For the big one."

"I'm beginning to feel more like I'm in some kind of computer game," I said. I wondered to myself whose thumbs were pressing the buttons on the console. I remembered that Charlie had been chess champion of his year for two years running, but since then I hadn't heard of him even competing. Why would I, though? I don't like chess.

"How often do you meet?" I asked.

"What do you mean?"

"I mean how often do you meet? We're here in school." We still were technically, though we were getting closer to the main gate. "So how often do you pop through your ways in and meet together? Once a week, or what?"

"We're always here, Angela. Every day we come to school, slip through the cracks, and end up in that room."

I stopped, and pushed Charlie's shoulder, making him spin round to face me. "Don't talk bloody nonsense, Charlie Seacole. The school would notice if twelve of its kids went missing every day. And I've seen you around the place. OK, I can accept that maybe this isn't really the school but somewhere else..."

"Oh it's the school all right, just kind of... shifted, you could say," interrupted Charlie. I waved him to silence with an impatient gesture.

"Whatever. But I have seen you around. I know I have. Janet too, and some of the others. So unless you've got a double..." My voice trailed away. Charlie was nodding.

"You saw my 'tulpa'," he said.

"Your what-the-who?"

He spelt it for me, and went on. "You were right, I have a double. We all do. Every time we come here, our tulpas take over, go through the school day for us."

"Hey now that's cool!" I said with a smile. "I'm in! If it means someone else does the work for me, I am so in!"

Charlie was silent for a moment. "It's not as good as it sounds. There is a price. The tulpas are supposed not to attract attention. So basically that's what they do. From the moment you become a Guardian Angel, you get to be Mr Boring, Miss Boring. Your exam marks fall, you end up somewhere towards the top of the bottom half. You're almost invisible. The tulpa makes sure the spotlight isn't on you. In your case, no more poetry prizes. In all our cases, when you get your report at the end of each term, you get a frown from your mum and dad."

That made me stop and think. I was always near the top. Dad always told me I only had one person to beat – myself. He would never be disappointed in me as long as I did my best. I could imagine his face when the mediocre marks gained by the tulpa came in. Charlie nodded.

"My parents give me the silent treatment," he said. "I hate it, but I put up with it. Because of this. Because this needs doing, and somehow I have been picked to do it."

"Come on you two!" called Janet. Everyone else had reached the gate. Charlie and I had lagged behind. As we walked, I fired more questions at him.

"So this is what we do, is it? Every day we come here, a Rising happens, and we go off and rescue someone, right?"

"No way," Charlie replied. "Risings don't come that often. More like once a week. We have been weeks without one sometimes."

"Some big war!" I scoffed.

"Yeah right, I hadn't thought of it like that," he said. "But y'know, you're right. Things have happened very slowly, and we spend a lot of time just sitting around." He looked at me and went on, "I think you being here means that things are going to speed up!"

"Why do you think that?"

"I don't know."

By then we had reached the gate, where the others had stopped and waited for us. Janet was getting impatient, so we wasted no more time in chatting, we simply walked off towards the town centre. As we walked, the outside world seemed to shift back into step with us. Or maybe it happened all at once and I didn't notice it. I only know that there came a moment when I realised that we had come out of the emptiness and were back in everyday. There were people about, lots of people. Cars. Buses. Noise. But all the questions I hadn't asked were buzzing round my head, and there were plenty, competing with the bustle; like were we the only ones, what happened to Guardian Angels when they turned sixteen or so, who was the other side, and most importantly, who the hell was in charge of all this? And oh yeah – could I get hurt?

Janet's voice brought me back to earth. She told us to spread out, keep our eyes open, and to make a sweep through the street. We had to find the woman.

CHAPTER 5
FISH ON A MISSION

I am looking back at all this. So maybe it's a little easier for me to describe now. All those unanswered questions, all the little details, everything that the other Angels seemed to take entirely on trust, all that was like when I watched a DVD once that held my attention all the way through, and then later when I read the book it was based on I could see that there were so many holes in the story the way they had filmed it. Right now I was being swept up in an adventure. I could see by the looks on the faces of some of the other kids that they were totally into it. The adventure seemed to give our lives meaning, we were special. Every time we met each other outside school hours, secret smiles would pass between us.

But that all came later for me.

An invisible cord held us together, more like a strong elastic, a steel spring, magnetism – who knows – but we were part of one another. Not quite like reading each other's thoughts, more like being able to pick up on feelings, sensations, excitement. For a moment an everyday thought ran through my mind – this was what it was like to be in a posse, to have a crew; the Guardian Angels were my crew. I felt the thrill that the bright-faced, excited kids felt, and re-focussed on what we were doing. We were flowing, swimming in a weird current like the one I had felt in and around the school, but this one was running around and through the bustle of the busy street, over and past the people. My mind wandered, as I had the sensation of being a fish in a river, or part of the river itself, swirling and eddying. Somehow I could feel Janet across the road, Charlie several yards behind me, the others weaving in and out of the passers-by; I knew that Janet was watching, searching, looking for signs, that the pulse-rate of the boy with the watch had increased, that Charlie was cool and casual, and that another of our number was totally calm. I knew that they could feel that I was jumpy, looking into the face of every woman who walked towards me.

Then suddenly I became aware that Janet was

focussing on me, looking across the road at me, and I couldn't tell why. She seemed to be aware that something had changed about me, though what it was remained a mystery to me. I was simply walking along as before, looking, searching, sweeping my gaze past the head of the woman a few paces ahead of me, matching my pace to hers in order not to catch up to her or barge into her. I had slipped into the same stride as hers, and now we were walking in step, almost marching, as I kept on searching and searching. I was almost annoyed each time I had to look past her bobbing hair, resenting the fact that her jacket was an eye-catching green. I didn't want to be distracted by her – I was here to do a job, and I was beginning to get angry at this. Why didn't she go away? Why didn't she take a side step into a shop instead of continually blocking my view. More and more I was looking at her instead of searching. I could feel Janet's increased agitation, and felt ashamed that here I was, failing in my task the very first time I was needed. Janet... Charlie... all the crew were beginning to focus on me, and my ears began to burn.

The trouble was that the woman was so familiar to me. Everything about her told me that I knew her, yet I was certain she was no one I had met. I had fallen into step with her, and now I couldn't break it – walking this way felt easy and natural. I had an urge to reach out and touch the woman on her shoulder, as she slowed slightly and looked from right to left.

That was the moment I recognised her, and a feeling of relief burst through me. The profile I had caught a glimpse of belonged to the woman I had seen in the Rising. I was right behind her. The feeling of relief turned to excitement, and that feeling immediately turned to something so close to panic that I didn't know what to do next. What could I do? Was I supposed to tap her on the shoulder, say, "Good morning, Madam, my name's Angela, and I am your Guardian Angel for today"? What good could I do by babbling to her about Armageddon and her being in great danger?

Everything stopped as she stopped. There was no more current. We were waiting. The other angels were waiting... were they waiting for me? I stood behind the woman, as passers-by stepped round us, some of them frowning and irritated by the way we were blocking the pavement. I was teetering on the edge of something, and my pulse was singing in my ears. What was going to happen? What was I supposed to do? No one had told me whether our missions... whatever... had ever ended in failure. Had we ever arrived too late to rescue someone?

The current was still, but there was a slight disturbance in it. I felt it, and quivered.

A bus had moved away from its stop a little way ahead of us, and was gathering speed as it came along the street towards us. I became aware of the roar of its engine as the driver shifted up another gear. Soon, within a couple of seconds maybe, it was going to draw level with us.

What happened next happened so quickly that I am sure my brain didn't take in all the details. A boy I hadn't noticed before staggered, going over on the side of his shoe with a yelp of pain. His shoulder caught the woman on her right arm and threw her off balance. To stop herself from falling, she took a step to the left, brought her foot down half-on the kerb, and fell directly into the path of the bus. No thoughts went though my head – I simply took a leap to my left and ahead, my arms reaching out for her, trying to catch her before she hit the tarmac. My hands gripped the green jacket, and the force of my leap knocked us both to the ground, where we rolled over and over. There were shouts, screams, the blaring of horns, the tortured rip of tyres as brakes were jammed on.

We stopped rolling a little more than half way over the road. I was aware that Janet was bending over us, pulling us both upright and dragging us out of the way of the traffic.

When we were on the opposite pavement, the woman slumped to the ground in shock, and leant against a lamp-post. I found myself kneeling by her side, but I wasn't paying any attention to her. I was watching a boy's head on the other side of the road, bobbing in and out of sight as he ran and dodged through the crowds. And there was Charlie, running after him.

The woman was starting to speak, but her voice was flat, like she was in shock. "Thank... thank you... you saved my life..."

As a crowd grew around us, and the bus driver leapt down from his cab, Janet tugged at my sleeve, pulling me to my feet.

"Angela, come on. Come away."

"But..." I began.

"Leave it. Leave her," Janet hissed urgently in my ear, pushing through the crowd and pulling me with her. I could see that some people were thinking of stopping us, not knowing whether we had been rescuers or had caused the accident. "There's nothing more for us to do here. They'll forget about us. Trust me, they will. As long as we just go. They'll forget about us. We're just like... like static on a CCTV camera, like we don't exist."

By the time we were back near the school, the crew had come together again. Charlie was the last to rejoin us, shaking his head in answer to Janet's questioning look. The boy with the watch nudged me, and said quietly, "Awesome, Angela." There was a kind of quiet elation amongst us – we were still buzzing.

When we reached the school, which we could see full of its usual bustle, Janet told us to split up and go in the way each of us knew. So I found myself at the metal fence again. Fine. If it had worked once before, it would work again. I simply stepped through.

Hello grey sky. Hello nagging wind. Hello crows. Hello weird current. Hello my fellow Guardian Angels, my crew. Mission accomplished?

The school was quiet. We seemed to be its only occupants again, as we filed down the corridor, into the classroom, and sat down. No one said much for the time that remained. In fact, hours and minutes didn't seem to mean much. I learned everyone else's names, and it seemed to be time to go. The buzz seemed to have left us, and we were subdued. Janet looked drawn, as though she had a headache.

"Is it always like this?" I asked; but nobody answered.

Janet shrugged. All she would say to me was, "Keep quiet about this when you get home, Angela. Don't say a word to anyone."

So we were a silent crew as we walked towards the school gates. Even the crows on the trees had stopped their racket. Charlie sidled over to me.

"You might feel a bit weird as you go through the gate this time," he said.

"How do you mean?"

"You'll see," He said. "It's not easy to describe."

But then, what the hell could be weirder that the day I had just gone through. I felt a bit fed up that I couldn't tell my parents that their girl had saved someone's life. It didn't seem fair, but it was expected of me, and when I thought about it, how could I explain anything that had happened today? Anyhow, I soon saw what Charlie had meant, because as we stepped through the large main gates of the school there was a kind of 'pop' inside my head, and suddenly I found myself in the middle of the noisy population of the whole school pouring out to the buses. I guess I must have merged with my – what did they call it? – my tulpa. The noises of the world returned and nearly deafened me. Not only that, but I jumped out of my skin as I felt a whack on my shoulder. Christine Cook and her hangers-on barged past me and hurried off, grinning back at me. I gave them my best scowl.

Oh yes, one more weird thing happened that day. I was up in my room, emptying my bag, and a sheet of lilac paper fell out of my English file. I don't use lilac paper. I didn't have any purple pens either, and the writing on this piece of paper was in purple. I had no idea where it had come from, and it never occurred to me at that moment that it could have been slipped in there any time during the school day. I was tired I guess, and puzzled, and annoyed that someone had been messing around with my stuff. The writing itself was simple enough.

"Please, don't go there again," it said.

CHAPTER 6
TEENAGE STUFF

I started dating Charlie Seacole. In the midst of all this adventure and weirdness I got myself a boyfriend, my first ever. I guess I did it partly because I needed something real to get excited about, if you see what I mean – something in the real world, the everyday world. To an extent he took my mind off the fact that I had just become part of something which was so 'out there' that it would have been easy for me, let's face it, to go mental, end up in a psychiatric ward. I had started to look up things on Google about the 'Last Days', and I guess I was a little freaked, so Charlie took my mind off that too. He had a nice smile. Neither of us knew how to kiss, but when we tried, that was nice too. I told you how the angels shared smiles and looks when we met – well,

Charlie and I just felt like sharing a little more. There was something that felt right about it.

Charlie had been dead right about one thing. That was that my marks, my performance in class, went right down as my tulpa took over things. Somehow, when I re-merged with it at the end of the day, I absorbed that day's lessons in a dull sort of way, and I was able to pick up a bit of pace when I did the homework. But overall, I found myself bringing home test results and reports which didn't look as good as they had.

My mum is status-conscious. What matters to her is that I am their only child, I was bright, and I ought to do well at school so I can get a good job. My dad is, to her, an example of someone who has done just that, and he is the yardstick by which she judges everyone. To dad, it isn't about status – he can take it or leave it – it is about making the most of your mind. Over the weeks that followed, I could see the smiles fade, the frowns become more frequent, the look of disappointment as my marks began to slide.

I have always been closer to my dad than to my mum. We were companions when I was nothing but a kid, swimming in the sea together, building sandcastles, all that kind of things. He could speak French, and he kept me in front of my class by doing things like going for a whole day when he only spoke French to me. He loved my poems and was thrilled when I won the poetry prize.

I hated hurting them, and there were times I just curled up in a ball in my room and thought about when I was little and everything seemed sunny. Mum and dad became irritable with me, and I started snapping back.

"You spend too much time on that computer, on Facebook or whatever you're on," my mum said one day. "Instead of studying."

She made the mistake of saying that when I was actually studying, and I just said, "Don't stress me, mum. Don't nag."

"I would never have dared say that to my mother," she said. "Oh God, I don't believe I just said that! Never mind not daring to say that to her, I'm turning into her. I promised myself I would never say that – see what you made me do!"

"Mum, I didn't make you do anything."

"You've changed," she went on. "You've changed since you've started seeing that boy, Charlie Seacole."

"You don't like him because he's black," I snapped, and instantly regretted that. Mum looked hurt, and I wanted to rush over and hug her. But instead I got up and stormed out, more angry at myself than at her. As I left, I saw my dad gently lay a hand on my mum's arm. I supposed he was going to give her the 'she's-only-a-teenager' talk, and suddenly it all seemed terribly unfair, because on the surface I had just become a moody teenager. It was just that my moodiness was because I was – I don't know – saving the world for them and I felt as though they ought to be grateful. But of course they couldn't know. And I felt so guilty about making out mum was racist. I had said 'black' very deliberately. I had wanted to hurt her. I know I was supposed to think about Charlie's colour, to be aware that his skin, more latte than black, had some sort of exotic history or other. Everything was supposed to be about diversity these days, but what was more important to me was that Charlie was a Guardian Angel just like me, and my boyfriend. It was so frustrating to be doing this sort of in the closet, because I felt special, grown-up, and important, but I had to wear this stroppy teenager mask for my mum and dad, and hurt them over and over again.

I think it was that day – yes it was – when I had stormed out of the living room and up to my bedroom to do my curling-up-crying trick again, it was that day I got the first of a run of texts on my BlackBerry. I had switched it on because I wanted to text Charlie or have a good moan to Janet, but as soon as it blinked into life I got the ringtone that told me there was a text message waiting for me. I read it. I stared at it.

"Pls dont go 2 skool by fence agen"

I read it three times just to make sure I had it right, and there was no mistake. I had pushed the matter of the note written in purple ink to the back of my mind, but this brought it right back. It was a warning, I guess, not to use my 'way in' to the weird and silent school. I checked for the return number. It wasn't one I recognised, but I keyed in a reply.

"Who r u & wot do u mean?"

My reply hung there for five minutes in my outbox, but didn't get sent. I cancelled it in annoyance, wrote down the number, and carefully entered it manually, repeating my message. This one hung in my outbox, and eventually timed out. I tried again, double-checking the number – it was correct – and hit the key to send it. Same result, it just wasn't going to go!

I could only think that Charlie was playing a joke

on me, so I rang his mobile.

"Charlie, did you just text me?"

"No. What would I text you about? I only saw you an hour and a half ago. What's the matter? Is someone bothering you?" His voice sounded concerned for a minute, and then he chuckled. "Hey, are you two-timing me, Ange? Some other guy texting you – is that it?"

"Don't be silly," I said, a little too quickly and a little too harshly. It was my day for being harsh. "Listen, it's OK, Charlie. No worries, right? I'll call you back – I just want to ask Janet something. OK?"

"OK Ange, no worries. Later."

Charlie hung up, and I dialled Janet's number. For about fifteen minutes we chatted about nothing at all. I didn't ask her what I wanted to ask her. I didn't say "Does anyone else know about us?" I didn't ask her whether someone other than a Guardian Angel could have our phone numbers. The questions which had worried me at the beginning, and which I had forced to the back of my mind, came forward again, just far enough forward to start worrying me again, but still I held back from putting them directly to Janet. We just chatted. Then she hung up and I dialled Charlie again, and we just chatted.

It wasn't unusual for us just to chat and chat. Although there were knowing looks and winks when we met, the subject of our missions wasn't often the subject of casual conversation. Chatting was, I guess, our way of relaxing. But this time, as Charlie and I did the boyfriend-girlfriend thing, I couldn't relax. I sat there thinking about all the Risings we had had, all the missions we had been on over the previous few weeks.

I had become used to Risings, adjusted to the weird way they felt. The adrenalin rush was still there during missions, but I was beginning to take them in my stride. They weren't always as dramatic as the first one where I barged the woman out of the way of that bus; sometimes we simply had to shadow someone as they made their way home, just to make sure they were safe. That sort of mission mystified me, but after one of them Janet said to me, "I think times like that are either like drills, to make sure we always go where we need to go and do what we need to do, or maybe..." she shivered a little and went on. "Maybe we're being watched, and the very fact that we were seen means we're doing our job, and the people are being protected."

Yes, of course I missed that opportunity to say

something too. Being watched eh? I was sure I was being watched. Someone was definitely watching me, slipping notes into my bag, texting me.

I began to keep an eye open for any sign of interest in the people we were sent to protect. Was anyone else shadowing them, or shadowing us? I saw nothing, nothing as blatantly obvious as the boy who had barged the woman into the way of the bus and then run off. Sometimes I felt an awareness of something, a presence, a vague suspicion, but nothing clear, nothing that seemed to come near us. Then I would check myself, tell myself I was being hysterical, paranoid, and for a while I would just lose myself again in the excitement of being special.

I would have shrugged any such feeling off, I think, if it hadn't been for the texts. They came thick and fast for a whole week. I couldn't reply to any of them. There was no threat in any of them, just a plea not to go back into our weird, shifted school. Eventually I stopped reading them, just deleted them as they came in. They stopped. It was as though the sender realised the texts were not being read.

Things settled down. We went for two weeks without a single Rising or mission. Then there was the man who drowned himself.

The Everywhen Angels

CHAPTER 7
SHE MOVES AMONG THE GROVE OF STONES

There was a Rising as usual. That's how I had come to regard Risings by then – usual. The whole business of being a Guardian Angel, of being special, of going on missions, of having adventures, had started to become usual. Not ordinary, just usual. I guess there is a difference. I mean I was totally into it again by now. It was part of my life, like Charlie was part of my life, like fighting with my parents was part of my life, like being a teenager was part of my life.

I say 'as usual', but of course we had just gone two whole weeks without one, so I suppose it wasn't as usual as all that. We were sort of lulled into a false sense of security, and had spent two weeks sitting in our room in our shifted school just chatting about normal things. We listened to our iPods, read something geeky, played games on netbooks or tablets, I sat close to Charlie, someone even passed the time doing the tai chi exercises which they had been learning at the weekend.

A Rising usually – there I go again – took us by surprise. One could happen at any time in the day, maybe as soon as we came into the room, or later in the afternoon. Something would alert us to it, and we would catch each others' eye. Maybe someone would sense a change in the weird current, or in the light, or in their own mood. Then we would all notice, and become still but excited at the same time, attentive, we would try hard to relax but it would have us on the edge of our seats. Even Janet was like that, and she had been a Guardian Angel the longest.

This time I think I noticed it first. I had been sitting very quietly, leaning my shoulder against Charlie's, and thinking. I had been wondering how long this whole Guardian Angel thing had been going on – how old one of us had to get before dropping out, how long Janet had to go and who would take over her position when she had gone, whether there were any former Guardian Angels still at the school, or off at university, or working – that sort of speculation had been occupying my mind. Later I confided all this in Charlie, and he listened without saying anything. But this time, at the point when these thoughts were making such an impression on me that I had almost decided to say them out loud to the others, I began to feel that difference in the weird current.

It was intense and sudden, and for a moment or two I thought I was the only person who had felt it. I looked around, and the others were pretty much as they had been for the last couple of hours. But I could feel, very distinctly, the current thicken and press inwards at us, at me, almost spiralling like water going down a plug, only more slowly, and with nowhere to drain. I had to call out – "Hey, guys!" – before anyone else caught on and paid attention. One by one, but quickly, everyone settled down to it, and the Rising became stronger.

The current was fluid, but thick. I was caught in a flow of molten glass, but it was cool, peaceful, green. I was floating in it, but moving steadily downwards, feeling it become heavier, darker green, hearing nothing but my pulse slowing in my ears, feeling nothing but a slight regret, a slight panic, both being overtaken by a willingness for the green to keep darkening to black and for all sensation to stop. Faces came and went, at first sharply but then more indistinctly. A woman I recognised, but at the same time I knew it was not me recognising her... two children, one of them mouthing something, perhaps 'Daddy'... all fading... fading... any moment everything would be black and still, and all my troubles would be over...

Suddenly light burst in, and I took a great gasp, gulping in air as though I had been holding my breath. I was back in the classroom, if I had ever been away, and the others were all gasping too. One person was coughing fit to be sick, and someone said "What the bloody hell was that?" We looked at one another.

"I felt like I was drowning. You OK, Ange?" said Charlie.

"So did I," said Janet, and there were nods from the others.

"Yeah I'm ok."

"Has anyone ever felt anything like that before?" said Janet, looking round us. "I know I haven't. I know it's stupid of me to ask, because I've been here longer than anyone, but I just don't know what to make of it. There was nothing I recognised, no clue about who to save, nor about where the person is. Help me out here, guys. Anyone?"

No one spoke for about fifteen seconds, then I took a deep breath.

"We have to get to the canal."

Everyone looked at me, then at Janet. She nodded, and we all got up to leave. As we walked down the drive to the gates and out into the town, I noticed that Janet was hanging back a little, letting me walk ahead and govern our pace, watching me. Usually – ah, usually again – Risings would happen, and we would go off on our mission confident that we would get where we were going on time. This one seemed, to me at any rate, to be more urgent, and the crew had to lengthen their strides to keep up with me. I heard puffs and pants and the occasional complaint, but when I looked back there was Charlie right at my shoulder, and Janet quietly urging people to keep up with me.

We have miles of canals round here. A hundred and fifty years ago, maybe two hundred, they would have been busy with narrowboats and barges full of cargo going this way and that. I had seen pictures in books, prints made from engravings, of boats being pulled along by patient horses on the towpath, and photographs of the later motorised barges. Then the railways got built, and after them all the main roads onto which convoys of lorries had hurried, and these canals had become disused, dried up or choked with rubbish and weeds. Then a few years ago they had been restored – the heritage thing – and for a while had again buzzed with narrowboats, this time hired by tourists, and the towpaths had become busy with cyclists and joggers. Now the canal had become more peaceful again and was slipping into a second period of neglect.

Somehow I knew where to go. It was a long way, and I was getting a blister on my left foot, but I kept going, feeling the others coming after me like the familiar shoal of fish. I thought I knew the way to a stretch of the canal where it went through a cutting. At each end of this stretch, about four hundred metres apart from each other, two bridges crossed the canal, leading walkways from alleys which connected the streets beyond. I knew I was heading for one of them. I only half-knew the way, but I felt as though I were being swept there. As we got close, filing down the alley to the first bridge one at a time, I slowed down. I deliberately walked past the steep flight of stone steps leading to the towpath, and made my way cautiously a little way onto the bridge, holding up a hand to stop anyone following me. I looked towards the second bridge, and then walked back again.

"Janet, if it's ok with you, I'd like you to step onto the bridge like I did, look to the left, and come back. Ok?" I said. I tried not to make it sound like an order, because everyone knew that Janet was our unofficial leader. But she nodded, and did as I had asked.

"What did you see?" I asked when she came back. She was calm, but her face was white.

"About halfway between the two bridges, about two hundred metres away, there is a man. He is sitting on the towpath, with his legs dangling over the side. I could make out one of his hands – it's down by his bum, flat against the towpath, as though he is about to push himself forward."

Janet was silent for a while, frowning. Then she went on. "I don't know what to do. I don't know how to handle this. It's different. If we all pile down there, he'll go in, and be under the water before we can get to him. We know it's deeper than normal just there... I'll take suggestions, guys!"

Silence again.

"I'll go down there," I said.

Janet nodded.

"Do it," said Charlie.

I turned and walked down the steps and onto the towpath. I tried to walk casually, not noisily and not furtively. I wanted the man to realise I was there, but not get spooked. I wanted him not to see me as any kind of threat. I think I must have been about twenty metres away when he suddenly realised I was there. He half-turned and stiffened slightly, relaxing a little when he saw me. I started singing a little song in French that Dad had taught me, and when the man looked up and met my eyes I smiled at him. He looked back at me without any expression, but at least he did look back. Maybe he had decided that I was a minor distraction, and that he would let me pass before slipping into the water. Maybe he didn't want to distress me by killing himself while a girl was there. Maybe he even thought of the danger he would put me into if I tried to rescue him. Whatever, he just sat there.

I made as if to walk past, but then stopped. I sat down at the edge of the towpath, just like him, just out of arm's reach of him.

"Hi," I said. "I often stop here. It's peaceful."

That was a lie of course, but I couldn't think of anything else to say.

"And your mum doesn't tell you not to talk to strangers?" he asked.

"Yeah she does of course," I said, grinning and making a few exaggerated punches in the air. "But I can handle myself. I'm a town girl – black belt in ooji-ma-fooji – Ah so!"

He looked at me.

"What was that you were singing?"

"An old French folk-song. I learned it from my dad. He's good at languages." I looked away from him, as though I was unconcerned. I looked over to the other side of the canal, where someone had made colourful swirls of graffiti on the brick wall of the cutting, and I turned my head this way and that, mouthing the words and names I could decipher from the tags. I felt him continue to watch me. Neither of us spoke for a while, until I met his eyes again. His face, which had softened when we were first talking, had become hard again.

"You won't stop me," he said. "You know what I mean."

"I can't stop anyone doing anything," I said.

"Even with ooji-ma-fooji. But will you tell me why?"

"Life. It isn't worth living. It just isn't worth living."

I kept eye contact, and remembered the faces I had seen in the Rising. I said, "Your wife... your two kids..."

"They'd be better off without me," he said. Then he looked at me more closely. "You know them? Do I know you?"

"I've seen them... around," I said.

"You still won't stop me," he said, after another pause. "You had better walk on. I'll wait until you are out of sight."

"Ok, if that's the way you really want it," I said, not knowing what to do next. Then I had an idea. "But listen to this first."

I fixed my eyes once again on the graffiti across the canal, and began to make up words and recite them, occasionally tracing in the air with one index finger, as though I were reading the tags and slogans on the wall, and translating them.

She moves among the grove of stones
In never-ending geas or quest.
In mossy-agate green she's dressed;
By peaceful smiles her face is blessed
To greet the newly-rising day
Among the grove of stones.

She seeks in each relief of bones
And in each in memoriam,
Each ad maiorem gloriam,
Mortality's thin diaphragm
Between the great and lesser way
Among the grove of stones.

She sings in sweet, melodic tones,
The treasures of discovered names
Of gone-before grandsires and dames;
And each life in her bosom flames,
And no tears in her eyes betray
Her in the grove of stones.

And though the fatal reaper hones
His quick, inevitable hook,
The lady with the joyful look
Records in memory's good book
Such names as in her mind will play,
Among the grove of stones.

I finished, and looked around. I was startled at first because he was no longer sitting by me, and I thought he had slipped in while I was speaking. But then I turned a little further, and saw that he was standing on the towpath.

"That was... remarkable," he said. "Where does it come from?"

"I just made it up. I'm a poet. It's... just words... doesn't really mean anything." Suddenly I felt embarrassed.

"You are a poet," he said, and then. "Ok, you win. I won't do it."

"I'm glad," I said.

"Goodbye, poet," he said. "And in future listen to what your mum says about talking to strange men."

"I will," I said. "Goodbye."

He turned round and walked down the towpath to the other bridge. I watched him all the way, right to the steps, watched him climb them, watched him cross the bridge and disappear, presumably into the alley. I was still watching the empty bridge when I felt rather than saw the other Guardian Angels join me, and felt Charlie's arm round my shoulder. Suddenly I felt tired, the blister on my foot stung, I just wanted to go home.

I heard Janet's voice. "What did you do, Ange?"

"I just talked to him," I said.

CHAPTER 8
IMPASSE

About two weeks later, one Saturday morning, I saw the man from the towpath again. I was looking at his face smiling at me on the front page of the local paper. 'Father of two drowned' ran the headline. I didn't have to read any more to know that he had gone back to the spot where I had talked to him, and had slipped away from a life which he still felt wasn't worth living.

"You're not saying much this morning, Angela," said mum.

She was right – I wasn't. I couldn't. I was dumb. I was a block of concrete. Blocks of concrete don't speak, can't speak. Mum shrugged and went back to what she was doing.

"Suit yourself."

It's funny how my mind works. Numb from the news about the drowned man, I had started thinking about the flood of spam emails I had received right after I had saved him. Let me back-track.

Charlie had walked me home that afternoon, his arm round my shoulder. I was limping badly, and I needed to lean against him. We passed the school a good ten minutes after the buses had left, and felt our tulpas merge into us with a pop. For some reason we never thought of catching an ordinary bus, we just walked and walked, and were really late getting to my house. Mum only worked part-time, and was always home by the time I got there. That day I hadn't given her any indication I was going to be late, in fact I told her I would be home at the usual time. I don't think she was actually too worried, but when she saw me coming towards the house with Charlie's arm round my shoulder she came to the door, scowling. Charlie was all for taking me right to the door, but I made him go back.

"If you're sure," he said.

"I'm sure."

Mum watched as I limped in.

"You are late. Where have you been?" she demanded, probably more harshly than she really wanted to. As I pushed past her to get a drink, she must have caught sight of my behind, where I had been sitting on the towpath. "And what the hell have you been doing to get your school clothes in such a state?"

I snapped. I was tired, I had just saved a man's life, and all my mum could think about was the dirt on my clothes.

"What the hell do you care what I've been doing? And if you think Charlie has been bouncing my bum against a wall, why don't you just say so?" I yelled at her.

"Don't you dare speak to me like that!" she yelled back.

"And don't you dare speak to me like that either!" I yelled back, before dashing into the living room, slamming the door shut behind me, and leaning against it, exhausted. I could hear mum talking crossly to herself in the other room, banging around getting ingredients for a stir-fry.

"Damn... I didn't want to say any of that. I so did

not want to say any of that!"

I thought, "Yeah, mum. And you didn't have to say it if you didn't want to, but you said it all the same."

I told myself I was blazing angry at her, but there was a guilty bit of knowledge lurking in the back of my mind, the knowledge that I hadn't had to say what I said either. When you get into this teenager-parent thing, it just kind of starts spiralling down, and keeps on spiralling no matter what you wish would happen. You can't stop it. It's like you have caught a virus. I was fuming when I sat down at the PC and logged on to my webmail. There was only one email waiting for me, and I opened it without thinking. This is what it said:

"You have to listen to me. You have to stop going into school doing what you're doing. I know you felt you were doing right today, but you have no idea what is going on. Please, please, please don't have any more to do with it. A friend."

I hit reply and typed:

"Oh yeah and you know better than me, whoever you are? You wanted me to let a man drown? Why? If I have no idea what is going on, why don't you tell me, 'Friend'?"

I sent the reply, and watched as the automatic postmaster bounced it. The 'friend' wouldn't get the reply. I set my spam filter to catch any mail from that address, but over the next week there was one email a day, with a similar message, but from different email addresses. Replies to all of them bounced. I was thinking about changing my own email address, but like I said, after a week the spams stopped.

On the Saturday morning, with the memory of the man's face smiling up at me from the newspaper still in my mind, I logged on to our chat room. Yeah we had a chat room, or rather a password-protected room in someone else's chat facility, which had been picked because it had no connection at all with what we were doing – I think it was a music site or something – and once the room had been set up everyone was given a 'back-door key', a shortcut to get into it without coming through the main chat lobby. It was a good way of getting together when we weren't in our classroom, and of talking when we didn't want to be overheard; we had rejected the idea of a Facebook page, and even Skype as being too open. Twitter was right out, of course. This time, when I logged on, I half-expected no one to be there, as we didn't have anything to discuss. But I was lonely, knocked out by the news of the man drowning that I had saved from drowning. I wanted to talk. I think I wanted to talk to Tinker – that was my name for the boy who had done the trick with the reflection from his watch face, and it was short for Tinkerbell, for obvious reasons. He was about nine months younger than me, and probably the Guardian Angel I liked best after Charlie. I guess that had something to do with the fact that he flattered me. Charlie teased him a little, saying he fancied me, but I felt that Tinker really did like me. I wanted to talk to him now because I remembered that he had made a remark in my hearing when we were at the canal; he said that everyone had expected Charlie to become our new leader when Janet left, but he thought I should be. Tinker wasn't much of a one for tact, because I knew Charlie heard that and I was pretty sure Janet did too. Over the past week I had let that sink in, I had been pleased with myself, thinking, "Yeah... why not?" The 'why not' had just happened. Now I had it in my head that maybe I would ask Tinker some of the unanswered questions.

I found company in the chat room, but it wasn't quite what I expected.

<Angel13> has entered the room

Skydancer: hi angel

Angel13: Hi Sky

Angel13: Not seen u in here before

Skydancer: used 2 come in some time ago

Angel13: mhm?

Skydancer: mhm

Angel13: Where u from?

Angel13: How come u don't come in here much?

Angel13: Only my friends come in here. I mean ppl I kno

Skydancer: I'm ur friend too

Angel13: Yeah? Do I kno u?

Skydancer: don't kno... do u?

Angel13: Cha is that u messing abt?

Angel13: Cha?

Skydancer: not cha

Angel13: OK so not Cha, then who?

<Skydancer> sent sound – whistle

Angel13: U don't say much do u

Angel13: Say something. U trying to scare me? Won't work.

Skydancer: no I'm not trying 2 scare u…

Skydancer: I'm ur friend, honest

Angel13: Do I kno u?

Skydancer: I'm not far away

Angel13: is it u sending me notes?

<Skydancer sent sound – gunshot>

Angel13: STOPTHAT!!!

Skydancer: Sorry sorry not trying 2 scare u just messing

Angel13: Yeah well stop messing too

Angel13: Honest if that's u Cha with another nick I'll murder u when I see u next

Skydancer: told u not cha

Skydancer: u mean charlie

Skydancer: this isn't charlie

Angel13: Yeah well who then?

Angel13: Is that u Tinker?

Angel13: Ur always messing.

Skydancer: no not tinker

Angel13: Look ur NOT scaring me ok? I don't like this but ur SO not scaring me

Angel13: If u don't tell me who u r I'm leaving ok?

Skydancer: sorry ok I'll tell u

Skydancer: well like I can't actually tell u but honest I am ur friend and I'm not trying 2 scare u

Skydancer: don't tell n e 1 I've been in tho

Angel13: Y not? Who r u?

Skydancer: can't tell u

Skydancer: they don't kno I can still get in

Angel13: "still"?

Angel13: R u the 1 who keeps sending me that note?

Angel 13: and texts and emails?

Angel13: Start telling me something or I leave

Angel13: Right. I'm outta here

Skydancer: yes

Skydancer: I sent u note and txts and emails

Angel13: Now we're getting somewhere

Angel13: Y u sent me them?

Angel13: WHY?

Skydancer: can't say

Angel13: Sod this

Skydancer: believe me I'm ur friend

Skydancer: prolly ur best friend

Angel13: Yeah... likely

Skydancer: please stay away from there

Angel13: Yeah I got the note and the text and everything, but that's all u ever say. U don't tell me why.

Angel13: Will u tell me why?

Skydancer: somethings gonna happen

Angel13: What?

Angel13: What's going to happen?

Skydancer: do u kno who the yellows are?

Angel13: No. Who are they?

Skydancer: do u know who the avenging angels

are?

Angel13: No.

Angel13: Who are they?

Angel13: Are they the enemy?

Angel13: Hello?

Angel13: U don't say much do you

Angel13: Speak to me dammit

Angel13: *hums a little tune while she's waiting*

<Angel13 sent sound – bark>

Angel13: Sky? Speak to me

Angel13: R u there?

Angel13: This is just going nowhere.

<Skydancer has left the room>

Angel13: sh1t!

<Angel13 has left the room>

Something was going to happen, was it? I had this on my mind the whole weekend. Things were happening all the time. They went on happening. They always do. The more things that happen the more you change. The more things happened to me the more I changed. The moment I plunged through the metal fence, I now realised, my whole life changed for ever. Things are supposed to change when you reach my age, but the speed with which things had changed since that moment was something else. This particular weekend at the end of this particular fortnight was one time that I really felt that I had really become the monster in my own dream. Everything I did was suddenly like the outspread arms, the moronic growling. I felt that I had been sucked into the whole thing, no longer special but helpless. I tried to fight it. I tried hard.

If failing includes spending the day googling everything I could find on the Apocalypse, the End Times, Armageddon, the whole thing, and trying to factor in Avenging Angels and Yellows, then I failed. I went through site after site that totally creeped me out, but I kept on going. If mum and dad could have seen the pages I was turning up – everything from fundamentalist Christian sects to Satanism – I swear they would have dragged me off the PC; but I always had a safe page minimised which I could bring onto the screen if I heard them coming. All day I sat there, and I know I was messing with my mind – badly – but the need to understand it all was taking me over.

For a couple of hours I was multi-tasking. I had about a dozen windows open, including one with the whole text of Revelation, and about three others on news agency sites where I scanned the headlines. I don't know why. It seemed to make sense at the time. Often I was driven demented by sites that would not close, sites that looped round and round to get you back where you started, pop-ups, you name it. I had to reboot three times and run my anti-virus software, to stop a message about blood coming on my screen, and a page I didn't want continually setting itself as my home page. I kept wondering, stupidly, whether Skydancer had got inside my PC. By the end of the day I knew two things. One: on the internet, insanity is never more than one click away. Two: there was nothing, nothing useful or that made sense, connecting "Avenging Angels" and "Yellows" to anything about the "End of the World". Beyond that, the need to understand was nowhere near being dealt with.

You don't want to hear about the dreams I had that night. Trust me.

The Everywhen Angels

CHAPTER 9
'FAIR IS FOUL, AND FOUL IS FAIR; HOVER THROUGH THE FOG AND FILTHY AIR'

I hadn't shaken any of this off by the time the next Monday came around. I dawdled over breakfast and getting my uniform on. Mum shouted at me that I would be late for the school bus and she wasn't going to take me in the car if I missed it. I had to run even though I didn't want to. I sat on the bus looking out of the window, passing places I vaguely recognised from missions and others that were part of ordinary life, and I felt disconnected from it all. I didn't get up right away when the bus stopped, but kept looking out of the window. A low chuckle behind me, as people got off, could well have been Christine Cook, and indeed there she was a few seconds later, smirking up at me from outside.

"You want to get off, love?" said the driver, loudly, when I was the only person left on the bus. It was what they call a rhetorical question, so I didn't answer. Hugging my bag to my chest, I got off the bus without another word, and walked slowly towards the school. I so did not want to be here today, but I caught sight of Charlie waiting for me. He beckoned, and I hurried a little.

"I'll see you inside, Ange."

I nodded. "Wait for me on the drive."

He went his way, I went mine – back to the metal fence – and pushed my way in. Yes, pushed. For some reason I found it tough going, and gasped with the effort, fetching up on the drive and nearly staggering into Charlie, who caught my arms and held me steady. He looked hard at me.

"Ange you look rough," he said.

"Oh thanks!"

"You know I didn't mean it like that. I mean maybe like you haven't slept, or you're really worried about something. Is something the matter? Tell me, Ange."

"There's nothing the matter," I said, but I didn't move, didn't make to move towards the school or anything. I just stood there, not even really looking at Charlie, how ever much he tried to catch my eye. Then I said, "Charlie, you would tell me if there was something going on, wouldn't you – something I don't know about? You'd tell me if there was something I needed to know but no one had told me? You wouldn't keep me in the dark? If you or the others knew more than you are letting on about this whole thing – the war, the Risings, the missions – you would tell me, wouldn't you? Charlie, I need to know you would tell me. You and I are more than just Guardian Angels together. We are. We're more. We're an item, and that means something, you know it does. If you know anything, you have to tell me."

I let him catch my eye then, and I searched his for something, some give-away. I could see nothing, only what I took to be concern.

"What's up, Ange? You look... I don't know... frightened. Has anything happened to scare you?" he said.

"No, I'm not frightened."

"I wouldn't blame you if you were. This whole

thing can sometimes seem weird – I don't pretend it isn't. There is so much Janet has never told me, and I don't think she knows herself. We all get like this some time, I know I do. But there is one thing I know, Ange, we have to keep doing what we're doing. That's all there is to it. We have to keep doing what we're doing."

"Just keep on doing it and never question it, whatever happens?" I asked.

"I guess so."

"Charlie, does your family get a local paper at home?" I asked. Charlie shook his head.

"No. Why?"

I set my bag down on the tarmac and unzipped the front compartment. I took out the weekend newspaper – I'd kept it – and held up the front page to Charlie. He looked at it, and looked at me.

"So?" he said. "What am I supposed to be looking at?"

"Recognise anyone?" I asked. He looked again, his gaze flicking between the few photos on the front page. Then he stopped and opened his eyes wide.

"This bloke who drowned... I mean I never got a good look at the bloke by the canal, but is this him?"

"Uh huh."

Charlie whistled, and then pulled the newspaper down from between us.

"No wonder you're spooked," he said, and I felt a bit annoyed, because 'spooked' was not what I was feeling. But I said nothing. I let him go on. "Look, put that back in your bag. Maybe we'll get a chance to talk the whole thing over with Janet and a couple of the others. We'll see, eh?"

I folded the newspaper, and put it back in my bag.

"Now I think I can see what's giving you grief," said Charlie. "You save a guy's life... and it was bloody brilliant, by the way, nothing can stop it being bloody brilliant... and then a couple of weeks later he's gone."

"That's it!" I said. "That's just it. We are supposed to be doing something really, really special, something big, or a little piece of something big. And so I do this, and now it's all been for nothing, or so it seems."

"You don't know that. You don't know where that guy had to be between then and now. You don't know what he might have had to do."

"No I don't. But anyway..."

I still didn't make any move to go into the school. I didn't do anything. I just stood there. It felt like there was something hard in my stomach.

"I can't tell you what this weekend has been like, Charlie," I said. "I think I'm going paranoid. I said I wasn't scared, and maybe that's true. But I do think someone out there is trying to get at me. Maybe trying to help me, maybe trying to scare me off, I just don't know. Did you know that on the web you can find just about everything you could ever want to know about the last war between good and evil, and a whole lot of stuff you never even dreamed of, and a whole lot of stuff you wish you hadn't asked about. But not one word is there anywhere which squares with what we're doing or think we're doing. It doesn't appear, it isn't there. Slice it as thin as you like, define a search any way you want, you get nothing. We don't exist. What we're doing doesn't exist. Unless I have missed something somewhere, the whole world's body of knowledge excludes us. Oh but the things that are there, Charlie... I mean yesterday I went for a walk, and everything I looked at I wondered whether it was a sign or a portent or something, or had a hidden meaning. I walked past churches when people were coming out, and I caught the eye of some of them, and I wondered if there was something significant about the length of time their eyes held mine, or the colour of their hair, or what they were wearing. I heard songs on the radio, and wondered whether the words had coded meanings. I looked in the sky for bloody cloud shapes. Nothing. None of it tied up. We don't fit in, Charlie. It's like we don't belong anywhere. We're supposed to be special and important, part of something that the whole of Western civilisation has been talking about and ranting about for two thousand years, and we don't exist. We don't fit in. We don't belong. We don't exist..."

I paused for breath.

"Charlie – who are the Yellows? Who are the Avenging Angels?"

Charlie looked at me for a while. Then he reached forward, put his arms round me, and held me in a hug. It was the best I had felt for two days. I didn't argue about it, I didn't worry that we were going to be in way later than everyone else. And for a while too I didn't care that Charlie hadn't answered my questions. I just let myself be held. I just lost myself in that for a few minutes, and everything felt all right again... well, sort of... as all right as it could be.

Suddenly Charlie's grip stiffened. He pushed me away and started looking around. Then he grabbed my hand. "Run!" he cried. "Quick, come on!"

I looked round too, but in increasing confusing, trying but failing to see some danger, an enemy bearing down on us, a tree falling, anything. There was nothing. I started to panic without knowing why. Something was wrong, something in the air, something in my mind was pulling me away from the school building, which seemed to be making peculiar angles with the sky and ground. I rubbed my eyes with my free hand, because they felt as though they had grit or sand in them, or as though I was struggling to become awake. Still Charlie tugged at my hand, pulling me towards the school, making me run.

"What? What?"

"Can't you feel it? The Rising?" he shouted, as though to make himself heard above a wind – and indeed there was a rushing in my ears, and a cawing from the crows that was almost like they were screaming. Yes, I could feel that a Rising was taking place, but unlike every other time, even the last one which had come to me first, there was something which felt badly wrong to me. This time Charlie had caught it first out here, and it had hit me unawares. I was scared and held back, even though Charlie dragged me along, the fingers of his hand digging into my wrist, towards and into the school building.

I had a sense of a great rip in time and space, of a hole that sloped gradually at its lip, but then its sides steepened sharply and plunged into nothingness, like a black hole. I felt in total peril, but not of being sucked down into it, and falling helplessly, but of something that was forcing its way up and out. The vision of the Rising was not clear to me yet, I could see nothing clearly, but I knew that there was a great horror about to happen. Was this what Skydancer had meant? My free hand clenched hard at my little Book of Common Prayer.

It was only when we reached the others, in the classroom, and our consciousness, our ability to see, joined with theirs, that things settled, swam into place, solidified in mind. What I saw, I knew the others saw too. There indeed was the pit, the hole in the dimensions. It was impossible to say whether it was tiny, dancing before our eyes, or billions of miles wide and we were hanging in space above it. But it was dark, and deep, and total, and that darkness, depth, and totality somehow... shone! Suddenly I could see something, some things, begin to crawl out of it. I thought at first it was spiders, and yes they did look like that; but as they got nearer or grew bigger – it was impossible to tell which – the legs, the bellies, the heads seemed to be made out of dry, burned, blackened bones, human ribcages and skulls. I wanted to run, but I couldn't. I could feel that the others were fighting fear too, and the mass of crawling, brown-and-charcoal-coloured bones wriggled and writhed out of the pit – more and more of them, until they were mimicking spiders no longer, but were just spewing out like sewage, in a huge, grey-black wave.

I could feel the relentless seething, rather than hearing the bones rattling. The fear that made me want to run was mixed with a horrible power which kept me rooted to the spot and commanded my senses – the senses of my vision – to watch, to hear, to smell and taste the choking dryness of the air, to feel the vibrations of this surging mass of filth. I have no idea how long it went on, but it felt like hours, and there I sat, thinking that any moment I would just let go of my bowels or the contents of my stomach.

All at once we became aware of something

different happening. The mass of bones was still rumbling out of the pit, but in the centre something bright was glowing. Small at first, like a star, but then growing or approaching, taking on human form. The figure was dressed in white, and it had the look of an angel, shining, almost blinding us. It seemed so wrong that such a saintly figure could be rising with and out of the filth that surrounded it. There was a look of bliss on its face, its hands were clasped in prayer, it seemed, and its eyes were raised to some distant horizon. But the more we looked at that face, the more its look was like one of those old paintings – the expression was fixed, artificial, a mockery of holiness – and as we realised that, we knew how come it could raise its head amongst all that filthy stuff.

The vision, the Rising, was suddenly snuffed out, but in the split-second before it was taken for us, I heard several people gasp, and one person cry out. In that split-second we had all recognised the face of the being in white. I could not take it in. I had seen exactly what my friends had seen, but I was sitting with my mouth open, wanting to say something, but as good as struck dumb. I looked from face to face. I saw disbelief, I saw growing anger, I saw fear... I looked directly at Charlie, and saw a look I couldn't fathom at all. Yes, I had recognised the face just as they had all done, I wasn't going mad, or maybe I was after all.

The face had been mine.

Some instinct took me over. My reason – what was left of it – told me to stay and question it. I listened to something quite different from my reason, and while they were still sitting, before anyone could say or do anything, I ran.

CHAPTER 10
BECOMING A HOODIE

I ran home. I had no idea where else to go. I sat in my room thinking. Over-thinking. Thank God mum was working late that day, or there would have been awkward questions. I didn't want to be asked awkward questions on a day when none of mine were being answered.

The next day I bunked off school. I had never done that before, I never saw the point. There is nowhere to go around here, nowhere you wouldn't bump into someone who knows you. This was different anyhow. I had just spent a sleepless night, lying in bed, convincing myself that I could project some kind of shield round myself so the Avenging

Angels, whoever they were, couldn't get me and the Guardian Angels couldn't find me. For all I knew, it worked – maybe I had even more powers I didn't know about. There were moments I doubted everything, those moments when I was actually falling asleep and jerked myself awake. Whether I tried to lie in the dark, or switched my bedside light on, there was always a moment when a figure seemed to loom over my bed, or approach me from the shadows – some kind of bogeyman, more or less human – or there were colours and shapes on my walls that shouldn't have been there. All I really knew was the Angels thought I was a Yellow, an enemy of some sort. I wasn't, I knew I wasn't, but to them it was as plain as day. All through the waking night, when I wasn't half-sleeping prey to the bogeyman or to the weird shapes and colours, I kept seeing that look in their eyes, the look of disbelief turning into hatred, and Charlie Seacole's look, which I had not been able to read at all.

And sometimes I would feel like wringing my hands, wishing I had taken notice of the note in purple ink which I had found when I had got home from my first mission... and of the texts on my Blackberry, and the of emails, and of Skydancer in the chat room. If only I could have turned back the clock to a time when my only worry was Christine Cook and the Patels, and to a time when a suicide in the newspaper would have simply been a sad story about someone who – thank God – I didn't know.

At other times I wanted to creep downstairs, boot up my laptop, and drive myself mental on the web again. I could feel an urge to log on to the chat room, see if anyone was there, and try to explain. I battled with this urge and beat it down. I so did not want to draw attention to myself.

When dawn came, I felt a little better, even though I was shattered for lack of sleep. I showered, and got into my school clothes. But I hid my books under the bed, stuffed my combat pants, trainers, and a hoodie into my backpack, and made some show of eating breakfast.

"What's the matter with you today?" said dad, not unkindly. I grunted, like a teenager is supposed to do, and instantly felt sorry. But it was too late. Once you hurt someone, even a little bit, you can't take it back. I kept my head down when he said goodbye to me and mum. What was one more broken thing right now? If I had tried to explain I would have booked a one-way ticket to the psychiatrist.

I headed off at the normal time, and it all seemed so easy. If you turn right instead of left at the end of our avenue you come to some allotments, and I had noticed months before that there is a space between two of the sheds where you can go and not be seen, unless someone actually comes to one of the sheds. That's where I made for, trying not to cast paranoid glances over my shoulder. Once I was there, in between the two sheds, with the scent of old, dry timber in my nostrils, I relaxed and waited, sitting on a plank balanced between a couple of rockery stones.

I waited beyond the time that the school buses went, adding a safety margin for stragglers having to hurry along by foot or with mum in the car. I waited beyond the time I knew that the school bell had rung, and when any teacher who had overslept would by then have shot all the amber lights on the way to the school car park and would now be cruising around grumbling about the lack of a parking space. I waited as long as I could – not too long, not long enough to give the Guardian Angels time to be given some idea of where I was by a Rising – and absurdly the thing that worried me was being spotted by someone's mum or dad on their way to work or shopping. And when I could wait no longer, I changed my clothes, out there in the open air, hoping that no one with more than a passing interest in half-dressed teenage girls was watching.

A count of fifteen – my hoodie, combats, and

trainers were laid out on the plank. Another look round to make sure I wasn't observed. A count of ten – my school shirt and tie came off. Five – my shoes, and I felt grit and stones under my socks. Another ten – my school trousers were round my ankles and I stepped out of them, shivering as the breeze touched my legs. Ten again – no, fifteen – as I grabbed my combats, got them the right way round, and stepped into them, the extra time being for getting my left foot jammed two-thirds the way down one leg, and having to hop about, pulling them down again. With my combats on I felt safer. Five seconds – my hoodie was over my head and my hands thrust all the way through the arms. Another five and I had stepped into my trainers and was lacing them up.

All that time, I had been counting, as though it was vital to my survival. But once I had all my casual gear on, I sat back down on the plank and breathed out. A big breath. I seemed to have been holding my breath up until then. I didn't exactly fold up my school clothes, but I took my time stuffing them into my backpack, the shoes first. Now I was changed, I didn't want to leave this temporary place of safety between the two sheds.

But I felt I had to move on. To be honest, I had no idea what to do next. Could I run away? Where to? How far could I go without being found, either by someone in this war that was supposed to be going on, or by the police looking for a runaway girl? I hadn't thought this through, and I didn't actually want to think it through. I couldn't have done so at that stage, anyhow. I just needed some time out. Time out before it all caught up with me again.

I stepped out from between the sheds, trying to fall into the walking pace of someone who was meant to be there. I didn't want to look furtive, hesitant, hurried, or anything. I had my hood up – that was a risk, because to many people a hooded youngster was a troublemaker. But there was the occasional spit of a raindrop on the wind, so I had an excuse. I walked out of the allotment gate, took a left turn, and headed in the opposite direction from the route to school.

The day was close, the streets seemed quiet, it was like everywhere was waiting for a thunderstorm. Or, as Skydancer had – what? – prophesied, for something to happen.

CHAPTER 11
MORE WARS, MORE RUMOURS
OF WARS

I walked until I came to a railway station, where I bought one of those rover tickets, the ones that mean you can travel anywhere in the city. I remembered not to ask for a half-fare, so that maybe the Customer Advisor would just assume I was a young-looking adult, not a kid bunking off school, and I... travelled. I went aimlessly back and forth across the network of underground and overground lines that make a coloured spider-web across the city, on those maps you see on station walls. Like I said, I felt like I wanted to run, just not very far, and I hopped from train to train. The city was a place youngsters are supposed to run to, not from, and I was too much of a coward to get out at a main-line station and take a train north... away. I suddenly wanted to leave myself the option, at the end of the day, to scuttle home and hide under my bedclothes, and pretend everything was ordinary.

As I rode the train, I rested my cheek against the cold window, and looked out. In tunnels, and in the long, underground stretches, I was aware of a little bit of my own reflection, and sometimes I could also see the reflections of people stealing glances at me, sometimes staring longer. I didn't care what they made of me – a druggie, some lost soul whom care-in-the-community had failed – I simply kept looking out of the window.

Passengers came and went, boarded and alighted, rustled newspapers and sandwich bags, listened to the hiss of iPods over tiny earpieces, made occasional banal conversation into iPhones, rattled on laptops, whistled, sighed, read The Girl with the Dragon Tattoo or some other dog-eared best-seller from a station book-stall, engaged in conversation – he said this, then she said that, then I said why don't you both shut up, and anyway, and so and so, and on and on. Sometimes the conversation was in a language I didn't understand, and I would sneak a look, and see two men in long, collarless shirts, baggy trousers, little caps of the same fabric, their lips moving rapidly above fringed beards. Their faces seemed forbidding and alien – although God knows I had seen Pakistani and Bangladeshi men before – until I caught sight of some kindliness hiding in a pair of dark eyes. Or sometimes it was a small knot of lean, tanned men around twenty years old at a guess, with rucksacks, chattering and drinking from water-bottles. Once a man with dreadlocks and intense eyes wandered in through the connecting door at one end of our carriage and out through the other, ranting without pausing for breath; scary, but his words I caught, as he passed, and I strained to hear him as he left the carriage. I almost followed him, but something, a leaden tiredness, kept me on my seat.

"...she shall dwell in the wilderness and be fed in the wilderness and be led out of the wilderness and shall bear a man-child who shall rule with a rod of iron and he shall ride upon a white horse and shall bear a name upon him..."

I recognised the words, but not the order in which they came.

I had been looking out at a part of the city I didn't recognise grey, high-rise blocks like oblong fingers pointing at a sky that seemed to be turning to the sort of colours I used to get when I was a kid and I played with my paint box, mixing yellows, reds, white. I was drifting, I think I was falling asleep, imagining heaps of brown, grey bones stacked up behind every façade.

"What's that you have there?"

I looked up. For the first time since I had got on any train that day, someone had spoken directly to me. For the first time since I had got on any train that day, I looked directly into someone's face. A man, in his forties I guess, clean shaven, neat hair, wearing a suit, a white shirt, a plain-blue tie. He had his arm tucked over a bulging pilot-bag, as though protecting something precious, and one leg crossed over the other, revealing an inch of leg above a sock which almost matched his tie. His shoe, dangling in front of him, was impossibly shiny; I couldn't see the other one, but the stupid idea came into my head that he hid it because it was the dirty one. I couldn't help smiling, and he must have taken that for encouragement, because he smiled back, and I saw two rows of perfect teeth. I saw he had one of those name-badges people wear at conferences and, for some reason, to and from their hotels; a simple cross, almost like a watermark, and over that, the words "Elder Phillips". We were alone in the carriage, and he had taken a seat opposite me.

"What's that you have there?" he repeated, pointing towards my right hand. I heard an American twang in his voice.

"It's a prayer-book," I said at last. "An Anglican Book of Common Prayer."

"You're bleeding on it," he said.

"Oh sh...!" I looked down and became aware of a small paper-cut on one finger, which was staining the edges of the pages red. I stuffed it in my pocket and fumbled for a tissue to wrap around the finger.

"Here," he said, handing me a clean, folded handkerchief.

"I couldn't," I said.

"You could," he said, still smiling. "And you will. My wife packs me dozens of the things!"

"Thank you, then."

There was a pause. I was about to look away again.

"Are you a believer?" he asked.

"Sorry?"

"Are you a believer? Are you saved?"

I paused before I answered. "I don't go to one of those churches where they all wave their hands in the air and look impossibly happy. In fact I don't go to church at all. I don't think I like preachers much – I'm sorry if you are one – I don't like the way they tell you it's all very simple, but then they store up all this knowledge in their heads which isn't easy at all..."

I was on a roll – never mind that mum had always told me not to speak to strangers, it was as though something was taking me over, something like whatever had made the man in dreadlocks rant through the train. Besides which, the not-talking-to-strangers rule was one I had broken already.

"...I've read the Bible, you know. We did Bible stories at school, and once I picked it up I couldn't put it down. It's weird, scary, wonderful, hard like iron sometimes, other times it is like poetry. I write poetry. And it's like a mystery. I hear preachers on cable saying such-and-such a passage means this, and such-and-such a passage means that, and I find myself saying, 'No it doesn't, it means something completely different, it's obvious it does, but what?' I know I believe in something."

He looked out of the window.

"Shall I tell you something I believe, and then you can tell me what you think of it?" he asked. Without waiting for me to say yes or no, he went on speaking.

"See all this out here? It's all going to end. It's not going to last much longer. It's all there, plain as day, in the Bible, in the Book of Revelation and in other prophecies.

"You're an intelligent young woman, I am sure you know your late twentieth century history. Right from the moment that the state of Israel was formed in 1948, and the Arab nations around it began to make war on it, Believers have known that we were moving towards Armageddon – the last great Battle. Then the European Community was formed, only back then it was called the Common Market, based on the Treaty of Rome. We have seen it growing and growing, until now we see it for what it is – the Roman Empire reborn. In 1995 the state of Israel negotiated associate status with this new Roman Empire, and entered into it on June first 2000. Soon the European Community will be one single nation, and it will have one single president – at first he will be elected, but then he will simply take over the reins of power as a charismatic leader. That president will be the Anti-Christ. He will promise world peace, and many professing Christians will flock to him; but he will lead them into all kinds of wrong things, and away from faith in Jesus Christ. He will create a single monetary system, like the Euro already is, and no one will be able to buy or sell without his mark upon them. The technology exists to do this already, by a tattooed QR-code, or a tiny micro-chip under the skin.

"This Anti-Christ will appear to be a great peacemaker, as foretold in the Book of Daniel. But he will impose martyrdoms on true Christians, who will be persecuted just like they were in the days of the Caesars; I mean he will really persecute them, they will be outcasts, punished by the law for their beliefs – you can see this happening right now. He will bring about some kind of global disarmament, but it will be a false peace. His ally will be the Great Harlot – a false religion which will seem attractive to many just like a whore is attractive to her customers. Excuse my language, but it's the only way I can say it.

"But then it will be fully revealed that this global peacemaker, this charismatic leader is possessed by the Beast from the abyss, and is himself the Beast, and by then it will be too damn late! He will unleash such persecution on the remaining Christians and Jews, many of whom will have converted to faith in Jesus Christ and will have preached the Gospel. Young lady, I have myself heard many a former Judaist preaching the Good News! This period of persecution is what the Apostle John called the Great Tribulation. And Jerusalem itself will be trampled, as he foretold in chapter eleven.

"It is prophesied that the Islamic nations will rise up against Israel, but as Ezekiel chapter thirty-eight, verse thirteen says - Sheba and Dedan, and the merchants of Tarshish, with all the young lions thereof, will say to you, have you come to take a spoil? 'Sheba and Dedan' means Saudi Arabia; 'Tarshish' was the old name for the city of Cadiz, but here it means the developed Western Nations; and the 'young lions', well they're the nations of the British Commonwealth. They'll be standing aloof from it all. And eventually the Anti-Christ himself will raise the greatest army the world has ever seen and invade the Middle East – you think it's all going to stop at Iraq? And there, right there at the valley of Meggido – Armageddon as it is called in the Bible – the last great battle will occur. Jesus Christ himself will come with his own great army and slaughter the Beast's army.

"All this was prophesied by the Lord Jesus

himself, when he said, in Matthew twenty-four, verses six and seven - You shall hear of wars and rumours of wars... for nation shall rise against nation, and kingdom against kingdom. Just look at the news, young lady. Since the World War of 1914, the whole world has been at war in one place or another, constantly. It is all one single war, constantly going on. And it is going on right now, right here. The Bible even predicted the invention of nuclear and biological weapons - And should destroy them which destroy the earth – Revelations eleven, eighteen; and – For then shall be great tribulation... and except those days should be shortened, there should no flesh be saved – Matthew chapter twenty-four, verses twenty-one and twenty-two. Missiles were prophesied – I saw the horses in the vision... for their power is in their mouth, and in their tails were like unto serpents, and had heads, and with them they do hurt – Revelations chapter nine, verses seventeen, nineteen.

"There is so much more – increase in population, plagues... well we have seen the threat of aids, and bird flu, what else might come along?... fear and anxiety..."

Eventually he stopped. I became aware that he was looking at me.

"Well, go on. Tell me I'm crazy for believing all that," he said with a smile. Not what I would have expected him to say.

"I don't think you're crazy," I said. "I've heard it all before. Many times. I only thought it was crazy the first time. No, you're not crazy."

"Thank you," he said. And then, "What do you believe in?"

"Angels. I believe in angels."

"Angels? Why, I believe in those too," he said, his smile broadening. "Be not forgetful to entertain strangers: for thereby some have entertained angels unawares. – Hebrews, chapter thirteen, verse two. They're everywhere. You never know when you're going to meet one. For all you know, I might be one. For all I know, you might be one!"

"Yes I might," I said, and I couldn't help grinning. He seemed like a nice man, but I had had enough of the conversation. "This is my station."

I got up from my seat and went out of the carriage onto the platform. As the train pulled away, I looked through the passing windows for the man. I didn't see him. It was as though he wasn't there at all. But I still had his handkerchief wrapped round my finger, so that was real enough. A gift from another stranger I wasn't supposed to speak to.

It wasn't my station, this one where I had got out. It was the next one up the line. I had started to recognise things through the window as we travelled along, familiar buildings had started to emerge from the dreamy, scary landscape. I wanted to go home now, no matter what was waiting for me. This station was as good a place as any from which to begin that process. I hoped.

CHAPTER 12
YELLOW IS THE NEW BLACK

People were filling the platform again as I made for the exit. Some of them had run down the stairs and looked crossly at the train as it pulled away. More people were coming down the stairs in a leisurely fashion, others were thronging the concourse, or queuing for tickets, or buying newspapers and Mars Bars from the kiosk. There were toddlers, mums with push-chairs, a crowd of people who must have been from the local offices getting home early. I had no idea this station got so busy. There were even a couple of nuns.

I walked out into the street, turned left, and headed along the pavement. A gusty, warm wind had sprung up from nowhere. It was too gusty, too warm, it tugged at my clothes, blew dust in my eyes, made me squint. Then I realised that this wind wasn't doing anything else. Nothing was affected by it. Litter stayed still, bushes didn't move, an awning above a shop didn't ripple in response. The wind was only happening to me, the dust was only in my eyes and no one else's. I was only vaguely aware of people's glances as I staggered and leant against a lamp post. Things in the street, began to blur, I could see nothing out of the corner of my eye except a grey sea-like swirling.

"Oh no," I thought. "Not again! Not now!" A Rising...

It came on me quickly. Suddenly I couldn't see a thing, as though I was staring into and down a dark tunnel... nothing except for one figure walking briskly towards me along the pavement. It was as though this one person, a man about dad's age in chinos and a corduroy jacket, had his own spotlight hovering in the air above him. It showed him and little bits of the pavement where he walked, and things he walked past. I couldn't take my eyes off him. There was a voice in my head, a silent voice but somehow it seemed to deafen me. It seemed to be saying, "Him... save him... stop him."

He came closer, closer, almost abreast of me, almost passing me. the voice, the compulsion to do something, took hold of me, would not let me go, would not let me do nothing. I took a few backward paces and dodged round in front of the man. We sidestepped. He tried to get past him, but I leapt at him and pushed him backwards.

"Stop, Mister, stop!" I yelled. "You can't go into the station, you can't get the next train!"

He staggered against the plate-glass of a shop window, making it bong like Big Ben. His mouth fell wide open as I shoved him back down the street, the palms of my hands on his chest. Then he recovered and pushed back.

"What the... you friggin' little maniac! Who the hell are you pushing? You little thug! Help... Police!"

He whacked at my head with his open hand, slapping at me. Every time he slapped he grunted through clenched teeth, his eyes blazing with indignation. Although I tried to duck, two out of every three slaps took me on the side of my head, and they hurt. My head fizzed, my left ear was hot and stinging, and I yelped every time a slap landed. People were looking, hurrying past to get to the station, but I kept on pushing at him, sometimes driving him back, sometimes being forced back myself. I wouldn't quit, I couldn't quit, the voice, the compulsion, wouldn't let me quit. Then suddenly, everything changed...

It was like that moment when I had first lunged towards that metal fence outside the school. The man and I both lost our footing, and as we fell towards the pavement, as I put my hand out to take what I knew was going to be an agonising, stiff-armed jar to break my fall, my vision cleared. Re-focussed. Changed.

I saw through someone else's eyes. I felt someone else's rapid pulse, someone in the already crowded train that was pulling into the platform I had left only a few minutes before. I knew what was in his backpack, I shared his thoughts of paradise, the nobility of what he was about to do, the holiness of his purpose, the sanctity of the wonderful cause he was about to die for, to kill for. And my own feeling flooding through me, shocking me, was one of utter pity. I wanted so desperately to be allowed to save him from this, to make him not do this terrible thing that was in his mind. I wanted to call out to him, "You're wrong... it doesn't work like that... you don't have to do this..." and to see the look of relief in his eyes as he clung on to life, crying. Here was a life worth saving, a person worth the struggle. But I was nowhere near, I was in the middle of a fall to the pavement, with the man whom I was saving from getting on that train. I was too far away even to share the consequence of what he was doing, too busy saving this other man who was still fighting me as he fell. This sudden, clear look into the mind of the man I couldn't touch, couldn't save, the man with a backpack full of explosives, the sharing of his thoughts and emotions, the cold, steel wall between mine and his, this was not a rising. This was something different. More beautiful. More terrifying.

I felt the suicide's last, calm breath, as he watched the second-hand on his watch close up on the hour. I heard the detonation and the explosion long before it reached the stunned ears of the man I was falling onto. I felt, from inside the heads of each person close to the suicide, dozens of lives wink out of existence. Then within a second, as my elbow thumped into the man's stomach and winded him, I felt the searing heat envelope those who died next, felt it go as soon as it came, as they too died. As I landed heavily on my stiff right arm, I felt the flying glass, the twisted metal, the blast, the moment of fear and pain that struck the next nearest group of people. Then that too was blotted out. As the jolt of the hard pavement shot up my arm to my shoulder, I felt the burning, crushing, sheering that did not go away so quickly. This blinding, the panic of pain, made me scream with their screams, as I rolled on the pavement. The crushing, the breaking of bones, the bursting of things inside people that seconds ago had been whole, the suffocation as the hot air shot upwards. The shouts, the half-choked words, the child's last terrified cry of "Mummy!" I felt myself murmur, "Hail Mary full of grace..." with one of the nuns, as a great weight forced the life out of her. I felt the terrible, crucifying pain of the dying, the maimed, the soon-to-die. I felt the fear, the bewilderment of those who limped and staggered, the panic of those who barged their way back up the stairs. Nothing but pain and terror.

Now I too was back on my feet, leaving the man I had saved gasping on the pavement. Clutching my wrist, ignoring the hurt in my shoulder, I ran, and ran, and ran – it felt as though I had been running for ever, as though I had never known anything but running. Would I ever do anything but run? Was I running from something or to it, and how the hell was I supposed to know any more?

The station was less than a mile from my school. I had only one thing in my mind, and that was to get there and to scream at the Guardian Angels for what they had made me do. I ran hard. I ran though my legs had turned to jelly, I ran though the breath hurt my lungs like a knife was being driven into them. I kept running on willpower alone, when I knew I had no strength left in my body. When I reached the school, I threw myself at the fence, felt myself push my way in though it resisted almost angrily, and rolled on the tarmac. If my wrist was broken, I couldn't feel it as I forced myself up to my feet. From somewhere I found the reserves to run again, into the deserted school. I wasn't even in the classroom where we met when I started to yell.

"Why did you make me do that? Why him? Why not all those other people? I know you all saw the rising. Why didn't you let me go and stop the man with the bomb? Why the bloody hell did they all have to die? Why the hell are we Guardian Angels if we can't bloody guard people? Why?"

The last "Why?" I had gasped out as I hung onto the door frame. I had crashed through it, almost wrenching the door off its hinges. No more energy, no more will-power, pain everywhere, my wrist in agony, anger now blinding me as I fought to raise my head on an aching neck. I looked up.

I looked up into faces I didn't recognise. But yes, they were kids from my school, but not the faces I expected. Then I saw. I saw a yellow prefect-badge here, a yellow headband there, dayglo yellow panels on someone's backpack, a sweatband on someone's wrist. I looked at all the faces in the enemy's camp. I looked at the face of Charlie Seacole.

The Everywhen Angels

CHAPTER 13
DEALING

"Wait, Ange... wait!" Charlie yelled at me as I ran out of the front door of the school.

"Why the hell should I?" I yelled back, turning round and walking backwards away from him, almost stumbling actually. I was trying not to cry... I was angry, and the tears were stinging my eyes, but I didn't want to let them out because I knew Charlie would think I was crying about him. Well, of course I would have been crying about him, but not like that.

"It's not how it looks," he said, spreading out his hands.

"Oh don't give me that," I said, still walking away

from him. "It walks like a duck and quacks like a duck, so as far as I am concerned it's a bloody duck..."

"It isn't how it looks, honest."

I pointed a finger at him. "Don't you dare say 'honest' to me! You... you let everyone think I was a traitor. I saw how they looked at me. You could have told them I wasn't. My life was in danger – it still might be. You knew it isn't me who's the traitor, and yet you let that Rising happen without saying a word!"

I was talking rubbish, of course. He could have saved me from everything which had happened after the Guardian Angels had seen me rise from the pit in the midst of all those filthy bones, of course he could. But it would have been at the expense of his own safety. He would have had to blow his own cover. But I was coldly angry. He hadn't needed to be so nice to me, he hadn't needed to go out with me. There was no reason for him to make me like him, to make me like kissing him. Even now, while I burned with anger about what he had done, part of me was worried about what would happen to him – and that made me angrier still.

We kept moving – me backwards, him keeping

pace – while clouds boiled in the sky like they were answering my mood. The more we argued, the more loudly the crows in the trees cawed. There was a current flowing away from the school, and one equally strong tugging us back towards it, and the wind hit us in gusts, first one way then another. It seemed to me as though the world in which the weird, empty school existed was straining, almost coming apart at the seams.

"How do you know I'm a traitor, Ange?" Charlie said. "How do you know I'm not working undercover in the Yellows? Not many people have the gift of being able to come in to the different... planes... of the school. How do you know I wasn't sent to spy on the enemy?"

"You could have told me," I said.

"No I couldn't. How did we know who you really were? Right now how do the Guardian Angels know that you're on their side? You came out of nowhere, when we had twelve people already. If both of us stood up in front of them right now, and said the other one was a traitor, who would they believe? Right now I don't know, myself, but they'd probably believe me before you. Would you risk it? Think, Ange, think! And you kept asking me if I knew who the Yellows were, and who the Avenging Angels were, and making all those comments about not existing. You could have been bluffing, you could have been testing. It could all have been a trick."

"Trick? Hah!"

I took a bad step at that moment, and landed flat on my bum. Charlie unhurriedly made up the distance between us, and stood looking down at me. Once again I couldn't read the expression on his face. He held out a hand to me. I took it and let him pull me up, but my eyes never left his face. When I got on my feet again, Charlie kept hold of my hand. I didn't want to let myself feel how nice that was, but I couldn't help it. Charlie Seacole... my boyfriend.

"Look, let's get away from here. Let's talk somewhere else, outside the school." He pulled on my hand.

"You are always pulling me, Charlie," I said, and twisted my hand from his grip, hating how empty it now felt and how it made me think I had suddenly lost all the nice things we had done in the previous few weeks. Nevertheless, I walked with him towards the school gates, and out of them. The clouds ceased to boil, the crows' racket died down, Charlie and I rejoined the real world. We didn't talk much as we walked, and we didn't touch. I knew I wouldn't ever touch him again. I couldn't. We just walked and walked, until we found a kids' playground with a few swings, a 'teapot-lid', and a see-saw. We took a swing each, and rocked ourselves back and forward a little. We were too tall for the swings – they were slung too low for us – and our feet dragged on the piece of bare earth scooped out of the bark chippings underneath. For a while we still didn't speak.

"What brought you back to school today?" Charlie asked eventually. "What made you burst in on... us? You were yelling something."

I looked at him.

"You didn't see it, did you?" I said. "You didn't share the Rising. It was hidden from you. You didn't see that I had to save one man from being blown up by a bomb that killed loads of other people. All that was hidden from you, because you really are a Yellow!"

Maybe it was a stupid accusation. After all, what guarantee did I have that anyone else had shared that vision I had, and the compulsion to save that particular man.

"I didn't see you do anything," said Charlie.

He sat and listened as I described to him everything that had happened since I had run out on the Guardian Angels, right after the Rising that had marked me out as a traitor. I described my tackling the man, and I told him every thought and feeling that had gone through me as the bomb had gone off and the train had crashed. More than once I saw him wince or shudder. The whole time he kept his eyes on the ground.

When I had finished, he said quietly, "No, you're right. I didn't see any of that."

"So why, Charlie? Why are you a Yellow? Why have you lied and lied to me?"

He turned a face towards me that was full of pain. "Honest, Ange, I haven't lied to you. Not about how I feel. I really, really like you. It's just... oh this thing takes you over... it becomes more important than anything else... you know that... you said so yourself."

He trailed off and looked away again. Then he turned back to me, his face still anguished, but his eyes suddenly bright.

"You have to believe me, Ange, because this is just so important. You're on the wrong side. Yes this last battle is going on, but you aren't one of the good guys. You're on the wrong side. These people you've been saving..."

"Don't tell me, they go on to do horrible things, yeah?"

"Not exactly. Not always," said Charlie. "But they each have a part to play, and it's not for the best. Sometimes it would have been better if... if they hadn't been saved at all."

He wouldn't look at me as he said all this.

"Charlie Seacole, don't you dare sit there and tell me that it's better to let people die, after I have just been through what I have been through. I have been inside people's heads who died. I have been inside people's heads who died, and took minutes to do it, and were in bloody agony while it happened. How the hell can it be better to let people die?"

"If it saves other people in the long run?"

"Yeah, right. But who made you the judge, Charlie? Who tells you who should be allowed to die?" I said. And then the simple answer came to me. "The Yellows have Risings of their own, don't they?"

Charlie nodded.

"But still, that doesn't matter," I went on. "Who has actually come to you and told you who is on the right side? Has anyone ever shown you what is good and what is evil? Or have you just been doing what the Risings tell you to do? I'm right, aren't I? No one has told you, no one has told the Yellows, just like no one has told The Guardian Angels."

Charlie said nothing, but kept on looking at the ground.

I went on again. "That first time I went out with the Guardian Angels, when I saved that woman from being hit by the bus... the boy who bumped into, the boy who ran away, he was a Yellow, wasn't he? You chased him, but your job was to let him get away, wasn't it? The Avenging Angels would have had to have... done something about him... if you had caught him. That's somehow... I don't know... in the rules of this war, right? The Avenging Angels are the ones who – how did you put it? – they 'deal with' things, right?"

"Yes," said Charlie, very simply, still not looking up. I grasped at a straw to save what I still really liked about him. Maybe he had wanted to protect me from everything. I gave him this one last chance to be the Charlie Seacole I really, really liked again.

"Skydancer really was you after all, wasn't it? That was you. You sent me the note, the texts, and the other stuff. Tell me that was you, Charlie. Tell me you wanted to protect me by keeping me out of all this."

He looked up, and stared at me. "What? What? I don't know what you're talking about!"

"Wrong answer," I thought to myself. Then while Charlie kept looking at me, I glanced around. I realised that there were other people in the playground who hadn't been there before. A couple of girls about my age were sitting on the teapot-lid, looking over at us. Someone else was standing in the gateway, and another kid was leaning against the fence. Out of the corner of my eye I could see a handful more coming across the football pitch, and a couple walking up the tarmac path. I didn't recognise them, except that they were kids from our school. I didn't have to count them to know how many there were. Twelve. The Avenging Angels. They were all around us. They had come to 'deal'.

I turned to Charlie, almost all my pity for him gone. Maybe if I got him to come clean, I could find more pity to replace what I had lost. It was a forlorn hope.

"You and I are special, Charlie, aren't we?" I said. "We can do things the others can't. That's why I was able to save a guy single-handed, that's why I found my way into the Yellows' place and found you. You can do things too, can't you? Were you a Yellow first and then a Guardian Angel, or the other way round? Because you can move freely between the real world and both places, can't you? It's almost like you can be in two places at once. And you didn't just see the Rising, where I came out of that filthy pit... you made it happen didn't you? You made us all see my face. What would have been there if you hadn't – yours?"

Charlie had his eyes fixed on my face as I spoke, and he was crying, his face screwed up into a distorted version of the boy I really, really liked.

"Ange, I would never have let anything..." His voice trailed away, though he kept looking at me. Then he seemed to catch sight of the people round us, and for a moment he seemed to grow very calm, though he had expected this to happen. Someone else walked up the tarmac path, through the gate, and over to the swings where Charlie and I were sitting. It was Janet. She put her hand gently on my arm.

"Angela, we have to go. We can't stay here," she

said.

I stood up. Janet started to walk back to the gate and I followed her. At the gate I turned round to look at Charlie. He looked at me, then at the Avenging Angels ranged in a loose circle around him, and his calmness deserted him. He didn't get up, he didn't run, he simply called out.

"Ange, don't leave me!"

But I did leave. Oh yes I looked back, and what I saw turned my stomach, but I did leave. I think I could have stood it if there had been something weird going on – dancing, chanting, magic signs – but there was nothing like that. The Avenging Angles looked exactly like what they were, teenage kids lounging in a playground. Some of them weren't even looking at Charlie – the two girls on the teapot-lid seemed to be engrossed in conversation. It was all so bloody innocuous and innocent.

But Charlie had slumped from his swing, and was propped against the frame, curled almost like an unborn baby. He called my name once, but I wouldn't go back. Part of me wanted to, to talk to him and tell him everything was OK, or to touch him, or something, but I wouldn't. I wouldn't go back. Soon I heard him babble loudly.

"And one of the four beasts gave unto the seven angels seven golden vials full of the wrath of God, who liveth for ever and ever..." he cried, his voice rising in volume and pitch. "And I heard a great voice out of the temple saying to the seven angels, Go your ways, and pour out the vials of the wrath of God upon the earth. And the first went, and poured out his vial upon the earth; and there fell a noisome and grievous sore upon the men which had the mark of the beast, and upon them which worshipped his image. And the second angel poured out his vial upon the sea; and it became as the blood of a dead man: and every living soul died in the sea. And the third angel poured out his vial upon the rivers and fountains of waters; and they became blood..."

Although I could see nothing, I could feel a current like there was in the school, that weird current that rippled and flowed along. But this was like an insistent whirlwind, and it was sucking at the fabric of the world, twisting itself round and round the circle of Avenging Angels, funnelling into the sky. At the dead centre was Charlie Seacole, still babbling and crying out, and even if I had gone back, there was nothing I could have done. I told myself that. Nothing I could have done. It was a lie, of course.

CHAPTER 14
BEING ABLE TO DO THINGS

But I wasn't scared. You could say I was still doing the monster-in-the-dream thing. In my mind, that's exactly what I was doing. It sounds crazy, but it was stopping me from going crazy. In my head, I could feel my arms hanging loosely, my fingers spread out to catch, I could hear my own voice growling. And it was working. All the paranoia, all the confusion, all the nagging ignorance I carried about with me – it was all turning to anger.

I walked along with Janet. I looked at her once or twice, and it seemed as though she was about to speak. But she didn't. It was like she was sacred of me. There was a look in her eyes which, when she looked my way, seemed to say that we both knew something, we shared a secret. But we didn't... or maybe we did and I just hadn't realised it. Maybe she could see or feel the monster-in-the-dream.

I noticed she looked away from me as soon as our eyes met – there was hardly any time to catch that knowing look. I suddenly lost the monster in my head, and felt like a dolphin in the ocean, every inch of my skin, every nerve-end, alive to the tiniest ripples in the weird current. The current had, up to now, seemed to flow at specific times and in specific places – the school, the street outside the railway station, just before at the playground. Now I knew it was everywhere, always, outside, inside, like a sea flowing in and out of every atom of everything. And I felt like I was a supertanker breasting through it, maybe strong enough to weather the worst waves it could throw at me, maybe at its mercy – I didn't know which yet.

I was shivering, and my bottom lip was trembling, but it wasn't from being afraid. It was more like I had triumphed over something, or pushed past a barrier, or come through some great pain. The current flowed round me, reforming behind me like a wake. For a minute or two I wondered if I actually had gone mad after all, and I laughed out loud about the way I had been swinging from one extreme to the other; but I didn't care either way now, and I still wasn't scared. If anyone was scared, it was Janet. Why?

Neither of us said anything. We walked back the way Charlie and I had come, towards the school, and when we got close I began to walk faster, so that I was ahead of Janet. I had suddenly become convinced of something, sure about something, and I wanted to see if I was right. With a hundred metres or so to go I broke into a run, with Janet still a few paces behind me. I didn't stop until I came to the metal fence in front of the waste ground that sat between the school and the builder's yard. There, I just stood and looked at the fence; Janet came up behind me, panting, and stood still too. As I looked at the fence, part of it directly in front of me began to ripple, as though I was looking at it through running water. I gave a sigh, or let out a breath or something, looked harder at the fence, wanting it this to happen. The more I wanted it, the more it happened. The rippling spread to a bigger and bigger bit of the fence, until a big oval patch, taller than me, was rippling, shimmering, changing shape. I wanted harder still, and the rippling part of the fence just ripped in two and spread back, like a hole torn in a wet paper bag. Beyond the rip was... somewhere else... indistinct, vague, but still and peaceful in a way too. It seemed to want me to be scared, but I wasn't, because I knew precisely what that somewhere else was. The main thing was this – I could see my 'way in', I could make it, I could cause it just by thinking about it.

I stepped through, reaching back and pulling Janet with me by the hand. She let out a little shriek, and we arrived on the path to the front door of the school. Janet's face was white. She almost looked as though she was going to be sick. I looked up at the crows on the trees. They were watching me.

"Hi, guys!" I said, and they all scattered, cawing loudly.

Janet and I almost seemed to surf the current, back through the front door of the school, along the corridor, to the classroom which the Guardian Angels must have felt they had made their own. As we went in, some of them raised their eyes, either to look at me with something like wonder, or questioningly at Janet. I let Janet take a seat, but I stood there, almost daring someone to speak. No one did. At last I broke the silence.

"I killed Charlie Seacole."

One of the others shook his head. "No you didn't. We saw. We had a Rising."

"It was the Avenging Angels," said a girl. "It's

what they do. It wasn't you."

"I killed Charlie Seacole," I said again, more loudly, pronouncing every word as though it was in capitals. "Don't tell me what you saw or think you saw. I killed Charlie Seacole as surely as if I had held a sawn-off to his head and pulled the trigger. I killed Charlie Seacole. You can say, if you want, that I let him be killed. But I could have stopped it happening, and I didn't. I don't know why I didn't, and right now I don't know how I feel about it."

"She's right," said Janet, still white-faced. "She could have stopped it. She can... do things. She can make her own way in. She pulled me in with her!"

"But no one can use someone else's way in!"

"I'm just telling you what happened."

I ignored this exchange. "When I ran away from you, after we had that Rising where you saw me on top of the pile of bones, you called on the Avenging Angels, didn't you! Didn't you!"

Janet and a couple of the others nodded.

"It's what we are supposed to do," she said. "But they couldn't find you – not until we had the Rising about what you did by the railway station, and then when you and Charlie went to the playground. They could find you and Charlie. We're not supposed to follow them or interfere, but I did, Ange. We knew by then we had been wrong. We knew Charlie was secretly a Yellow."

"It's what we are supposed to do," I echoed, mocking Janet's voice. "Who has ever told you what you are supposed to do? Tell me that. You can't, can you? You don't know, do you. You don't know why you do what you do any more than the Yellows know why they do what they do, or the Avenging Angels know why they do what they do. You 'save' people... the Yellows allow things to happen to the same people, or stop you from saving them... the Avenging Angels go out and do their thing, and never come back without 'dealing with' someone. That's true, isn't it? And if they hadn't found Charlie, or if I had protected him, they would have tried to work their thing on me. That's true too, isn't it? And none of you know why. No one has ever come and explained to you exactly what is happening. You're just caught up in this because you're having an adventure, and it makes you feel special. You don't really know if there is a war going on between good and evil. And if there is, you don't really know which side you are on. You just assume you're the good guys. And the Yellows probably assume the same. And for all I know the

Avenging Angels do too, but I haven't bothered to ask them, and I don't think I will bother."

I paused and looked at them. Some were staring at me, others were looking away. Janet had a couple of tears rolling down her cheeks.

"You're special, Angela," she said. "You can do things."

"Yes, I can 'do things'," I said, spreading out my hands in front of them. I wanted the light in the room to intensify, to take on an amber colour – it did. I wanted the current to surge and roll around the other Guardian Angels – it did. I was making it happen. I was 'doing things'. I was powerful. I was really special. Really, really special.

I looked down at them all. I had come to think of them as my friends. We had seen Risings together, gone out on missions together, and between times we had talked to each other, texted, emailed, hung out in chat rooms. We had smiled secret smiles, exchanged secret looks. We had been special, we had had adventure. And they had sent the Avenging Angels after me. And I had let the Avenging Angels 'deal' with Charlie Seacole.

"I can do anything," I said, making the current

swirl faster round them. "Anything I want. I can make all kinds of things happen. I'm special. I'm having a fine adventure. And do you know what I am going to do?"

Janet shook her head. So did one or two of the others.

I lowered my hands. The light returned to normal, and the swirling current died away.

"Nothing at all. Because just like you, I'm a failure, a fucking failure. I'm out of here."

I turned and left the room. If any of them wanted to stop me or wanted to follow me, I neither knew nor cared. Neither did I care what they might be saying about me behind my back. For all I knew they would get over this, and the next day they would be out on missions again, having their adventures, feeling that they were special. For the last time in this sidestep-in-space I pushed open the front door and stepped out of the school. For the last time, I walked back towards the main gate, giving a quick glance to the silent, sullen crows ranged on the trees. For the last time I stepped out of the front gate and back into normality.

And straight into Christine Cook's face.

"Someone's out of uniform," she said, blocking my way, flanked by the Patel sisters.

"So what?" I said, poking a hard index finger into her shoulder with each word. "You have a problem with that, Christine? You have a problem with me? 'Coz let's face it – you are the one with the problem here, and if you want to make it a bigger problem, just keep on doing what you are doing!"

For maybe as long as a minute, we stood facing each other in silence. Then she smiled.

"Nah, no problem at all, Poet," she said. "You want to come down the Costa with us, for a latte or something?"

"Cool," I said.

So that's what I did. Sure that was weird, but I'd done and seen weirder. I went for a coffee with my new friends.

CHAPTER 15
THE STUFF WHICH HAPPENED AFTERWARDS

And that's it, really.

Except for the stuff which happened afterwards. Sometimes I regretted the fact that I no longer pushed through the metal fence. Sometimes I was tempted to do things with the current that I still believed I could feel. Sometimes I missed Charlie, missed the boy I really, really liked. Sometimes I pretended that boy hadn't been content to see me 'dealt with' by the Avenging Angels, and I cried a bit.

Mostly I just hung out with Christine, Lakshmi, and Kesha. They were ok. I could talk to them once I got to know them. I could chill out with them and talk about ordinary girl-things, and then maybe step the conversation up a bit. They even asked me about my poetry.

Kesha became my closest friend. No longer just a bully's hanger-on, she was actually really nice. Once I asked her to explain her name. We have loads of girls at school whose parents or grandparents came from India, but I had never heard her name before.

"It's short for 'Dhakeshwari'," she said. "And you're right, it's an unusual name. It means something like 'the pure woman' or 'the shining woman' I think. I hardly speak one word of mum and dad's language anyway."

Then one rainy day, after school, Kesha and I were at my house, doing homework together. We had got round to it slowly, coming to it through a little meaningless girl-talk which gradually died down to the occasional remark. Then my ball-point ran out; I swore quietly and asked Kesha if I could borrow one from her. She reached into her schoolbag, got one out, and handed it to me. I had written a whole sentence before I realised that I was writing in purple ink. Then I stopped and stared at this pen in my hand. It was like my brain had stopped. I had a heap of facts in front of me, and yet they were stubbornly refusing to organise themselves into a conclusion. I looked over at Kesha.

She was lying on her tummy on my bed, propped up on her elbows, frowning at something in a book. A silver chain round her neck had flopped out of her school shirt, and on the end of it a silver figure was spinning slowly, catching the light.

"What's that on your chain?" I asked. She looked down.

"Oh!" she said, and brought up a hand as though to tuck it away. But then she left it. "Funny thing, that is. It's a Buddhist thing, and we're Hindus. But it was a present and I like it, so I wear it."

"Yeah, but what is it?"

"It's called a 'Dhakini'. It's a kind of a... I don't know... I guess you could call it a 'cloud fairy'."

"It looks like..."

"...an Angel? Yeah, it does."

I took a deep breath.

"You're Skydancer," I said.

"Yes, I am," said Kesha.

"You wrote me the note."

"Yes I did. And I sent the texts and the email."

"And you came into the chat room to warn me off."

Kesha nodded, smiled briefly, and then looked down. I took another breath, and then went on, taking a chance on some speculation.

"You used to be a Guardian Angel. You got sick of them, of the way they had no idea what they were doing, and you left," I said. Kesha said nothing, and I went on. "You found you could do things they couldn't. Things started to happen to you more than to them. You started to ask questions. Right?"

"Something like that. I could do some things – not like you can, I think. But I can still... well... move around things, get things done. Like, it was easy to get the note into your stuff, and getting texts and emails and things you can't trace, that's ordinary geek stuff really. But the Guardian Angels, yeah they don't like questions. They'd rather be left alone to do what they do. Sometimes I think it's an excuse to skive schoolwork, more than anything else. I think that they feel questions sort of cancel out what they're doing. I know they really believe they're doing good. When I got too many questions in my mind and found out that they wouldn't or couldn't answer them, I started googling for answers. That's how I found out what 'tulpa' meant, for example – it's a Tibetan word, I think. I found loads of stuff about 'End Times', most of it really weird, but nothing about the Guardian Angels, the Avenging Angels, or the Yellows. Not a thing. Then one day I told them I wasn't going to be with them any more, and I walked out. No one tried to stop me, and that's weird too, because sometimes I wonder if I am still being played with, messed around with, kept in the dark. Anyhow, I knew you had become involved, because I saw you go through the fence that day we were chasing you. Or more like I kinda felt it. Funny, I didn't like you back then, but I still didn't want you to get involved. I don't know why, but I'm glad I did."

I was nodding like anything, and grinning too, when Kesha got to the bit about googling for information and finding nothing. Somehow it made everything so much better to have found someone who had been through more-or-less what I had been through.

"I'm glad you did too. Do you believe there really is some kind of battle going on between good and evil? I mean, it's not like we imagined it, but do you believe in all this 'End Times' stuff?"

"The Book of Revelation?"

"Yes."

"We're Hindus, like I said," said Kesha, shrugging. "It's not one of our myths. How about you?"

I turned round to face her fully, and she sat up on my bed.

"Funny, I've never really thought about it much. But I do. Yes I do believe in it," I said. My thoughts went back to the preacher on the train, the man who had given me the handkerchief and had talked about never knowing when you're going to meet an angel in disguise. "You know, there have been hundreds of weird sects who believed that the world was coming to an end at one time or another. One of these days one of these sects is going to be right, if only by accident... and that wouldn't make them any less weird, and their weirdness wouldn't make them any less prophets... do you see what I mean?"

Kesha nodded. We sat and looked at each other for a while.

"Show me your angel," said Kesha, her eyes

bright. I pulled my Book of Common Prayer out of my schoolbag and handed it to her.

"Cool!" she said, then: "What's this stain on it?"

"Blood."

"Ew!"

"It's only mine."

"Ew anyway. Where did you get it?"

I told her all about the man in the bookshop, how his sister had passed it to me.

"This is something I don't understand," said Kesha. "You got yours from the bookshop man who died, I got mine from my uncle Dinesh just before he died. And I know Janet got hers from an old tramp or a bloke in the fairground or whatever, and she never saw him again. Is this how it works – there's always an old man involved?"

"I don't know," I said. "One of the boys had a tattoo – how would that fit in? And do we really want to know, you and me?"

I said this, but when I did I had to push down a

kind of curiosity in my mind. I had to pretend that I wasn't wondering whether the preacher on the train was part of it, or the ranting man with dreadlocks, whether there really were signs and portents all around us. Most of all I had to pretend that I wasn't aching to reach out, to feel the ripples in the weird current which – I knew, I was sure – flowed in and around the whole world. What would I feel? What would I touch? Who would I touch? Would I find myself feeling bands of Guardian Angels in other schools, for example? I began to feel a little scared – at last. What if what I felt was really, really big? What if I had underestimated everything, and Armageddon was happening right now, and I touched it? Or worse, what if what I felt was piddling and small, like a practical joke played on a handful of us? No, Kesha and I had made a promise to each other that we wouldn't go into this. I still felt a failure somehow, and I wanted not to feel that way. I was looking at a page in the middle of an unfamiliar book again, and this time I didn't want to turn one page forward or back – it might have explained why and how so much could exist in the same place at the same time, and I might not have liked the answer.

We sat in silence again for a few minutes, and then I thought of something to say to make me feel better.

"If I believed the world were to end tomorrow, I would still plant a tree today," I said.

"Nice one," said Kesha, smiling. Then she frowned a little. "That's famous. I've heard it. Who said it?"

"Martin Luther," I said.

"The American guy?"

"No, that was Martin Luther King. This is a German guy, centuries ago."

"He sounds wise, even if he is ancient."

"Yeah," I agreed. "Except he probably didn't actually say it. It's probably made up about him. He was a monk or something, but he rebelled – kicked against the church because it wasn't doing things right. That's kinda like us."

"It's still wise, even if he didn't say it," said Kesha. "It's like a slogan, a catch-phrase."

"A mission statement," I said. "He said a better one, simpler. 'Here I stand – I can do no other'. He really did say that."

"That's cool too. We could have that as our motto, you and me!" said Kesha, and then she said what I had been thinking. "It would make us feel less of a failure."

"Yes, I guess so," I said, slipping the little prayerbook into my pocket, and gripping it tightly.

And that is about it, except for two very last things out of all the last things. One: I went to Charlie Seacole's funeral, and I hugged his mum and dad. They told me I was very brave, the way I took his death; it turns out he hadn't died in the playground, but he had suffered an aneurism and slipped into a coma, and his parents had made the terrible choice of asking for his life-support to be switched off. They told me what a lovely son he had been, what a cheerful and good boy, and I nodded. Two: I started to get really good marks at school again, and my mum and dad were pleased.

PART TWO
WHICH WAY SHALL I FLY?

O 1

I dreamed I opened my eyes, because I was asleep and dreaming that I was awake. I dreamed I was awake. I was awake, but it was a dream. Let me get this right...

I thought I opened my eyes. I remember shutting them. That was last night. I went to sleep. Now I am awake. I woke up. I must be awake. But I'm not. I must be dreaming that I'm awake. If I am dreaming at all. No, I'm awake. I must be awake. It's just a very weird awake.

Sod it!

Okay, okay this is what is weird about being

awake, if I am awake. I'm on the ceiling. I can feel the ceiling against my back. It's hard. And I know which way is down. That way's down. Down towards the bed. There's a kid lying on it, fast asleep, just as I was before. No he isn't asleep, he's... this must be a hospital, right? Okay that bed he's on is a hospital one, and that machine just there, with the screen and the wires going to the kid, that's an EKG measuring his heartbeat. That other one going to a tube in his mouth... that one's making him breathe. There's a drip in his arm. There are other machines.

He isn't moving. I can feel nothing about him at all. I can usually read people by the quark stream passing around their chi. I can't read him, though. I'm getting nothing. Nothing coming from his brain. That's like a deep, dark pond. I feel nothing. He must be in a coma, and a pretty deep one at that. The light seems wrong, but he looks really sick.

How long have I been awake? How long have I been looking down? I don't know. Long enough for me to get used to it being weird. It isn't logical, but it isn't weird any more. Who knows what's logical? The ceiling is hard against my back, and that is right, because ceilings are hard. I can't hear anything. Why can't I hear anything? I should be able to hear something if I can feel something.

What's happening below me? I'm looking down at the top of a man's head, I can see his shoulders, and when he moves I can see that he has a white coat, because it is flapping. He's a doctor. This is a hospital, he has a white coat, so he's a doctor. There are two other people – they've just come into the room – a man and a woman. The man has his arm round the woman's shoulders. They're talking to the doctor... at least I can see that they are facing each over and seem to be shaking, moving, gesturing... it's not easy to make it out from the ceiling, but I think the doctor is pointing towards the kid on the bed, so they must be talking about him.

Now the doctor has left the room, and the man and woman are just standing there with their arms round each other. Just standing. That's all they're doing. Standing and rocking each other gently. Now they've moved to the bed. The man has sat down in a chair at the bed side, and has taken the kid's hand in his. The woman is leaning over, kissing the kid's face. It's like they're saying goodbye to him. Now they're standing again, facing the kid. Just standing. Standing a long time. Now they're turning, going...

The ceiling is always so hard against my back, but I still can't hear. Here comes the doctor again, with two other people in white. Nurses? The doctor is picking something up. A clip-board hanging at the end of the bed nearest the kid's feet. He's writing something on it, hanging it up again, and talking to the other two people. Now he has gone again, and the nurses are moving around. They're taking away the leads to the EKG and turning it off, taking the drip out of his arm, stopping the breathing machine and taking away the tube, packing everything away... wheeling the machines out of the room.

Everything is still now.

I'm getting nothing from him. Nothing is moving in or around him. Nothing is moving at all.

Except maybe me. I can't feel the ceiling on my back any more, and the way I can see the room is changing. I am floating down from the ceiling, and as I float down I am beginning to hear again. Voices outside the room, the sound of a – what? – maybe a floor-polisher, a soft electronic bell and the footsteps of a nurse answering it, a trolley or a wheelchair being pushed past.

Now I am standing at the foot of the bed, and from this angle at last I recognise the kid lying there. I don't need to pick up the clip-board to read the name. Charlie Seacole. No surprise. Me.

Why doesn't this surprise me? It ought to. Maybe

having woken up on the ceiling was enough of a surprise for one day. I still wonder whether I have woken up at all. I still remember closing my eyes last night and falling asleep. It had been a big day for me, a lot had happened, new responsibilities had come my way, things had entered a new phase. I had been excited.

Let me try closing my eyes now, and opening them again. There. No, still standing here looking at myself on the bed. Try it for longer, count to thirty. There. No. Still standing. Try it for longer still, try to drift away, thinking of nothing, thinking of Angela maybe, think of waking up later, and getting toast and cereal, and getting ready for school. There, opening my eyes again. No!

Maybe if I go and find Janet, she'll know what to do. Or Angela. No, that would be impossible.

I am turning away from myself on the bed, and walking out of the room. Down the corridor I go, past doors to other rooms and wards, past the nurses' station. No one is bothering me, but then it's always visiting time in hospitals. This must be the doctor I saw in the room, and the man and woman he was talking to are my mum and dad. Mum and dad are wiping tears away and being very brave. The doctor is being kind. Perhaps I ought to stop and talk to them, but it doesn't seem relevant to me. It doesn't seem important. It seems more important to see Janet and find out what is going on. I can try to talk to mum and dad later, when things are sorted out. Things have to be sorted out, because they can't go on like this. I have to prepare myself for my new responsibilities. Things are going to start happening really soon – big things – and I need to make sure the others are ready for them.

02

I am beginning to wish I still couldn't hear. This is the room where we – the Guardian Angels – meet. Only right now it is full of year-eight kids, still new to the school, waiting for their teacher to turn up. And they are chattering, and banging books on the desks, and arguing about who sits where. I'm just leaning against the wall. I'm not used to this room being full. I used to come here for lessons when I was their age, but for more than a year now I have been used to it being quiet except for the little bit of noise the GAs made while we waited for something to happen. I am not really sure why they are all here now, and why I am here and not with the GAs. I'll figure this out eventually, when I figure out whether this is a dream, a Rising of my own, or what.

Over there, in that corner, is where I used to sit with my mate Christo. I'd have my pocket chess set on the desk, and he'd turn round to face me and we would have a quick game until the teacher turned up. Then I'd put the lid on it until later, and hope the pieces hadn't jiggled loose when the next little gap between lessons turned up, or it was break time and too wet to go outside and play football. Christo was a laugh, and every time he took one of my pieces he would make a noise like an explosion with his mouth, or say "Banzai", or "So perish the enemies of Lo-Kar!" The stupid things you do and say when you're a kid! He didn't know much more than Ruy Lopez and stuff like that, but sometimes he'd make wild moves that threw me and made me think. I liked that. I think I'd like to find him some time and have another game. Yeah I'd like that. Maybe later.

Here comes the teacher now. "Settle down!" he's saying loudly. It's Mr Callister. I know him. He has only been out of university for two years and this is his first job. I heard he used to go to this school before uni, but he would have left here while I was still in junior school. He's not ancient like the other teachers, he always wears dark blue shirts and those chino trousers, and never knots his tie up to his neck.

He's looking over to where I am standing, and he seems puzzled, and like he's going to speak to me. No... his frown is relaxing and he's turning back to the class. I hear him say, "Open your books at the chapter about Australia."

It strikes me that although the room is absolutely full, I can still read no one, I can't feel the quark stream or sense anyone's chi. By rights I shouldn't be here at all. I must have missed my way in. The room should be quiet, and the only people here should be GAs or...

Yes, the room should be like it was last time I was here, and it's bloody annoying that it isn't. I had walked with Janet from the playground, the quark stream bubbling round us, sullen and tepid. I will have to find my way back again. Maybe if I go out and come in again. I'll try later. What was I saying? Oh yeah Janet and me. We had walked from the playground where the swings are. We walked silently. I didn't want to say anything, and I could feel that even if Janet did, she couldn't think of anything to say. When we got to the corridor outside this room she stopped and put her hand on my arm. I looked at her. She didn't say anything, but I could tell what she was thinking.

"They're yours now, Charlie. I can't do this any more. Look after them."

We came in here, and the rest of the GAs looked up as we came in. We were twelve again, and that felt right – tragic but right. The next day, when Janet had gone, we would be down to eleven, but who knew whether someone else would find his or her way to us. It had never felt right with thirteen, it had always felt out of balance.

I kept on my feet, but Janet sat down and looked out of the window. She looked sad. I kept looking at her, catching her mood, but losing what she was actually thinking. Everyone else was looking at me, waiting for me to speak. I took a breath.

"I couldn't save Angela," I said. "I tried. I fought hard to keep the quark stream neutral for her. I tried to reach out to the Avenging Angels and get them to stop. But once they've been called out, they can't stop. Something has to happen. They can't go back with a job not done."

"You did what you could, Charlie," said someone. "We had a rising. We saw."

I shook my head. "Did you see them come for her? They had seen how badly she had failed, how she had let all those people get killed in the bombing. They had seen that she didn't fit in. Oh she was brilliant, but she was number thirteen – and there should never be a number thirteen. They knew that, and they came for her."

I looked out of the window, where Janet was looking.

"You loved her, Charlie," she said. "She was your girlfriend."

I think that was the only time I had felt like crying about what had happened. But when you get caught up in the GA business, even dating and stuff like that seems not to be important any more. Yeah of course I loved Angela. I had fancied her ever since our first day in school together, though back then it was puppy-love. I always used to sit at the back in class, not just to play chess with Christo, but also because I could look at her from there. Okay, so winning the year chess championship twice running was important to me as well, and a load of other guy-stuff, but when we kind of got thrown together by both being in the GAs, it just seemed really easy to hit on her. I had enjoyed dating her, even though she could sometimes be moody.

"That doesn't matter," I said. "She was number thirteen, and that was wrong."

I don't want you to think I'm hard-hearted. I'm not. It just that I was the leader then, the new leader. I looked over at Janet. She was resting her head on her arms. It was as if she wasn't there any more.

Later on she would merge with her tulpa one last time, and we wouldn't see her again. A leader has to be decisive, and I was going to be a leader and a half for the GAs, and do things they had never seen before.

"Something big is going to happen soon," I said. "It's going to be bigger than anything we have ever done before. More important than the bomb in the station. A complete change is going to happen. I can't tell you any more than that at the moment. You're going to have to trust me."

Ben Gillett stood up. Ben is in my class. He's a centimetre or two bigger than me, and broader across the shoulders. Before we both became GAs we hadn't got along. Since we became GAs he had accepted me, maybe a little more grudgingly than the others, as though he didn't quite trust me, or didn't believe a chess-player could become a GA and have adventures. He never smiled, and he wasn't smiling now.

"I trust you, Charlie," he said.

"Thank you."

I didn't ask him to like me, and I didn't care whether he did or he didn't. I simply needed him to do whatever I asked of him. No one said command was going to be easy. It's more difficult than doing as you're told. It takes Officer potential, like in the Army I guess. It's a talent – born leader – that kind of thing.

One by one the others stood up and gave me their support. Soon they were chanting my name. No one was smiling or grinning. The occasion was too serious for that. But for the first time that I could remember – and I had seen three leaders of the GAs since I became one – they were greeting one like a Roman Emperor. Me. Hail Caesar.

"Char-lie! Char-lie! Char-lie!"

I let it carry on for a few minutes, and then I raised my hands to silence them.

"Let's sit it out for the rest of the day," I said. "I can't see there being another Rising today."

We sat down until it was time to go. No one said much. I wondered if they had noticed what I had noticed: Janet had already gone, slipped out while the chanting was going on. I had hardly been able to sense her in the quark stream as she went down the corridor, and by the time she got to the main door of the school, that was it. She had lost it.

All that was yesterday. It must have been yesterday, because it is so fresh in my memory. Same as going to bed that night, tired, excited, my sadness about Angela fading. She wasn't important any more. She was history. Janet too. Both of them history. Now was important. The future was important. What was coming was important. What I was going to have to do, leading the GAs was important.

A bell has just gone, and the kids from Year Eight are filing out of the door. I am standing here a bit surprised by the things I remember happening here yesterday. Now there is no one left in the room except Mr Callister. With just him and me in here, it feels more like it ought to, emptier, quieter.

I can't get a handle on this, though. Mr Callister is looking round the room. He looks sad. No, it's not just sad, it's something else, but I don't know what. It's like he's looking for something, or trying to remember where he put something. There's a frown on his face, but it's not an angry frown. He's frustrated – that's it – as well as being sad, he's frustrated about something.

"Just for a moment there, I thought..." he is saying, and then nothing else.

He's just standing there now, looking at the floor,

his hands on his hips. He's shaking his head, sighing, and picking up his briefcase. Now he's walking out through the door into the corridor. Teachers are weird.

Who cares? He's not important.

Now he's got me at it. I'm standing here as though I have lost something. I haven't lost anything. Have I? There is noise outside the classroom, but it is getting less and less. It's going-home time. Kids are leaving the school. Time for me to leave too, so that's what I'm doing.

03

Something else weird – leaving the school now – I've been waiting for my tulpa to merge with me. I can always feel it coming, and it's a bit of a laugh, like when your ears pop. But I am way out of the school now, and it's like I'm straining, hunched up, waiting for it, and it's not happening.

I mean, strolling through the last of the kids leaving school was kind of weird, but no one took any notice of me anyway so that was cool. But the no tulpa thing? I just so did not expect that, and it's got me... I don't know... I'm not, like, worried or anything, but...

Okay, what I'll do is this. I'll make my way to the playground, the one with the swings and the little roundabout, where I last saw Angela. It isn't far. Maybe I'll pick something up there. The Avenging Angels really manipulated the quark stream there, and there's bound to be some echoes. Watching the AAs at work is so awesome. Not everybody gets to see them, and totally no one gets to go up against them. They're kind of on our side, but they're kind of neutral too. They do what they have to do – I like that in them, and like I told the GAs, once they go out to take care of someone they never go back without a job done. It's hard, but I understand that.

Okay, let me get it straight in my mind what had happened up to that point. Angela had no idea I was following her. She just seemed to want to run and run until she got to school. I wanted to get there ahead of her, but there was just no way I could do that. She had a head start on me, and she was a bloody good runner – those long legs of hers – and it was like she was possessed by a demon or something, and couldn't get tired. And then I saw suddenly how I could beat her there...

...She had to use her own way in, and that was down by the builders' yard. Mine was on the nearer side of the school main gates, and if I kept up running at this pace I would get to it minutes before she got to hers. So I ran like a maniac, and threw myself at it, coming out almost with a bang on the path to the main door of the school. I almost tripped and fell but I just kept running, and I was sure I made it to the front door, and inside, before Angela had got through her way in. The quark stream was like white-water rapids down the corridor. I don't know when I have ever seen it so disturbed. And when I got to the classroom and burst in, there were the Yellows. Not the GAs, the Yellows. And they were so not expecting me, so when I sat down on the nearest chair, and they looked at me – boy, did I grin!

Yeah, and I was still grinning when Angela got there. I was going to tell her everything, let her in on the whole secret. I admit it - I was really right up myself, totally full of myself, I had even forgotten about what had happened to the train-load of people. But that's the way I am. Oh man you should have seen the look on her face when she came into that room – she was ranting on and suddenly she stopped when she saw me and realised she wasn't supposed to recognise anyone in the room. It was like she really didn't recognise anyone, and couldn't get her head round why I was there. And of course I was grinning still. Okay I know it was silly to grin, but I couldn't help it because the whole situation was like totally random, yeah?

Well, I don't know where she got the energy from, but she turned round and bolted down the corridor again, and of course I had to jump up and run after her. By the time we got outside the school she had run out of steam a bit.

"Wait, Ange... wait!" I shouted to her.

"Why the hell should I? Give me one good reason," she said, turning and walking backwards away from me. I could see that she was crying, but trying to pretend she wasn't.

"It's all over, Ange. The game's over," I said.

"It isn't how it looks, Charlie," she said, spreading her hands out wide. "Honest it isn't. I can explain."

"It's too late for that. We all saw what we saw, Ange. There's no getting away from it. We all saw you tackle that bloke outside the station. Sometimes – argue it any way you want – if it walks like a duck, and quacks like a duck, it needs longer in the microwave!"

"What?" she said, with a blank look on her face.

"Never mind... stupid joke," I said, and I thought to myself, "Yeah, the kind you used to laugh at, the kind you thought were cute." But I went on.

"Ange, you got it all wrong. You got it all so wrong, and you know it. You screwed up, you screwed up badly. You know I'm right."

Then she said, "I could go back to the Guardian Angels and tell them exactly what I have just seen – Charlie Seacole sitting with their enemies. I could tell them you're a traitor, Charlie."

"No you couldn't, Ange. Right now how do the Guardian Angels know that you're on their side? You came out of nowhere, when we had twelve people already, and everyone knows that thirteen doesn't really work. If both of us stood up in front of them right now, and said the other one was a traitor, who would they believe? Right now they'd probably believe me before you. Would you risk it? Think, Ange, think! And you kept asking me if I knew who the Yellows were, and who the Avenging Angels were, and making all those comments about not existing. I know you were bluffing, and testing me. It was all a trick, wasn't it."

It was at that moment when she tripped backwards and fell on her butt. She fell heavily and I could see that it had hurt. She just sat there, all her energy drained now, as though the run and everything had caught up with her at last. I didn't need to rush, I just walked up to her and held out my hand. She took it, and I helped her up. Our eyes met. Her hand felt good in mine. She was my girl.

"Come on Ange," I said, gently pulling her by the hand. "Let's get away from here, away from the school. Let's talk. Let's talk everything through, eh?"

For a moment I thought she was going to smile. I thought some magic was going to happen and she would come and lean against me and cry, and I would make it all better for her. I could have done that. I could have taken her back to the GAs, and made her part of everything again, and she could have been part of the big thing that's going to happen very soon. I wish she had done that, because her hand felt so nice in mine. My girl. But that didn't happen. Oh it so could have happened, but it didn't. Instead she twisted her hand out of mine.

"You're always pulling me, Charlie," she said.

I hated how empty my hand felt now. It felt suddenly as though all the being-together we had enjoyed up to then had just been rubbed out. She had rubbed them out, just like that. But we kept on walking, out of the school and back into the outside world. We just kept walking and walking, side by side, not saying a word, until we got... here.

This is the place. I'm standing at the railings of the little playpark. There are a few mums with toddlers here now, a couple chatting on the bench, one of them just gently joggling a push-chair with a baby in it. It's gone sunny. It's quiet. And no, I can't feel anything of the quark stream. It's like it totally died. That is so unlike how it was last time I was here, with Ange.

I remember we both sat on the swings, and we did talk. Not a lot of what we said seems to make much sense now, though. I know I explained to her how there was more to all this than she could possibly realise, that 'choosing sides' in this battle wasn't as easy as she thought, and that in reality we are chosen. I explained to her how every action we take has its consequences, and how if we save someone it is difficult to see what they went on to do; and if we let someone die it was just as difficult to see the good that might come of it. I don't think she got it. She got angry with me at one time. The idea was too big for her to take in, and I felt really, really sorry for her.

Our talk sort of stopped for a while, and she swung back and forward for a while, trailing her feet on the ground, making tracks in the bark chips. Then she looked at me again, and she seemed to be begging for something with her eyes.

"Charlie, you tried to warn me about this, didn't you!" she said. "The note I found in my bag... the texts... the emails... those were from you, weren't they? You're Skydancer. Please tell me you're Skydancer. It would mean such a lot to me to know that."

I looked her straight in the eyes and said, "Yes, I'm Skydancer. I tried to warn you, without letting you know who I was. You're number thirteen, Ange. Thirteen just doesn't work. It's wrong. You were special too, and that's what makes it all such a pity. You could move from one place to the other, you could come into the GAs' school or the Yellows' school. Not many people can do that."

"You can too," she said.

"Yes I can," I replied. "There's a reason for this. Something so big is going to happen, and I'm needed. I know how special I am, Ange. I am going to have such a big part to play in it, and it needs someone like me, who can move about in the quark stream, and move from place to place... Listen, Ange... I can square this for you. I can make it all right again. Just come with me, back to the Guardian Angels, I'll talk to them. There'll be a way that we can work round there being thirteen of us. Maybe it's time for one of us to go anyway, and there'll be twelve again. Come with me, Ange, come now while there is still time."

She looked up.

"What do you mean 'still time'?"

I looked at her, and was about to explain everything, when I saw a frightened look come into her eyes. She began to glance around. I felt it too, before I even looked. I realised we were not alone. I didn't have to count them to know that there were twelve other kids around us, kids from our school, kids with tulpas taking their place in lessons, kids who would not go back without a job done. Avenging

Angels. I could feel where each one of them was, by the disturbance each one made in the quark stream. Two girls were sitting on the little roundabout thing, another person was by the gateway, and another by the fence to my left. Two more were coming up the path from the pond, and the rest were walking towards us over the football pitch, fanning out to make a circle round us. I could feel the quark stream begin to swirl.

"Ange," I said, urgently. "I won't let anything happen to you. I won't let them get to you. Come with me now, right now, let's make a run for it!"

But Ange had curled up on the swing. Her eyes seemed to have gone out of focus. Her lips were moving, but I could barely hear her. She was singing one of her French folk songs. She was out of it, she was gone.

I could feel and now see that the AAs were all around us, the disturbance they were causing in the quark stream was making a vortex, like water running out of a bath, only this was rising, more like a tornado, sucking stuff in from four straight streams, like points of a compass, and organising it into one terrible storm, with us in the centre of it.

I stood up and looked round at them.

"No!" I yelled, and shut my eyes. I concentrated as hard as I could, drawing in every stray bit of the quark stream I could, using my mind to drag theirs away and set up another vortex in the middle of theirs, spinning in the opposite direction. I was strong, very strong. I am strong, I know I am. The two vortexes pushed at each other. There were sparks as though metal was grinding against metal. It felt as though the world was coming apart at the seams. I gritted my teeth and carried on, and for a while I felt as though I was winning – not just holding my own, but pushing them back. But then they were like a spring, and pushed back at me harder still. For Ange's sake I tried to hold on, to fight back; but suddenly I felt like I had been climbing a mountain, and my hands had been ripped away from a hand-hold, and I was falling. I lost hold of everything. The sparks stopped, the grinding stopped, and I felt myself flung through the air... no, it felt like I was being flung through millions of miles of space for millions of years... but the next second I found myself rolling over and over in the grass, fifty metres or more from the swings, outside the circle of Avenging Angels. From here, I could never hope to get back inside.

I could see that Angela had stood up. She was looking over at me. I could feel the vortex getting stronger and stronger. She was fighting it now, but she was so much weaker than I was. I heard her scream "Charlie!"

I am not very proud of this next bit. I almost feel a coward. But on the other hand, there was nothing I could have done, and I had to save myself. I had important work to do.

I realised I was not alone. Janet was there.

"Come away, Charlie – you have to come away now!" she insisted.

And that's what I did. I turned my back on my Ange, my girl as was, and walked back, back to my own destiny, without looking back at the playground, without listening to any sound that could be heard coming from there, ignoring the tugging and straining of the quark stream. Sometimes you have to make hard decisions.

Janet suddenly said, "Me miserable! Which way shall I fly infinite wrath, and infinite despair? Which way I fly is Hell; myself am Hell; and in the lowest deep a lower deep still threatening to devour me opens wide, to which the Hell I suffer seems a Heaven."

I recognised it – Paradise Lost – we were doing it in English. I knew she understood... what Angela had gone through.

That was then. Right now I am sitting on the end of the bench. The two mums are chatting, ignoring me. Good. I want to be ignored. This hasn't been a good memory, and the fact that the quark stream is as still as a mirror is a good thing. It helps.

04

I don't think the answer is here. Something seems to want to keep me here, but there is too much pain, too much sadness. I shall move, I don't want to, but I shall. I shall go back to the station and see if I can find an answer there. It's funny, though, because I am not really sure what the question is, unless it's "What the hell's going on?"

That's the question – I remember – people were asking the day after the bomb on the train. Or one of the questions. I think I know where to find the answer. I'm walking along, out of the park, towards the station, and I'm thinking. It's all becoming clearer to me, much clearer. Things that didn't make much sense before are beginning to come together. I remember grabbing Angela's hand...

There was something in the way she behaved that day. She got off the school bus and dragged her feet along the pavement, looking down. I had almost given up waiting for her, thinking she wasn't coming, but then I felt her familiar shape, her signature, in the quark stream. She didn't seem to want to look at me, didn't smile, hardly said a word. When we used our ways in, she staggered and I had to catch her, and support her for a minute. Still she didn't seem to want to look at me.

"You look rough, Ange," I said.

"Oh thanks, Charlie!"

"You know I didn't mean it like that," I said. "I mean you look like you haven't slept, or you're really worried about something. Is something the matter? Tell me, Ange. You can trust me – you know that."

For a while she just stood there, like she was trying to make her mind up about something. I thought she would want to come inside, but she just stood there.

"There's nothing the matter," she said, still avoiding looking at me. Then she said, "Charlie, I think you have been keeping secrets from me. I think there's something going on – something I don't know about, right? You ought to tell me if there was something I needed to know but no one had told me? It's not right to keep me in the dark. If you or the others knew more than you are letting on about this whole thing – the war, the Risings, the missions – you would tell me, wouldn't you? Charlie, I need to know you would tell me. You and I are more than just Guardian Angels together. We are. We're more. We're an item, and that means something, you know it does. If you know anything, you have to tell me."

Then she did look at me at last. There was something in her eyes I couldn't make out – they seemed to shift, as though she was looking for signs in my face. But I kept calm, and kept my expression neutral, except maybe I frowned a little – not cross but more, like, concerned. And I was concerned. Just then she seemed a little crazy, paranoid, really hyper.

"What's up, Ange? You look... I don't know... frightened. Has anything happened to scare you?" I said.

"No, I'm not frightened, I wouldn't call it that," she said.

"I wouldn't blame you if you were. This whole thing can sometimes seem weird – I don't pretend it isn't. You think there are things I'm not telling you. Well, there is so much Janet has never told me, and I don't think she knows herself. We all get like this some time, I know I do. But there is one thing I know, Ange, we have to keep doing what we're doing. That's all there is to it. We have to keep doing what we're doing. It's important – really, really important."

"You mean we have to just keep on doing it and never question it, whatever happens?" I asked.

"I guess so."

She was silent again, and stopped looking at me. She seemed to be thinking.

"Charlie, does your family get a local paper at home?" she asked.

"No. Why?"

She put her bag down and bent over it, unzipping it and rummaging through the stuff inside, looking for something. Then she brought out the local freebie, neatly folded so that the top of the front page showed, and held it up to me.

"Recognize anyone, Charlie?" she asked.

I looked at the headline – "Father of two drowned" – and at the smiling photo beside it. Of course I recognized him. How wouldn't I recognize him.

"It's the bloke from the canal," I said, steadying her hand so I could read the story. I gave a whistle – it seemed he had waited a fortnight, then gone right to the same spot and into the water. He had left a letter. The paper said that he had told his wife and children that he loved them, that's all.

But I knew what it had said:

"It's been here inside my head since I was a boy, and now I spend the whole of my waking life, looking over my shoulder, or rather not daring to because I would rather not acknowledge what is following me. I am like the person to whom Coleridge refers in the Ancient Mariner, who '... walks on and no more turns his head, because he knows a frightful fiend does close behind him tread'. I know I am a coward; where I am going I should have taken you and the children with me, to save you from what is happening. But I can't. My life is not worth living, as a consequence. Forget conspiracy theories, darling; what is wrong with the world, and what is happening to it, is bigger than the biggest conspiracy theory ever dreamed up. I can't face it, and yet I have left you to face it. I'm sorry."

There's a note to that, saying the guy was paranoid. That shows how much whoever wrote the note knew! I knew because I had seen it on the internet. I did it from an internet café via loads of servers so no one would have been able to tell. It was like the quark stream told my fingers where to go. It wasn't hacking; it was part of the battle, part of the game. There was a pdf file of it, in an official report...

Anyhow, there I was with Angela.

"No wonder you're spooked," I said. "Look, put that back in your bag. Maybe we'll get a chance to talk the whole thing over with Janet and a couple of the others. We'll see, eh? I think I can see what's giving you grief now – we save a guy's life... and it was bloody brilliant, by the way, nothing can stop it being bloody brilliant... and then a couple of weeks later he's gone."

"That's it!" she said, and her eyes were really big and wild by now. "That's just it. We are supposed to be doing something really, really special, something big, or a little piece of something big. And so I do this, and now it's all been for nothing!"

"You don't know that," I said, trying to calm her. "You don't know where that guy had to be between then and now. You don't know what he might have had to do."

"No I don't. But anyway..." she said, just standing there. I had never seen her looking so miserable, like she was undecided or torn about something. She went on. "I can't tell you what this weekend has been like, Charlie. Maybe I'm going paranoid. I think someone out there is trying to get at me. Maybe trying to help me, maybe trying to scare me off, I just don't know. Did you know that on the web you can find just about everything you could ever want to know about the last war between good and evil, and a whole lot of stuff you never even dreamed of, and a whole lot of stuff you wish you hadn't asked about. But not one word is there anywhere which squares with what we're doing or think we're doing. It doesn't appear, it isn't there. Slice it as thin as you like, define a search how ever you want, you get nothing. We don't exist. What we're doing doesn't exist. Unless I have missed something somewhere, the whole world's body of knowledge excludes us. Oh but the things that are there, Charlie... I mean yesterday I went for a walk, and everything I looked at I wondered whether it was a sign or a portent or something, or had a hidden meaning. I walked past churches when people were coming out, and I caught the eye of some of them, and I wondered if there was something significant about the length of time their eyes held mine, or the colour of their hair, or what they were wearing. I heard songs on the radio, and wondered whether the words had coded meanings. I looked in the sky for bloody cloud shapes. Nothing. None of it tied up. We don't fit in, Charlie. It's like we don't belong anywhere. We're supposed to be special and important, part of something that the whole of Western civilisation has been talking about and ranting about for two thousand years, and we don't exist. We don't fit in. We don't belong. We don't exist... Charlie – who are the Yellows? Who are the Avenging Angels?"

I didn't know where to start. How could I answer all these questions? There was so much she didn't realise, too much to take in. I could start telling her things, but she would have been even more spooked by the time I was halfway into the story, and I didn't want that. All I could think of doing, just then, was hugging her. So I did that, and let her nestle into me.

Suddenly I felt a change, a surge, a boiling in the quark stream. I recognised the signs that a Rising was beginning, but there was something wrong with this one. Angela was still nestled in my arms as though nothing was happening, and I wondered how she could possibly have missed what was happening.

Her arms were locked round my waist, and I had to push her to get free. Then I grabbed her hand and yelled at her to run, pulling her along behind me as the quark stream whipped itself up into a storm. There was something big about this one, and I didn't want to be caught out here. I wanted us to be inside with the other GAs. I ran like hell, Angela almost a dead weight behind me.

We made it into the room and into a couple of seats just as the Rising really took hold. I suddenly felt sick, and there I was flying right above something – a deep, dark hole, hundreds of metres across... no, kilometres... I didn't know. All I did know was that it was so deep that it made me dizzy. Even though it was dark I could tell there was no bottom to it. And the darkness was so solid, and there was stuff piling out of this hole like water from a backed-up drain, and it was foul and filthy.

Then this thing started to rise up out of it, and the sickness in my stomach began to rise again. I looked over at Angela, and she was looking at me. She seemed to be smiling. That's when I realised! Angela – my Ange – had been totally aware of the Rising, but she had tried to keep me away from it. Why? Why? Because she was making it happen! She was that special, that friggin' dangerous! Not only was she making it happen, she was making us see what she wanted to see. She was making us see someone rising out of the foul, filthy hole... someone in shining white, someone with the face of an angel, but someone totally evil. That face, that angel's face – mine!

I had to fight this, and that is what I did, mind-to-mind with Ange, stripping away the picture she was sending to the others, and replacing it with what was underneath, what was really there. The true face of the being who was rising out of the pit. Hers.

My head ached like it was going to split. I could hardly hold on. It was like I was being driven insane. But I did hold on.

05

What I really want to do now is go and talk to mum and dad. They looked so sad in the hospital. I want to tell them everything is all right. I couldn't tell them before. Now I think there isn't anything stopping me from telling the whole story if I want to. They have a right to know. They'll be happy – relieved – to know their boy is part of something this important. They'll smile. They won't be sad any more. It'll be like the chess thing all over again, when I was younger. Maybe I'll do that next. Next, right after I visit the canal.

The last time I was here the Yellows had sent me. We had had a Rising, it was just like the Rising the GAs had – the one which had touched Angela first – the thickening of the quark stream, the swirl of water as thick as molten glass but cold. I felt it as green and cold and heavy as she must have felt it the first time, deadening my ears, slowing my heart, filling my lungs. And then the great gasp for air. All of the Yellows, right up to Aidan Kavanaugh the oldest one of us, gave a yell when the Rising broke. I was on my feet like a shot, but the other Yellows didn't follow me. Why should they? They had no idea what was going on. To them there was no clue in the Rising about its meaning, where the thing was going to happen, or anything. I knew – oh sure I knew. I knew because I was used to there being separate Risings for the Yellows and the GAs, and that mattered because I would be there. I would be there... see if I can explain it now... because it was the right time for me to do a job one way or another, whether it was stopping somebody from doing something, or making sure they did it. I would be in the right place at the right time, to see the right Rising. Because that was what my job was, my role. This was the first time that exactly the same Rising had happened for both the GAs and the Yellows . Okay it was some time later, but it was the same thing, and that meant I knew where to go.

"Where are you going, Charlie?" asked Aidan – he was our leader, but I knew that was going to change very soon, it just had to – and there were puzzled looks on everyone else's faces too. I was half-way out of the door. I had to stop. Was it worth trying to explain to them? I didn't think so.

"Look... trust me," I said. "You all know me. There isn't time to explain. It'll only take one person to see to this. If we all go it won't work. Let me deal with it?"

That wasn't how it was supposed to work. Aidan was supposed to get us all together, and we were supposed to make our way to wherever we had been shown, fanning out, covering an area until we saw the person we were looking for. Then we were supposed to make sure they went where they were supposed to go, did what they were supposed to do, without anyone getting in the way or interfering. But this time the Yellows trusted me, they listened to me, they let me go on my own. So I headed straight for the canal, straight to the little bridge where Angela had first seen the man who drowned himself. I got there sweating, my heart thumping, one trainer nearly off because I had tripped while hurrying. I edged onto the bridge very slowly. I didn't want him to see my reflection or anything like that. I didn't want him to see me at all. I didn't want him to know I was there. I felt really big against his skyline, even though I was by then only just poking my head round the corner of the wall of the nearest building. It was like I was totally scared of him. But what did I have to be scared about? He was sitting right where he had been before, and I could see he was putting stuff in his pockets – I suppose it was stones, little ones which were lying around loose on the path. He was doing it slowly, like he was thinking. I didn't move, because he was turning his head while he reached for them. I only began to move down the steps and onto the path when he stopped putting stuff in his pockets. I walked slowly towards him... very slowly.

I've just thought of something. It's something Angela said to me right after she asked me "Who are the Yellows? Who are the Avenging Angels?" This memory of me coming up to the man is so clear now, like it is a pivotal moment in my life, so important, and that's why Angela's words are coming back to me.

"Charlie, how come you recognise the drowned man's photo? You never got up close enough to him."

She didn't know – how could she know? – what had happened here, on the same spot on the towpath where she had persuaded the man not to drown himself. Right now I don't know if the thumping heart and the sweat is a memory from that day or the fact that Angela asked me that question. It's all mixed up, because now I am alone here I'm like totally calm.

But while I was slowly walking up to the man, trying not to startle him, I know that my pulse was like screaming inside my head. I wondered how come the man couldn't hear it too. But he seemed to be miles away. He was staring at the graffiti on the wall at the other side of the canal. He was humming, as though trying to remember a tune. And then he spoke out loud, and I jumped and almost gave away that I was there, coming up behind him. I thought he had heard me coming and was talking to me. But what he said made no sense.

"She moves among the groves of stones..."

He shook his head, took a deep breath and spoke again.

"She moves among... the groves of stones... in never-ending... No... it's no good, I can't remember it."

I took one careful, quiet step closer to him, being careful not to let my reflection appear in the water. He spoke again, more quietly this time, and with a lot of sadness in his voice. He was so, so sad. I felt sorry for him, really sorry. Really sorry about the burden he carried in his mind. If I could take it away from him, I would – I knew this.

"Like one that on a lonesome road doth walk in fear and dread, and having once turned round walks on, and turns no more his head, because he knows a frightful fiend doth close behind him tread."

I froze. I didn't move.

"That was easy enough to remember," he said. "So no more looking back. There is no point."

That was when I saw him take his weight on his hands, lift his backside clear of the ground, and begin to slip forward, feet first, into the canal. I think he went in straight, holding himself stiff, because there wasn't much of a splash, just a zoosh, a sucking noise almost, like the canal was swallowing him. He seemed to bang his head or scuff it on the edge as he went over.

My heart was still banging like hell, as I ran the last few steps to the edge and knelt down. The water was green with weeds, slow, whirling slightly. I could see the top of his head, his shoulders, and his arms seem to have floated outwards and upwards. His whole body was turning slowly clockwise, spinning round, and soon he would be facing towards the bank again, towards me. A great bubble of air burst from where his face was, but he wasn't sinking. In fact he was beginning to float slowly upwards again, his hands and wrists breaking the surface. I pushed up my left sleeve as far as it would go, leaned forward as far as I dared, and reached down. My arm slid into the water, found the right shoulder of his jacket, and held on tight.

"Don't worry," I said. "It'll be all right. You'll be ok. You're safe now. I've got you."

And I held him there.

His face turned up to me, and he looked at me through the green water. He opened his mouth, and another great bubble of air came out. I could feel and see his whole body shudder, and then his hands gripped hold of my left arm, the arm that was holding him. For a moment I thought he was trying to pull me in with him. But then I realised that he was struggling. He wanted to come up again. I stiffened my arm, and held him there.

"It's all right. Everything is all right, just as it was meant to be," I said again, as I held him and looked into his face. I knew how it felt. I knew what the deafening, deadening water sounded like in his ears, because I heard it as he heard it. I knew what the water felt as it filled his lungs. I knew what it felt like to have his heart slow down, for the panic and the will to live to go away gradually, and that quiet calm to come over him.

By the time he let go of my arm, and floated down and away, you see... I was completely calm.

My heart had stopped banging, and my pulse was slow and easy. I was breathing okay. I wasn't sweating any more, it had dried and my shirt, which had stuck to me, was flapping a little bit. That felt comfortable. Once my arm was out of the water, that began to dry as well, and by the time I reached the steps again, I could pull my sleeve down. I was calm as I climbed those steps, totally cool as I looked around to make sure that no one was watching. Everything was all right again. The world was as it should be. The thing that was supposed to happen had happened. Maybe it was a bit late, but better late than never.

I felt cool about it then. How do I feel about it now?

06

Okay I am putting off finding mum and dad for a while, although I still really need to talk to them. But instead I have come here because it isn't actually all that far from where I was before at the canal. I wanted to see this place. It's so busy. They call it City Road, and it starts here at Three Lane Ends, where the roads from two other suburbs join, and heads off uptown. It's got like a shopping centre and pubs and things like that and it's always heaving. This is where Angela first came on a mission with the GAs.

I am not likely to forget it. I'm not likely to forget Angela's first day at all, because I couldn't take my eyes off her. I can still see her. She was about one metre sixty-eight tall with legs that went on for ever. Her hair was brown, but that doesn't really do it – I tried to find the exact shade on the net and the best I could do was "chestnut", but that is a colour horses are – it was beautiful, kind of straight but curling under at her shoulders, and it hung down each side of her face. That's about how long it was – shoulder length. Oh yeah and her face was long and pale. I think if anyone had sat and looked at her for a long time they might have said she was plain, because there wasn't one feature of her face that you could say was beautiful or even pretty, except maybe her blue eyes. But she wasn't plain at all. I think she was one of these girls just on the right side of plain who don't know how good looking they really are, so they don't pose and they don't strut. And I bet she didn't realise she had such a figure either. She had a long, straight neck, and shoulders which were broad for a girl, but not too broad. If you drew a line from her right shoulder to her left, and then from there to her right hip, and from there across to her left, you would have a long, perfect Z. I could see this even though she was wearing school uniform. Of course I knew who she was. She was in my class, and I knew she wrote poetry and kept herself to herself a lot. I had been looking at her since Year Eight, but when she walked into the room and joined the GAs it was like seeing her for the first time all over again. And when we dated... you know I can remember how she felt when I put my arms round her, what she smelled like, everything, but that was later. She was gorgeous.

And she was totally wrong.

There was something just not right about her, and I nearly lost sight of that because of how great she was. Oh I could see right from the beginning that there was more to her than any of the other GAs. She was made from the same stuff as I was, she was different, she could do things that I could. She was different from the rest, way ahead of them if she had known it. Maybe that was what was wrong – there shouldn't have been two of us. I wish I hadn't been in love with her sometimes.

Tinker, the youngest GA, he had a crush on her too. You could see it in the way he looked at her, the way he laughed when she laughed. He played a silly trick on her – I think Janet put him up to it – with the glass in his watch, making the reflection of it dance round the room, and she laughed when she saw what a feeble trick it was. And after she had pushed the woman out of the way of the bus on her first mission, who had gone up to her and called her "awesome"? Yeah, Tinker. I could never understand why he didn't just leave her alone. She was way out of his league. She was way out of everyone's league. Except mine. But when she had walked in to our classroom, everyone had gone quiet. No one had expected her. We all sat and looked at her, and she stood and looked at us. I smiled and winked at her. I don't know why. I think it was because fancying her had taken over from the feeling that something was not right here.

Angela almost backed out. ""I'm sorry, I'm in the wrong place," she said.

Janet couldn't see that of course, I'm sure no one else but me had any doubts. Janet said, "No, you're okay, Angela. You wouldn't be here if you weren't supposed to be here." Then she asked Angela how she had got there, and some twonk called it "having her platform nine-and-three-quarters-moment" – I mean how nerdish is that! But then it was her first time and it must have seemed as weird to her as it did to any of us the first time. Then Janet asked her if she believed in fairies, and Tinker pulled his stupid trick with the watch glass, and the next thing we knew she was sitting down with us and was one of us, and hearing all about what we do. And then the Rising happened.

So we were all here that day, right where I'm standing now at City Road, fanned out, moving through the crowds of shoppers and people rushing and dawdling and getting in the way just the same as they are today. The GAs were busy looking for the woman they had seen in the Rising, all focussing on locating her. What they didn't realise – and they never did realise this – is that the Yellows were all there too. Each one of them was marking a GA, moving along with them, tuning in to them in the quark stream so it was less likely that the GAs would know they were there. It's so cool how the Yellows can do that. This didn't always happen, because we never got the same Rising; but sometimes we got... a different Rising about the same thing, if you see what I mean. This was one of those times.

It was difficult for the Yellows, because there was a kind of overlap. They were down to eleven because I was in with the GAs that day, and the GAs had someone extra – Angela. So basically I was shadowing Angela, or I thought I was. I hadn't been there for the Yellow's Rising, I just saw they were there. That's how it seemed to work. At least no one had to shadow me.

I think I became aware of the woman at the same time Angela did. I felt the quark stream swirling round both of them, joining them, and like a little current joining me to both of them, growing stronger. I moved closer and closer to them across the crowded pavement. It was difficult because in crowds people move at different speeds, and you have to keep side-stepping round them. As well as the connection in the quark stream between me and

Angela, which was getting stronger by the moment, and the web of links which stretched between all of us, I could feel one of the Yellows very close. I couldn't see him, but I felt him closer to Angela and the woman than I was.

All the time this was going on, it was like time was slowing down. On the way to City Road I think I'd totally lost it, because I walked along with Angela just talking and talking and telling her all sorts of things about the GAs and what we were supposed to be doing, and letting her in on all our secrets. And of course I was hitting on her like anything! So all this was running round and round in my head, and I was calling myself a retard for thinking and acting like that. And at the same time it was like the pressure of the quark stream was building up like water behind a dam and it was going to burst.

Then something seemed to be glowing red hot in the quark stream up ahead. I knew that it must be someone fairly small, because I couldn't see them with people in the way. It was like the stream suddenly collapsed, went sideways, became confused as the streams round the woman, the other Yellow, and Angela kind of collided. At that moment it was like time slowing right down, and the crowd ahead of me parted, and this is what I saw:

There was a kid. I could only see his back view, but I knew him. His left ankle was twisting under him, and he was going over sideways with his shoulder heading straight for the woman. There was a bus coming towards them, and I knew that when he hit her there was no way she was not going under those wheels, and maybe him too. But the amazing thing was Angela. She had already started to move, not towards the woman, not towards the kid, but to the woman's left. She was already throwing herself in front of the bus, like she could see ahead exactly where she ought to be. To me, right then, it seemed like she was deliberately trying to kill herself. But when the kid did knock into the woman and send her flying, Angela was already there to grab her and roll, pulling them both clear, past the off-side wheels of the bus. I could see the driver's face totally white with terror, pushing himself back with both hands on the steering wheel, as though that would stop the accident. He must have had his foot hard on the brake. I could see the kid – he seemed to have bounced off the woman and was staggering forward, turning the stagger into a run. I caught a glimpse of Janet, over the other side of the street, running out to drag Angela and the woman onto the pavement. I saw in a flash about twenty or thirty different reactions from everyone around the scene. And then I set off running after the kid, dodging round people, catching hold of metal posts and swinging round them to change direction, ducking and diving in and out, and away from City road into the back lanes, round loading bays, workshops, and lock-ups.

We both slowed and stopped when we were sure no one was following or could see us. The kid leant against a wall and looked at me. He was the youngest Yellow, Aidan's brother Simon.

"You want to tell me what the hell you thought you were doing?" I said to him. He didn't say anything, he was trying to get his breath back. So I went on.

"We just aren't supposed to do that. We can't do that. We are supposed to make sure things happen – not make them happen. We can't just kill people."

"It didn't happen like that," he said. "Honest. I just went over sideways on my ankle. I didn't mean to, and it hurt like hell anyway. But Charlie, anyhow... look... maybe it was supposed to happen like that. Maybe my falling into her was supposed to happen the same as all the other stuff we've seen. It was just this time one of us was actually meant to be there and meant to be involved by accident. That's possible, isn't it?"

"If it is, it's the first time I've seen anything like

it," I said. "And I don't like it."

"I don't like it either," said Simon. "And I don't like the way the place was full of Guardian Angels. It didn't happen, Charlie, did it though? Bugger – my foot hurts! It didn't happen because of that girl. It all went wrong."

I'd seen this a few times before, times when Yellows and GAs were out together. Sometimes there seemed to be no reason why we were all there, almost like we were all making sure the same person made it where they were going. Sometimes we had the same person in view, and up to now when that happened the GAs seemed to get the better of the Yellows. Maybe it was because they didn't know the Yellows were there, and so they weren't distracted. But what Simon was saying had me worried. You see I don't think Angela could have reacted that quickly. She had dived to save the woman before she had fallen in front of the bus. It was like she saw ahead. Not only had time slowed down for her, she had moved ahead of it. I didn't like to think about this. That was another reason why she was all wrong, and the wrong things were beginning to pile up.

"You get off back," I said to Simon. "Go a long way round."

Simon groaned, and took a few steps with his bad foot. He said, "I think it's swelling up."

"Too bad," I said. "Anyhow, you managed to run fast enough before. You can manage to walk back to school now."

So off he went, limping a bit too much and trying it on, leaving me to find my way back to City Road and on towards school again, because by the time I got to Three Lane Ends everyone else had gone. All that was left were some black skidmarks from the bus's tyres.

From then on I stuck to Angela like sick to a blanket. When I wasn't with her as part of our dating, I was right behind her, or close by, watching her. I even found somewhere near her house where I could watch through a piece of broken fence. I would stand there sometimes, and catch sight of her. Not that I got much chance to do that.

Then there's the scary bit. I forget when she told me she was having bad dreams, but right at the same time I started having dreams too. In these dreams I was always following her, about two steps behind. Sometimes it seemed to be somewhere sunlit or full of people, but mostly it was somewhere dark. So awake or asleep I was always following her. And in some of these dark dreams I felt like I wasn't really me, and when I was awake I kept remembering the piece of poetry the man who drowned was saying. There was something about a grove of stones, and then there was this:

Like one, that on a lonesome road

Doth walk in fear and dread,

And having once turned round walks on,

And turns no more his head;

Because he knows, a frightful fiend

Doth close behind him tread.

Sometimes in these dreams, Angela and I seemed to be walking amongst standing stones, like a stone circle packed tight, and it was dark like midnight, or like a closed-in space. And I was always right behind her, never more than two steps. Sometimes I wasn't myself – I said that – because sometimes I was a monster with my arms stretched out to the side and my fingers spread, ready to catch her and crush her. But I was the one who was afraid in the dreams, in case she turned round and saw me and screamed.

O7

Perhaps I should go and talk to Angela's mum and dad first, before my mum and dad. I want to very much. But I have been round there before, once or twice, and they have this book on the coffee table in their lounge, and it's full of these weird drawings by a guy who saw himself as a man with a bull's head. And it's like there's nothing left of him that's human – you've got to pity him – but his eyes are hard and brutal, and his horns curl round, and his hair is like a mass of wild, weird curls drawn with a fine-tipped pen, and it freaked me out to see these pictures but I couldn't leave them alone. I couldn't take my eyes off them. When I had been reading that book, and Angela's mum came into the room to talk to me, I was tongue-tied. She was being really polite to me, which was nice, but I couldn't think of anything to say; and so she probably thought I was just a dork, and wondered what her precious daughter saw in me. Angela's dad just didn't like me from the off.

But there are things I would really like them to know about me, and about Angela – things they wouldn't guess at if I didn't tell them. It is really hard to tell people things. Particularly things they don't want to hear. People spend their whole lives believing what they want to believe. They kid themselves that such-and-such a thing is true, and then they go on believing it, no matter what anyone tells them. I don't know that Angela's parents would want to hear what I have to say, but they ought to.

Kesha Patel was like that.

We arrived in the GAs at about the same time as each other. I can't remember which one of us actually walked through the door first, so it was probably her by a couple of days. Anyhow at first we got on ok. She was really witty, and nice-looking too with that black hair almost to her waist. We often found ourselves together, talking and stuff. We weren't dating or anything like that, we were just really friendly, but people used to joke that we were an item. I didn't mind. I didn't mind being one half of "Charlie Seacole and Kesha Patel" one bit, so I never denied it.

But I think Kesha began to resent it after a while, and she would turn her pretty face into a frown.

"Why don't you say something, Charlie?" she said eventually. "We're not together, and every time I tell people that they grin and say – Well, Charlie doesn't exactly deny it."

"What's the big deal? Let them talk." I said.

"It's not right," she said. "What if it got back to my mum and dad? They're so... Indian. Indian girls don't have boyfriends just like that. It's not what we do."

"You mean I wouldn't be good enough for you? I wouldn't be good enough for your mum and dad? Oh thanks a lot!"

"It's not that, Charlie. You know you would, Charlie... well you probably would... I mean they're old fashioned about some things but not others."

I suddenly began to feel pretty disrespected by all this.

"Kesha," I said, while she shook her head at everything I said. "What you're trying to tell me –

pretty bloody clumsily – that this is all about colour. I'm not Indian, and I'm not white, and I'm not black. What is the big deal? What you're telling me then is that isn't about colour but it is, or something, is that it? The more you tell me it isn't, the more it is."

"Stop, Charlie."

"You stop. You stop digging yourself deeper into this hole!"

"Bloody stop it, Charlie," she said, gritting her teeth.

"All right, all right. I was out of order. We both were."

This conversation hurt, and that's why it is such a clear, sharp memory. I don't know if I really thought Kesha and I would become an item, but that was the moment I knew we wouldn't. We stopped fighting, and she stopped frowning, but it was like something was broken and couldn't be fixed. We still talked, but not like we did before.

Okay, I guess I did have a crush on her, sort of. If I hadn't, I wouldn't have done what I did next. I found she had made her personal web-profile private, and I couldn't get into it any more. When I mentioned it to her she said, "Oh yeah, I'll add you when I get a moment", but a week later I still couldn't get in, then two weeks later still nothing. I didn't bother asking her again, but I really wanted to see what was going on, what she was telling people and showing them. Don't let anyone tell you it's impossible to hack into Facebook or Myspace or things like that. It isn't – it isn't any more difficult than getting official reports about people who commit suicide – I did it. I hacked into Kesha's private profile.

You know, it's strange, but before I became a GA I wasn't all that brilliant with computers. It never occurred to me to think that being a GA would change that. Maybe it did.

I was able to see all her new stuff, and all the comments from her friends. It was like getting close to her again. And another thing I did was hack into her chatroom account for a laugh, and I appeared a couple of times in our chatroom as "Skydancer". It was cool, being able to get close to her this way, to be able to read things she kept for friends. She had said she was going to add me anyway, so I didn't feel like I was doing anything wrong. Then I saw someone had written something on her wall about her and me, saying she was sorry we weren't dating any more; and Kesha had said "Excuse me! We were never dating in the first place, if you don't mind! LOL". So that was that. You can say something to people over and over and they won't believe you, but put it on the web and it's gospel.

Then we had the fight.

It was one Saturday. I was just cutting down between Woolworths and the building next door, taking a short cut, when I heard running footsteps. I thought it was just someone in a hurry back on the pavement, but suddenly I felt my shoulder being grabbed, and there was Kesha, right in my face and boiling mad.

"What are you, Charlie Seacole? Just what are you?" she said.

"What? What? What did I do?"

"You know bloody well what you did. For a start you hacked into my private profile. You read all my private stuff..."

"Well you said you were going to add me to your friends list and you never did," I said.

"Oh yeah and what if I didn't?" she shouted. "How does that make hacking me right? What if I had decided not to add you?"

"Why wouldn't you want to add me?" I asked, spreading my hands out.

"That's not the bloody point!" Now she was nearly screaming, and I could see faces peeking into the alley as people passed. "It doesn't matter why I did or didn't add you. It matters that I didn't, or I hadn't. It matters that you just decided to hack into my private world, Charlie Seacole. And..."

"Okay I'm sorry. I won't do it again."

"... I haven't bloody well finished! You hacked into my chatroom account too. You pretended to be me. You are nothing but a stalker!" She was well angry by this time.

"Oh come on," I said. "I was just having a bit of a laugh."

"A bit of a laugh?" she said. "Oh ha bloody ha! Are you the kind of scumbag sicko they let in the Guardian Angels? Are you the kind of person they let protect humanity, and fight in the battle between good and evil?"

Now she was calling me names I stopped trying

to calm her down. I was riled too.

"At least I have a proper angel!" I spat at her. "Not some bogus Indian fairy like yours."

"Yeah?" she spat back. "At least mine was given to me. At least I didn't steal mine like you did, Charlie Tealeaf Seacole. You're just a thief. You stole your angel like you stole my identity in chat!"

"I didn't steal mine – I found it!"

"Yeah, yeah" said Kesha, turning away. "Talk to the hand, sicko-loser, because the face just logged out! In fact, talk to my back!"

That did it. I think I roared at her. I am sure that the quark stream blazed around me and I sent a hot, angry wave at her. She must have felt it coming, because hers flamed too. And suddenly there we were, still in the alley, but outside it too, facing each other, eyes locked. Around each of us, the quark stream whipped like a whirlpool; arms lashed out from it, waves of it battered at each other, all the energy we could conjure up pushed and shoved, like continental plates rasping at each other. It was like we were standing on nothing, and the whole world was disappearing around us. Everything was all this energy battering, battering. I could see Kesha's face, as angry as one of those statues of Kali. She was beautiful, terrible, dangerous, no longer like a human being at all, her eyes were blazing, cold green in the middle of red fire. I knew she wanted to crush me to nothing, and I wanted to do the same to her. Steal my angel? Steal her identity? I wanted to steal her life! There was a roaring in my ears almost too loud to bear. The air was hot, like in a desert sandstorm. I could feel dozens of thin tendrils from the quark stream, like steel whips, lashing out from my body, trying to get to Kesha; and for each tendril snaking out from me, there was one from Kesha, each one looking like a striking King Cobra. Mine and hers battered against each other, twisted round each other, looking for a way through. I felt fear choking me, and realised that one was coiling round my neck. I felt anger, and knew that one of mine was tightening round hers too. I had never felt anger like this, and I was loving it. I felt pain as one of Kesha's steel whips slammed against my face, and I felt joy as one of mine lashed hers. The air space between us seemed to be screaming, but then it could have been our voices, each one full of fear, joy, anger, pain. It was like... it was like everything one did to the other was done right back, lash for lash... it was like... it was like we couldn't stop it, we were both pushed on by our burning anger at each other...

It could have gone on for hours. I have no idea how long the quark stream thrashed around us. But suddenly it wasn't any more. Kesha and I were standing, looking at each other, in the alley by Woolworths. I didn't even know whether our battle had actually happened. We were just a teenage boy and girl standing, looking at each other. For a moment, it seemed like all I had to do was say something to her, maybe apologize for everything and make us friends again. But when something is broken, it's broken, and I said nothing. Kesha turned round again, and walked out of the alley.

She didn't come back to GAs, either.

08

It's funny when I think about it, but one of the really cool things about being a GA – for me anyway, at the beginning – was afterwards. I mean after we had been out doing what we did, or even sitting around in our empty classroom. I got a buzz from going on line and going into our chat room to talk about it all. I can laugh about it now, but it was at times like that that we became just a bunch of mates. We were ordinary teenagers again, all with geeky screen-names and all this LOL and LMAO stuff.

I was Chessman, Kesha was Skydancer – the original Skydancer – Tinker was poshrat, until Angela came along and he did his nerdy trick with the watch, and then he called himself Tinkerbell. I think I preferred poshrat, whatever it meant; Tinkerbell was just so... so... Anyhow, that's how he got his real-life nickname – Tinker. I told him he was a gypsy, and he just grinned. Janet told me not to make fun of him, but she'd got me wrong there; he didn't bother me, he was just some kid hanging on to the edge of the GAs as far as I was concerned. Anyhow, Ben Gillett was BigBen, Janet was xemojanx and so on.

Janet used to be like this mega-goth wannabe. Her deep red hair used to be wild, with a bit of black ribbon in it, and she would try to make her eyes up with dramatic, black eye-shadow, but she was always getting shouted at by the teachers for that. If she could get away with something that wasn't school uniform, something red or black like a leather wristband or something, then she would; and she would deliberately wear the opposite of whatever was fashionable amongst the chavettes. If they all wore their ties loose and their shirt collars open, she would button her collar up to the neck, even make it stand up and bend the points over, and her tie would be knotted so tight, with a tiny little knot.

"It's a Windsor knot," she told me once. "My granddad showed me how to do it."

Then when the chavettes got all smart, Janet would open her shirt collar wide, and wear the tie inside it. Like I said, she was always getting shouted at by the teachers for not wearing proper uniform, and had notes sent home. She would always put on this bored, sour expression, and her best mate – until she joined the GAs – was a girl who cut herself regularly. I mean!

But I began to notice that she had toned it all down. I thought, when I looked back to before I became a GA, that it had just been her tulpa blending in, not being noticeable; but I realized eventually it was that being a GA was making her serious, I mean really serious, not just some girl playing at being a depressive emo.

Kesha had been a bit "little-miss-Hindu", like her mum had dressed her, and that had made her stand out a bit. But she got more westernized. Just a little bit. She stood out a bit less. I guess we all did. But it was like in secret we all walked tall.

One day, Jan had told Kesha and me and some of the others, in the chatroom, how she had got her "angel". Hers wasn't really an angel, it was a couple of earrings, made like silver wings, and she got them at the fair at Chart Heath. For me the fair is always the thing that always tells me autumn is starting; it always turns up on a weekend in late September or early October, and the heath fills up with brightly-painted artics and mobile homes, in a big ring like wagon-trains make in the old Westerns my dad has on DVD. The fair is usually there for two or three days, and sometimes it rains and the Heath gets shin-deep in mud, but more often than not there is low sun shining off all the crappy paintwork, and it goes on into the evening, when all the red and yellow lights come on. There's always a smell of trampled grass, diesel generators, and fajitas. Anyhow, Jan was at the fair, wandering round, looking bored and gothic I'll bet, when she heard a sound. She told it like this, typing away, sending it into the chatroom in a long stream, and mostly we didn't interrupt her. Mostly.

xemojanx: i cud hear this sound sort of a sharp smack and a ping and it just got inside my head and i cudnt ignore it. i kept looking round for where it was coming from and it was driving me mental...

xemojanx: then i realised what it was like it was coming from this shooting gallery it was the sound of air rifles going off...

xemojanx: you load them by kinda folding them in two, putting a pellet into the bit in the middle and then closing it up again...

xemojanx: the smacking sound was when the rifle is fired and the ping is the pellet hitting the target or the metal plate behind it and it was like i just cudnt resist it...

xemojanx: it was so weird like i was being pulled towards the shooting gallery...

xemojanx: and it was like i knew i cud... i cud hit all those little ducks that go along from right to left, it

was so weird. well not weird like everything that has
happened since...

BigBen: BRB

Skydancer: hb

poshrat: hb

chessman: hb ben or ul miss it all

xemojanx: hb ben...

xemojanx: ... neway it was weird all the same. so
i went up and asked if i could have a go and the guy
said yes, and i paid my money. he gave me a rifle and
showed me how to load it – i knew nehow – but when
i put it up to my shoulder...

xemojanx: ... i could tell that there was sumthing
wrong with the sight, so if i wanted to shoot straight i
had to look to the left of it and neway i had to shoot
ahead of the ducks...

xemojanx: ...becoz they were moving, right?

poshrat: it's called deflection shooting

chessman: duh p-rat!

poshrat: what? what?

chessman: nm nm

xemojanx: ... so i took aim and squeezed the trigger and bang down went the first duck...

<marco has entered the room>

BigBen: back

xemojanx: hi marco wb ben   (((((((marco))))))

BigBen: ty jan. hi marco.

chessman: wb ben and hi marco

marco: hi guys (((((((jan)))))) (((((((kesha)))))))) what's up?

Skydancer: (((((((marco polo)))))))) and wb ben. jan is telling us about how she got her wings. at the fair on chart green.

marco: ok kewl.

marco: *pulls up a chair and listens*

BigBen: ty ty ty ty and LOL @ marco

xemojanx: marco i was telling everyone how i felt i had to go to this shooting gallery and try to shoot six of those metal ducks with an air rifle. u with me?

marco: *nods*

xemojanx: k lol... neway six times i loaded the rifle and six times down went a little duck. i knew that the bloke behind the counter was looking at me and i wondered...

xemojanx: ... if he was frowning or nething becoz he didnt want me to win but he wasnt becoz when i looked up he was smiling with like one eyebrow raised...

xemojanx: ... and hes like – pick nething from the second shelf – and theres teddy bears and dolls and ornaments and weird stuff like torches and sets of spanners and screwdrivers...

xemojanx: ... but there was sumthing shining in between i dont kno it might have been in between a car-wash kit and a teddy but it was bright and sparkling and just like i cudnt ignore the ping noise...

xemojanx: ... i cudnt take my eyes off this shining thing. it was only little and i cudnt see wat it was, so i asked the bloke and he went to get it, and it was a little card with 2 earrings on it in the shape of wings...

xemojanx: ... and he said they were renaissance angels wings and i just looked at them and they were SO beautiful i just wanted them. i dont kno why i wanted them so much – well i didnt kno why then, its kinda clearer now – i just did...

xemojanx: ... so i took them as my prize. i didnt think they were valuable or anything or special...

xemojanx: *pauses for breath and sip of coke LOL*

xemojanx: ... and thats how i got them. of course like theres always a little shop in stories where you go and buy sumthing weird and then the next day you cant find the shop of course the fair packs up and leaves...

xemojanx: ... dont kno wat else to say.

marco: I never hrd how u found ur way in to school – u kno – ur special way

poshrat: your platform nine 3/4

chessman: duh!!!! :D

xemojanx: LOL

xemojanx: well u kno the big gates at school the ones which are always open and every1 walks thru them...

xemojanx: ... well u kno the little gate at the side which leads to the footpath we are all supposed to walk on becoz the drive is where cars and vans come in...

xemojanx: ... but they locked it becoz people were jamming into it and making a big crowd outside the gates i heard ...

xemojanx: ... well one day I was just like trailing my fingers on it and i felt i ought to push at it. yeah I had my earrings on for the 1st time and it was like hearing the ping or seeing the earrings shining for the first time...

xemojanx: ... there was sumthing telling me i shud push at the gate and sumthing else like running water like i was standing in a river and my feet were being sucked at but of course i was dry...

xemojanx: ... and i just pushed and it opened but not like a gate opened more like i was pushing a curtain back or it was soft and melty and i was pushing a hole in it...

xemojanx: ... and i stepped thru and took 1 or 2 steps and turned round to say to everybody like hey look at this but...

xemojanx: there was no1 there and just this tugging at my feet and the rest u all kno LOL becoz i met the gas

BigBen: LOL @ the gas

xemojanx: the bloody GA s you nerd LOL

chessman: kewl!!!!

marco: indeed molto cool

<poshrat> sends the sound applause

BigBen: awesome jan tyvm

xemojanx: yw

xemojanx: ne1 else tell how they got their angel

thing?

    xemojanx: charlie? mark? ne1?

    chessman: L8R maybe ok

"Later, maybe, ok?" I said; but I don't think I ever told anyone in the chatroom. I told Jan later when I bumped into her in a café in town, and I think she must have told Kesha, because how else would Kesha have known? I don't know if she told anyone else.

We were sitting there, and Jan was slurping at a glass of coke. She was using a straw loudly, because there were chavettes at another table, and they were sipping their drinks from their glasses, trying to look cool and sophisticated, and Jan as usual was in chav-baiting mood and trying to annoy them. I started to tell her about my angel key-ring. I was looking out of the window, and the weather on that day was just how I remember it before.

I was walking along the tarmac path through the park. It was autumn – that I remember too – because there were leaves blowing across, and I had my jacket zipped up against the cold wind. The sun was low and in my eyes, flashing through the branches of the trees, and there was a spit of rain from time to time. I could see where the path ran straight past the playground, and just to one side of the football pitch, and I could make out a woman sitting on the bench; but she got up and left when I was still about two hundred metres away, maybe more. When I got to the bench I happened to look underneath it – I don't know why – and I saw a leather handbag. I thought it must belong to the woman I had seen sitting there, so I picked it up. I looked for her, but I couldn't see her anywhere. She would have left the park by then, and could have turned left, or right, or gone straight on; and anyway I hadn't got a close-up look at her.

I put the bag on the bench and opened it. I looked for something with her name and address on it. There was a wallet full of credit cards, and there was a driving license with a name on it, but nothing with an address. There was about fifty or sixty pounds in the wallet, and a load of other stuff like make-up in her bag. There was a mobile phone – I picked that up and thought about switching it on – but who would I have called, if her phone was here? I could have tried one of the numbers in her phonebook, but I could imagine the reception I would get – "Who's this? Why have you got her phone?" – and the next thing you know the Old Bill would be round to arrest the black kid with the lady's handbag!

There was a bunch of keys on a ring. Several rings, actually, all linked together, about three of them. One of these keyrings had a fob on it, and I held it up to look at it. There was a dull, metal medallion on the end of a piece of chain. On it, slightly raised from the surface, was the figure of an angel. It had jointed armour and a spear, but wings spread out from its back. It looked grim, but I was certain it was an angel. I grinned and called it "Lucifer", thinking it looked like the rebel angel. I turned the medallion over and read what was on the other side; it was in a flowing kind of writing, like I had seen on the price-tags and signs in a shop that sold New Age stuff. In the centre of the medallion were the words "Christ Michael" and "Aton", and around the edge, like the inscription on a coin, were the words "Creator God Michael of Nebadon". I thought this was weird, and I thought about a kid in my class at school who was a Jehovah's Witness, and how he used to say that the archangel Michael was the same as Jesus in the Bible. I remember I laughed a bit, because here was a picture of someone people thought of as Jesus, but I had just given him a devil's name.

I took the fob off the main keyring, and I looked at it. Then I jiggled it up and down in my hand. I liked the weight. I don't know why I liked the weight, I just did. The metal seemed heavy and soft, so that it didn't jingle, but more like absorbed it when I banged the chain and the ring and the medallion together. I put the bag back down on bench, and closed my fingers over the medallion. It felt good, it felt right; it felt like I had been meant to come across it.

I put it in my pocket, put the bag under the bench, and walked off.

I'd got to this bit of the story, and Jan said "Why didn't you take it in to the police station?"

"Oh yeah, right," I said. "Like I am going to walk down the street with a handbag. Apart from anything else – like I said about the phone – who would have believed I didn't nick it?"

Jan by then was sucking noisily at the last millimetre of coke in her glass, and the chavettes had got up to leave, looking daggers at her.

"You know what, Charlie," she said. "It's a different story from the one everyone else tells. We all got our angel things from a man we never saw again. Like me and the fairground man, and Kesha and her uncle Dinesh. You're the only GA who got one from a woman. That's weird. I don't know. It might be special."

That's what I thought too – it was special, I'm special. I knew I was special even then, different from the other GAs.

Here's one thing I never told Jan, or anyone else, though:

The far gate of the park was about four hundred metres further on from the bench. When I got there, there was a woman coming into the park. She was walking very quickly. I looked at her as she passed me, and I could see that she was frowning, and staring ahead like she was trying to see into the distance. I wondered if she might be the woman who had left her bag under the bench, and was only just coming back for it. Anyhow, she didn't seem to notice me, and I didn't say anything to her.

I did look her up and down, though. She looked nice. A bit younger than my mum, somewhere in her thirties, with thick hair that bobbed and swung as she walked. And she was wearing a smart, green jacket.

That's the other special thing. Everyone else got their angel thing from a man they never saw again. I thought I wouldn't see the woman again, but then how was I to know one day would come, the GAs would have a Rising, and Simon Kavanaugh would shoulder-charge her in front of a bus, and Angela would save her life.

O9

I'm walking through the park right now. I'm walking along the path that cuts diagonally across it, and goes in between the playground and the football pitch. The weather seems like it did on the day when I got my angel, but I may not be remembering right – everything seems so mixed up today. I don't know what is going on.

I need to see mum and dad, and I need to see the Guardian Angels. I think I need to find Janet, or Mr Callister maybe. I definitely need to see the GAs. Definitely. And I need to come back here, and sit on the swing where Angela died. Definitely.

But I need to go and look somewhere else first.

There's a big, oblong building near here that old

people call the Tithebarn. It's Victorian, but they say it's on the site of a much older building going back to the Middle Ages, or to Saxon times or something. The side of it facing the street has had all its windows filled in – you can just about see where they were – and the whole lot covered in cement. At one time it was painted red, then pink, but people objected. That was back when I was little. I can just about remember it being pink. But then they had to paint it cream, and nowadays it looks grey. A doorway seems to sweep inward, right in the middle of the big slab of a wall, and there's a door set back, painted purple. Over the doorway there's a neon sign saying "Pandemonium", and there are posters on the curving recess with the names of DJs – big black letters on a yellow background. It's a nightclub.

I've never been in there of course, because it's licensed. Maybe I could pass for eighteen now, because I'm tall, but not back then. I've walked past outside it during the day, and wondered what it was like inside. I've walked past it during the evening too, and when the door swung open there was often the sound of Trance music coming out. My mum and dad didn't like me being out too late when I was young, because there were a couple of gangs in town and talk of boys going tooled up; but this place fascinated me, and I used to walk home from Christo's house the long way round, just to pass by that door, hoping that it would open and music would come out, and maybe I would catch a glimpse of flashing lights or something.

One evening it was like I just found myself there. I had been at Christo's, and we had been playing chess and talking about it, and he had brought out a chess problem from his dad's newspaper. I couldn't solve it, and it was on my mind as I walked home. It didn't even register with me that I was walking past Pandemonium that time, I was so caught up in the chess problem. I only realized when I had just gone past the doorway, and I kind of stopped and looked back, and wondered about walking back and forth past it a few times. But there was a bunch of people dressed for clubbing coming towards me, and I didn't want to look stupid, so I kept on. There was one bloke in the bunch of people who seemed to have everyone's attention. I guess he was about nineteen or twenty, and two girls were holding his arms and laughing, and I could see he was loving that. The rest of the people – blokes and girls – were all laughing and joking, maybe a bit too loud, like you do when you want to make out you're one of a gang. Anyhow, as we got close to each other he saw me, and stopped, and got his right arm untangled from the girl on that side.

"Hey pal," he said. "You want a present?"

"Sure," I said, trying to look as cool as I could.

He reached in his pocket, and took out something small. He passed it to me, and I saw it was one of those smiley badges with a pin on the back – just a yellow disc with two dots for eyes, and a curve for a mouth. It wasn't much, but it made me feel good having it.

"I won't need it where I'm going," he said. "I'll be in Afghanistan by Monday."

"You in the army, then?" I asked.

"Yep."

"Cool. Good luck... and thanks for the badge."

"No worries, mate," he said, and turned to go. The girl on his left arm had been looking me up and down. I heard her say, "He'll be gorgeous when he turns eighteen!" and someone called her a "cradle-snatcher", and they all laughed. I walked home wondering when my face would stop burning.

There was a point when I realised that my heart was thumping not because of what the girl had said, but because of having the badge in my hand. I was holding really tight to it, and the side with the pin was digging uncomfortably into my hand. But I didn't want to let it go, I didn't want to put it into my pocket and forget it was there, or accidentally drop it. It just seemed so special. Part of my mind was telling me I was being silly, being a big kid, but still I held it really tight. I forgot all about the chess problem, and began to hurry to get home.

When I got home I ignored my mum calling "Charlie? Want some supper?" and went straight to my bedroom. I couldn't think what to do with the badge – should I hide it in a drawer or something? – but then it seemed the right thing to do to pin it to the lapel of my school blazer. So I did that, and I hung the blazer up to look at it. Then I unfastened it again, and re-pinned it, but this time on the underside of the lapel, where no one could see it. The next Monday, when the soldier was due to fly out to Afghanistan, I wore it to school.

I remember that the nearer I got to school the more I could feel something, like a rushing and a pulling. No, it was more like something was working on my mind at that point. There's a wooden fence, really high, before you get to the school railings, and then just where the fence stops and the railings begin, there's an old tree. It's like the fence grows out of it one way and the railings the other, and you can't see that they are three separate things, because of the shadows made by them. Well, it was like something was telling me to go and look right into those shadows. No, not pulling me, not yet, but like there was something inside my head making the decision – part of me but not part of me – and I was getting scared. I had stopped by the tree, and people were walking round me, not paying any attention to me. Their voices started to sound like they were coming from a long way off, and their faces and figures, that I could see out of the corner of my eyes, seemed blurry. I moved closer and closer to the shadows, and they seemed to grow; and I began to feel like I did once when I was a really little kid and I got lost, and I was close to panicking. The shadows seemed to grow and grow.

Then I found myself touching the pin on my yellow smiley badge, and suddenly I didn't feel half as afraid. The shadows stopped being frightening, and seemed more – I don't know – impressive, important. I walked into them, and there was a moment when everything went very cold, and after that moment I found myself standing in the corner of the school grounds, on the grass.

Yes, that was when I began to feel the rushing and pulling.

Into my mind came the word "quark". Apart from chess, the other thing I was into was atoms and sub-atomic particles, ages before we were supposed to do them in school. I was into hadrons (I remember telling Christo about them, and he called them "hard-ons" and laughed, and I punched his shoulder) and stuff like that, and how quarks were these unknown particles that made up hadrons, but they were impossible to see and they only existed in theory except for the "top" quark which decayed too quickly to be measured. But maybe they were floating free at the time of the Big Bang at the beginning of everything, and that's almost how it seemed to me now... there was a stream flowing, like water, from the spot where I stood, straight across the grass to the front door of the school. The hypotenuse of a right-angled triangle. It was like I could see these particles, even though they're incredibly small – a different colour for each of the types of quark... up, down, strange, charm, top, and bottom – making a strong current, tugging at my legs and making me move my feet.

It didn't register with me until I was moving, surrounded by this stream, that I was all on my own. No one else from the school was to be seen, anywhere, and the whole world seemed really quiet. When I got into the school it was like an exam day. Everything still, no one talking, but you know everyone is there. Only they weren't. I couldn't see anyone, anywhere. But still the quark stream kept tugging at me, until I came to the classroom, and there were the Yellows, waiting for me!

There were eleven of them, and I was the twelfth. I was the missing piece, that made it all perfect. I was a Yellow before I was ever a GA, and I was the twelfth GA too. All of it was perfect.

The Yellows were totally cool, and welcomed me like I was their long-lost brother or something. Aidan Kavanaugh explained to me how it was a great adventure. No, The Great Adventure, he called it, the last great adventure, the last battle the world was ever going to see. And we were the good guys. We made sure that things happened that were supposed to happen. Aidan told me it was all a part of a big plan.

I could see it. To me it was all like a big chess board. I could see in my mind's eye how all the pieces went together, how they moved. And the more I took part in the Yellows' work, and then when I knew I had to become a GA too, the more I could see how perfect it could all be.

It was like I had invented a new form of chess in my head, where the King had become a super-piece, able to move anywhere, like the Queen, but also to jump like the Knight. And I felt that I was so close to being like that new King. Just a few more things needed to fall into place for everything to be right. I wasn't a kid any more. I was going to be a King, in a perfect world, a world made new. A world where everything that was meant to happen happened, and happened because we saw to it that it did. Where I saw to it.

Because things have to happen. The way Aidan explained it on that first day, it's a 'dynamic universe'. To me it was a totally cool adventure. It was even cool in its own way, but sad too, that the bloke who gave me the smiley badge was killed after two weeks in Afghanistan. It was in the local paper, and on TV. I had been thinking that I would find some way of thanking him, maybe when he got home on leave. But I guess that wouldn't be right. I won't ever see him again. None of us see the people we get our thing from again. That how it is. That's right.

But now... I don't know. I've got as far as the park gates, where I saw the woman in the green jacket. I've stopped here. It feels like there is no point going on to Pandemonium. I'll turn round. I'll go back towards the playground. Maybe. For now.

The Everywhen Angels

10

So here I am, sitting on a swing in the playground. It's cold, and I know it's cold, but I don't mind. I can feel the cold, but I don't feel cold. It's dark too, but there are lights here now, because the new skate ramp is open, and there's a handful of hoodies using it. A bit of skateboarding, yeah, and a lot of just hanging. And I am sitting here, and like everyone else they are ignoring me, but that's cool, because I want to be ignored. I don't think I am any closer to knowing what's going on, though. And you know what? It's beginning to get to me.

Suddenly I just want to go over and talk to the chavs by the skate ramp. I want to talk about anything, anything at all. I don't mind what it is – football, TV, school, girls, something nerdy, anything will do. I am sick of being on my own. It was cool at first, now it's getting to me. I don't like it any more. I would go over to them and talk to them if I thought it would do any good. Maybe I'll do that anyway. I could lean against the side of the ramp like a couple of them are doing, and mutter, and nod, and laugh when they do. I could pretend I'm one of them, and pretend I'm joining in, and when one of them says, "Let's go to the Spar and get some Coke", I can say, "Yeah, c'mon lads, let's go do that!" What the heck, though, I can't be bothered. I could go and do that anywhere, I could spy on people doing anything, go into houses, no one will stop me. That should be good. But... suddenly it doesn't seem worth it.

It's all beginning to get to me, but it's just like not feeling cold. I don't really feel anything much, just flat. I am beginning to feel like I am a figure in a photo or a drawing. Flat. That's it. I'm becoming flat. I don't want to be like that. I want to hold on to all my feelings. I want to laugh. I want to get really mad. I can still feel them a bit, but it's like they are slipping away.

One of the boys in hoodies is coming over to the swings. He's making straight for me... No he's sitting on the next swing. He's pulling back his hood.

It's Tinker.

I didn't know he hung out with these guys. Maybe he doesn't. Maybe he just knows them. He's looking at my swing.

He's looking at me.

"Hello, Charlie."

"Tink? You can see me?"

"Yes I can see you, Charlie. Of course I can see you."

"And you can talk to me and hear me too!"

"Yes, Charlie."

"Tink, this is amazing. Wow! You of all people. Tink, I have no idea what is going on. Things have got confusing for me. But I am SO glad you are here – it's great that you can see me, and we can talk. But why can't I talk to anyone else? Why is it only you who can talk to me?"

"I think that's because this is my dream, not yours, Charlie."

"Huh? This is a dream, then? I'm dreaming, right?"

"One of us is, Charlie. I'm sure about that."

"Weird. Cool too. What's going to happen next?"

"I don't know, Charlie."

"Tink, I have to get to the GAs. There's so many important things to do. There's stuff they need to know, stuff they need to do. I'm supposed to lead them, Tink. I am supposed to lead a whole army of GAs, and join up with all the Yellows too. There's a big battle coming up, Tink, and we're in it, and I am going to lead a whole army, Tink. I've got to get to the GAs right now, but it's difficult and I don't know why. You've got to help me, Tink."

"It's not going to happen like that, Charlie."

"Come on, Tink. I'm your leader."

"No, Charlie, not any more. You never really were."

"Someone else has taken my place? No way, Tink. I can't have that. They need me, they need the things I can do. No one else can do the things I can do. Help me get to them, Tink. You can do that. I'll make you my second in command."

"It's not going to happen, Charlie."

It's like I am beginning to feel again, at least a bit. There's like a desperate bit of the flatness, the bit that won't let go to all the other feelings.

"Oh bloody Hell, Tinker," I am almost growling this. "It's got to happen. It must happen. It can't NOT happen! Help me!"

"I can't, Charlie. You know I can't."

"But look, I still have my angel. I still have the key-ring with the medallion in it!" As I say this, I am diving my hands into my pockets, searching everywhere for it. Where is it? I can't find it.

"You haven't got it any more, Charlie," Tinker is saying.

"What... where has it gone?" Now I'm looking on the ground beneath the swing for it. "I need it so I can use my way in! I know – I've got my... my... other thing."

"You don't have it, Charlie, you don't have either of them. You won't find them. You can't use a way in any more."

The flatness has come back, and I am just sitting here, saying nothing. Tinker is still sitting by me.

"I really wanted to lead that army!"

"I know you did, Charlie."

"I want my angel."

"You can't have it, Charlie. You know it's gone."

"Why?"

"You stole it in the first place, Charlie. And you don't need it anyway."

"I want my smiley badge, then."

"You can't have that either, Charlie. You don't need it."

"I so wanted to lead that army."

"I know, Charlie."

"Or just the GAs."

"I know, Charlie."

"I can't?"

"No, Charlie."

I am sitting, thinking about this. The world seems flatter and flatter. I seem flatter and flatter.

"Tink, am I dead, or dying, or something?"

"That's what I think, Charlie."

"I don't want to be."

"Who would, Charlie!"

I am shaking my head, trying to think straight. This is wrong. All wrong. This is not happening. It's not how things were supposed to be. I must explain this to Tinker. Got to make him understand.

"No, Tink. You've got to be wrong about this. I'm not dead. Angela's the one who's dead, not me. She was the Thirteenth Angel. Thirteen is no good. There were twelve tribes of Israel, twelve disciples. Twelve is good. One and two make three. Three is good. Twelve and three – they work. There should be twelve Guardian Angels, not thirteen. One and three make four. That's bad. Four is bad, somehow. The thirteenth person at the Last Supper was Judas Iscariot, the traitor. Thirteen is wrong. If anyone is dead, it's Angela. That's definite, Tink. Not me!"

Tink is thinking... I think. He's thinking what to say. Maybe.

"Look, Charlie," he is saying, very slowly, very deliberately. "When there are thirteen of anything, it doesn't matter where you start counting. You could start anywhere in the Last Supper, and finish anywhere. You could start with Judas, and count until you got to Peter, or anyone. You could start anywhere in the Guardian Angels, and count until you reached thirteen. You could end at Angela, or me... or even you, Charlie."

"Me? I could be the thirteenth?"

"Yes, Charlie. But anyway, thirteen, twelve, eleven, it doesn't actually matter."

"It doesn't?"

"No, Charlie."

"It's all so confusing. There is so much I don't understand."

I am just sitting for a while, staring at the ground, trying to take all this in. All the things I believed to be so, just aren't. Everything seems to be upside down. Angela isn't dead, but I am? How does that work? But on the other hand, how would I know what it's like to be dead? I feel like crying, but I can't.

"So you think I really am dead? Like... checkmate... the King is dead?"

"Yes, Charlie."

"What can I do?"

"I don't know, Charlie."

"Tink, if this is your dream, can't you do something? Make me alive or something?"

"No, Charlie. Even I can't do something like that. Even though it is my dream."

I am sitting, silently, swinging. I go on like this for a while, but I can't count seconds or minutes any more. Even time is beginning to get flat.

"This sucks. This really sucks!"

"I guess so, Charlie."

"I don't know what to do, Tinker. I don't know what to feel. I don't know where to go or anything. What do I have to do now? Tell me what I'm supposed to do."

"I don't know, Charlie. I'm sorry."

"That's all right, Tink. No worries."

"Thanks, Charlie."

"I suppose I could go back to the hospital, and check out where I'm lying on the bed. If I'm still there. I could do that, couldn't I, Tink?"

"I suppose you could do that, Charlie."

He's pulling up his hood.

"You have to go now, don't you, Tink?"

"Yes, Charlie. I have to go."

"Why?"

"Even dreams can't last for ever, Charlie. At least I don't think they can. Sooner or later I have to wake up."

"Do you think I'll ever wake up from this?"

"I can't say, Charlie."

"I might, though?"

"I don't know, Charlie."

He's standing up, putting his hands in his pockets. I am so flat I can't think of anything more to say.

"Bye, Tink," I say.

"Goodbye, Charlie."

He's walking away, going towards the tarmac path. He's calling out to the other guys by the skate ramp. They're waving to him. Now they are leaving too. I'll leave in a minute. I'll go to the hospital again...

The bunch of them are walking away over the football pitch, out of the glare of the lights. I can hardly see them any more. There's Tinker. I can still see him, walking down the tarmac path. I can still see him. Just about.

I am sitting on the swing. I am so flat. Everything is so flat.

Where's Tinker? I can't see him.

I am sitting on the swing. I'll go back to the hospital in a minute.

The world is so flat.

So flat.

I am sitting on the swing...

PART THREE
THE POSHRAT

CHAPTER ONE, IN WHICH I ALMOST LOSE A DOG AND ALMOST MEET A KING.

My name is Ashe Sobiecki, and I was nearly thirteen when Becks, my Staffordshire Bull Terrier ran off while I was taking him for a walk. It took me by surprise when he did that. Normally he walks along at heel, and I talk to him, and he cocks his head on one side and listens. I talk, and he answers with grunts and growls, and sometimes a bark. He's good like that. I sometimes sing rock songs to him too, and he barks like anything.

Becks always listened when he was a puppy. I've had him since I was nine. Dad said having a dog and having to look after him would teach me responsibility. It was dad who called him Becks. So I thought that Becks having me would teach him responsibility too, and I was right. Becks is a very responsible dog, and he always was. Which was why it surprised me when he ran off. I have never known him to pull at his lead, since I first taught him what walking to heel meant, not until that day, and not very often since. Dad made me use the lead, and said I had to do it. It was the law or something, so anyway I did, and Becks never minded.

There's a place where you notice our suburb begin to thin out. It's a bit further now, because I think the car-park for the new garden centre reaches there. It's not exactly the countryside, not yet, but it's like the town isn't holding on to its place any more, it's beginning to lose its grip. There are buildings that aren't quite farms, but might have a few sheep and ponies. There are stands of trees which aren't quite woods, and there are tracks which aren't quite lanes. You mustn't be surprised to see ducks turning a flood-puddle into a pond as if by magic, or rabbits here and there; and once, one cold day when there was still snow on the ground, I saw a stoat in its winter ermine. I have even seen a sparrowhawk take a pigeon. When I was younger, I always liked to think that this area had a magic to it, because it was where something became something else. I used to notice things, I had my own little landmarks which told me whereabouts on a scale I had in my head, between town and country, the exact spot was. When we did percentages in school I used them in the scale. I graded the places by smell too. There's a place where it smells of sheep droppings, and that's about eighty percent countryside, and another where I can smell some sort of lubricating oil, and that's seventy-five percent town. And sounds too. You never quite lose the noise of the traffic in the background, but it's definitely louder the closer you get to the main road – well it would be – and in the opposite direction there's the place where you can sometimes hear curlews in spring. That is so cool, that sound.

Well, I like it round there. It's not just the landscape, not just the smells and sounds, and the birds and stuff like that. It's a feeling I get. I have always had it. It's being right on the edge of something. I know it is only the countryside it is on the edge of, but it's the edge that counts. It's like one of those graphs that go along in a kind of gradual slope and then shoot up suddenly. It's like that only upside down, so that the slope wants to pull you. I like being right where the pull is strong. It feels dangerous. But it's a dangerous idea, not a real danger, if you see what I mean.

So it wasn't just a surprise when Becks suddenly tugged hard on his lead, which I had been holding loosely, and ran away. It was more like an adventure. He headed down a track which curved round into a stand of silver birch trees, like they have in our local park. Only these were scrubbier and some of them had fallen over, and were making letters and Viking runes with each other. Well, I had to run after him, even if I was on what they call the knee of the graph, even if I was going to slip down the big slope. Becks had got way ahead and round the bend. I couldn't see him any more, and couldn't hear his scudding paws, but I could hear him barking, and then even that stopped. As I ran up the track, I could see something white beyond the trees, but I couldn't make it out until I got round the bend myself.

It was a fairly ordinary sight for an adventure. It was a group of caravans. There were three of them, and they were large, and they weren't new. Neither were the LDV van and the old Volvo parked to one side. There was a line of washing strung between two of the caravans, and maybe a wisp of smoke coming out of an aluminium chimney on the top of the first one. The caravans, the car, and the van were pulled round in a horseshoe shape. Between the opening and the dead centre of the shape, Becks stood still. Another dog was facing him. The other dog was bigger, but skinnier, grey, maybe a cross between a border collie and something else. Maybe a bit of greyhound. It was baring its teeth, and the hair along its back was standing up. Yeah, Becks' adventure had already taken off.

I got the thought that if I talked to the other dog, like I talked to Becks, it would listen to me. So I looked right at it, and walked towards the two of them. I walked slowly so as not to spook the other dog or make it attack me, but also I stayed relaxed, so it wouldn't think I was afraid. I don't think I was. I was more – well – interested to see if my idea worked.

"Hello boy," I said. "What's your name? That's my dog there. His name is Becks, and he's a Staffordshire. Are you guarding the camp? You're a brave dog, aren't you. A good guard dog."

At first the dog's eyes didn't leave Becks'; but as I got nearer, they kind of flickered between Becks and me, until I could tell that it was getting just a little nervous. That's where I stopped. I put my hands in my pockets and kept talking to it. I was wondering whether to sing to it, when the door of the first caravan opened, and a boy stepped out and looked over to us. He was about as much bigger than I was as the difference between Becks and the other dog. He came towards us, and I didn't like the look on his face.

"Hey chavo!" he shouted, and then something like, "Jal avree!"

I knew he wanted me to go away, but I stood where I was. He hesitated, then called back over his shoulder, to someone else in the caravan.

"Dad... gorjo!"

A man's head appeared round the door. He was about halfway between my dad's age and my grandad's. He looked at me, then said something quietly to the boy. The boy whistled for their dog, who turned and trotted after him, occasionally giving a look over its shoulder, like it was telling Becks they had unfinished business. Becks turned and trotted over to me, well pleased with himself, wagging his tail. I picked up his lead. I felt it might be a good idea to go, but the man called over to me.

"Av akai!" he said.

I went over to him, with Becks walking to heel.

"You speak Romany then?" he asked me.

"No," I said.

"But you came when I said."

"Well I kind of knew what you meant," I said. "You said something different from what the boy said, and he wanted me to go away. I just understood it."

"You understood it. That's interesting," he said. "You want a cup of tea?"

I thought about it. Here I was – I knew that the man and the boy were Romany, what some people, like my family for instance, still call gypsies – somewhere I had never been before, being invited into a caravan. About four years before, when I was at junior school, a police sergeant had come and given us a talk about not going into strange buildings, or getting into strange cars. No one had said anything about caravans.

"Have you got coffee?" I asked. "I'm a coffee man myself."

"Are you indeed," said the man, raising an eyebrow. "Well I am sure we have coffee, though it'll only be instant, if that'll suit a coffee man like yourself. Come inside my home, and excuse the state of the place. We don't often entertain visitors. Bring that fine Staffordshire with you – he'll be housetrained, I've no doubt – he's a good dog, and you have him trained well, apart from the running-away. I can see he listens to you."

I stepped up inside the caravan.

"I'm King Shaw, by the way," said the man, offering his hand. I shook it.

"Pleased to meet you," I replied. "I'm Ashe Sobiecki."

"That's a Polish name."

"Yes. My granddad came here from Poland when he was very little."

I looked all around me, checking out the inside of the caravan. I didn't know what King Shaw had meant by excusing the state of the place. It was very tidy, and smelled of washing and ironing, and spicy food, and all kinds of comfortable, family smells. It smelled like a house rolled up into one room. It felt like lots of things had been put away, stashed behind other things, folded up into the walls, tidied into cupboards. You could touch a secret spring and everything would change, beds would come from nowhere, curtains and partitions would unfold. In here, in this caravan, there was a whole little world on an edge, like it was outside but squashed down, like a lump of coal made into a diamond. But this was much more, because you could hitch it up to a big car or a four-by-four and head over the other edge, the edge outside where the suburb and the countryside can't make up their minds where one other ends and the other begins. This was an exciting place within an exciting place.

King Shaw sat me at a padded bench on one side of a fold-down table, and I watched him while he put heaped spoonfuls of instant coffee into two mugs. He had a face that looked like it had been carved from wood, lined with the weather, and thick, dark hair with grey streaks. His dark jeans and sweater pushed up to his elbows made him look lean. A woman about the same age as he was came from the other end of the caravan, where she had been folding clothes, picking up a boiling kettle on her way. She filled the mugs – well, nearly filled them because King Shaw added milk – and smiled at me before going back to what she had been doing. King Shaw sat opposite me, putting a mug in front of each of us and a plate of biscuits in between us, and I looked round the caravan as he began to speak. Becks sat on the deck and looked at us both.

"We don't get many visitors, Ashe. And those we do fall into three kinds. One: those people who come in here sticking their noses in our business, telling us we can't do this and we can't do that, and we must do the other thing. For that kind of visitor we put on all the Romany cant we can, and say words that make the dogs bark. They tell us they're only doing their job, but you know what I think? I think they should get proper jobs, making something, doing something useful to help folks, instead of jobs that mean you have their noses stuck in other people's business. Some people like to give us the reputation of thieves, Ashe, but I never knew any Gypsy lad who didn't work hard at something, if only mending lawnmowers or trading ponies. Laziness is not the Romany way. You can't jaul down the drom by standing still, eh?"

I nodded, because I got what he was trying to say. He looked at me very hard when he said those Romany words, then he pushed the plate of biscuits towards me and went on.

"Two: the kind of people who come to us because they are 'interested'. We're fashionable, we're politically correct, we're 'sexy'. They want to hear of our laws and customs and folklore and all of that. Frankly, chavo, I don't see anything wrong with telling people like that a complete pack of lies. They'll believe anything, and people who will believe anything deserve what they get. Things like this come in waves. Before we were ever called thieves and turned out and moved on, we were the 'Kings of Little Egypt', and people would come to us for dukkering and charms, and for dancing and entertainment. Now it's come round again full circle, and folk want us for their entertainment, although they are very polite. Patronising is what I call it. Know what that means?"

I nodded.

"They insist on our 'proper' name – 'Roma'. I don't mind being called a Gypsy, though, because it harks back to the Kings of Little Egypt."

"Are you a real Gypsy King, then?" I asked, sipping my coffee.

"No," he said with a chuckle. "King is my given name, my baptismal name. But... I suppose I am the boss of our little group here... my own family, my five boys – you met my youngest, Connor, outside, the rest are working – and my brother's family too. And I'm generally harkened to amongst a wider group. So I suppose I am a kind of Gypsy King."

The woman was chuckling too, and shaking her head at the same time. Becks was wagging his tail, pleased that everyone was happy. King Shaw glanced over to her.

"I am forgetting my manners," he said. "Like I said, it's been a while since we have entertained a visitor. This is my wife Kathleen. She doesn't agree with me about the word 'Gypsy', do you Kathleen?"

"Pleased to meet you, Mrs Shaw," I said.

"Pleased to meet you, Mr Sobiecki," she said. "And no I don't."

I looked round the caravan again. I saw all sorts of things like they had suddenly appeared out of the gloom. Someone had made a shelf all around any wall-space that didn't have cupboards. It was high up, and narrow, and full of ornaments. They must have been set out specially now the caravan was stopped here, because they would not have been safe when it was on the move. I could see a little statue of the Virgin Mary, and pictures of Pope Francis and Pope Benedict, and lots of decorated plates. One that caught my eye had a picture of the Archangel Michael... like a knight with wings on his back, and a sword in his right hand, with the point touching the ground. My eyes met Mrs Shaw's; she was watching me as I looked round the caravan. I turned back to King Shaw.

"What about the third kind of visitor? You said

there were three kinds. What's the third kind?"

"Ah, the third kind," said King Shaw. "The third kind of visitor, Ashe, are the people who are meant to come here. And we don't know anything about them until they do come. But I can tell you one thing – you're one of them. People like you... we make sure they go away with more than they came with."

CHAPTER TWO, IN WHICH I HEAR OF BAAL AND ANATH, AND GO AWAY WITH MORE THAN I CAME WITH.

My dad says I learn things by imitating. That's not it. I learn by looking and listening. I choose to imitate things if I want to, and I don't always want to. Sometimes I do things because it seems like a good idea to me, and sometimes I just do things. There in the caravan I was looking at Kathleen – Mrs Shaw – and looking at King Shaw and listening to him as well. Mrs Shaw was nearly as tall as King Shaw. I looked at her hair which was long and shiny, and I looked at her shoulders and hips, which were broader than my mum's. I looked at her sweater with the high neck, and her sheepskin body-warmer, and her long skirt. I looked at the grey socks on her feet, and at the slippers she had kicked off. I thought the sweater and the body-warmer looked snug .

"Folk used to say we were devil-worshippers, you know," said King Shaw.

I took my eyes off Mrs Shaw, looked again at the statue of the Virgin, and the pictures of the Popes, and over to a crucifix hanging near the window, and then at King Shaw.

"Why was that?" I asked.

"Two reasons, mainly," he replied. "Firstly, we speak a very old language, and our word for 'God' is 'Devel'. There is nothing strange about that, it's just a different word, but folk who didn't know our language... well... you can see how they could take it. Secondly, we are a very old race, and we have stories that go way, way back before even the Bible was written. And I guess there is a third reason too. Everything comes in threes. It's just that people find reasons not to like things they do not understand."

"I want to understand things I don't understand," I said.

"That's because you're different."

"Am I? I hadn't looked at it like that. I don't feel different. Different from what?"

King Shaw didn't answer. Instead, he pushed the right sleeve of his sweater further up. There was a tattoo on his arm. It had faded, but I could still see the deep blues, and greens, and reds that had made it up when it was new. There was a heart, and behind that two daggers or swords crossed, and there was a ribbon with a word that I couldn't read.

"How would you like one of these?"

I looked up at him. He was smiling, but I could tell he wasn't pulling my leg.

"It's illegal, isn't it? Until I'm sixteen."

"Not if I we do it with henna. Henna's painted on – no needles. And it is supposed to fade after about fifteen days, but we'll see how long this one will last." His smile got wider. "Only don't show your mum and dad, okay?"

It's funny... I don't know how to explain this... I know how wrong all this sounds. I remember that policeman warning us that adults sometimes want things from us, and make us keep it secret, and that's usually a sign that what they want us to do is not right. You know what I mean, no need to draw a picture for you. Well, here was King Shaw, a man I had never met until today; I was sitting in his caravan, and I was going to say yes to something he wanted me to keep secret from my parents. What did I feel? Edge stuff! Tipped over the edge into an adventure, and sharing something with an adult in a way I had only ever shared with a friend when we were both eight. A secret, like swearing an oath, being blood-brothers, Sicilian bandits, the Men in Black. The policeman hadn't known about edge stuff. I knew how he saw things – you draw a line, and one side of it is so, and the other side is not, no percentages, no part-country-part-suburb. He would have put taking a tattoo from King Shaw on the 'not' side, along with getting into cars. But I knew that he would have been, to the Shaws, one of their 'first kind' of people – the sort that stick their noses in, and say you can't do this, you can't do that, you must do the other. And in a way he was right. But today, right here amongst the edge stuff, he would have been wrong.

I rolled up my sleeve.

Mrs Shaw came over to the table, carrying plastic pots and bottles, little paintbrushes and sticks, some cloths and a roll of paper towels. King Shaw slid along the bench a little to make room for her, and she sat down, arranging her things precisely on the table between us.

"Lean your elbow on this pad," she said, putting a folded cloth down for me. "Keep still, and tell me what you would like me to put there."

I looked up at the Archangel with the sword.

"Please may I have an angel like that?" I asked.

King Shaw gave a low whistle.

"Can you manage that, Kathleen?"

"Course I can," she said, stirring something in one of the plastic bottles. "But it'll take a while. Why don't you tell Mr Sobiecki one of your stories, King, to keep him occupied while I work?"

"Why don't I indeed! Hmmm... ah, I know. Ashe Sobiecki, my young friend, you shall hear the story of Baal and Anath, to whom henna is sacred. It is very, very old."

When he said those two names, Mrs Shaw glanced over at him very quickly, and then crossed herself. But she said nothing. King Shaw began.

*

Far away in the land of Canaan, many years ago, beyond the city of Ugarit, where they sang psalms to the creator El long before the Children of Israel came and stole not only their land but their psalms too, there stood a mountain. The mountain's name was Zaphon, and it was the home of the great god Baal, son of Dagon, called 'Lord of Thunder', 'Almighty', 'Rider of the Clouds', 'Lord over the Earth'. Some folk called Baal by the name of Hadad. Baal was never still – he could never rest – and thunder could be heard daily from Mount Zaphon, and flashes of lightning played around its summit.

From the summit of Mount Zaphon, where he ceaselessly paced to and fro, Baal could see the Mediterranean ocean, home of the god Yamm. Baal became angry. His kingdom now felt small, because he could see its boundaries. And in his anger he called out to Yamm, insulting him continually in his loud voice, hurling thunderbolts and making great winds, so that Yamm's kingdom was constantly in turmoil, tossing this way and that in the storms and winds that Baal sent.

"Come out and fight me, Yamm, you coward!" shouted Baal, in a voice that echoed in a peal of thunder so loud it was heard beyond the southern border of Canaan. "Stop skulking in your slimy kingdom. Show yourself!"

And at last Yamm came up from the sea, his dark face rising like a tidal wave, and he set his great, green foot upon the shore, upon Baal's kingdom. And he shouted back to Baal in a voice like the crashing of breakers against the cliffs.

"Here I stand, you blustering bully! Are you nothing but noise? I challenge you! Who's the coward now?"

Baal saw that Yamm was indeed mighty, a great enemy, strong and fearsome. Baal himself was no coward, but he was very cunning, and so he went to Kothar, the blacksmith god, skilled in making any object a god could need. He asked Kothar to make him mighty weapons with which to fight Yamm. Kothar took all the metal that lay under the ground between Mount Zaphon in the West, and the Indus river in the East, and he worked it into a great, bronze sword. And he scooped up a huge piece of the Earth and made it into a stout shield; and the hole it left became the Sea of Galilee.

Armed with the sword and shield, Baal charged at Yamm. The battle between these two gods lasted twelve whole years, during which time there were such thunderstorms and tides as had never been seen in the Mediterranean. Baal pushed at Yamm with his shield, and battered at him with his sword; and with every push of the shield and stroke of the sword there was a huge peal of thunder and flash of lightning. Yamm whipped Baal with waterspouts and showers of stinging rain and hail.

In the city of Ugarit, and throughout Canaan, the poor people cowered in their houses, only coming out when the two rival gods paused between rounds.

Eventually Yamm began to gain the upper hand, and roared with delight, beating Baal further and further back inland. One lash with a mighty waterspout was enough to send Baal's shield spinning from his hand, to land on its edge in the sea, where it became the island of Cyprus.

By this time even the gods themselves had come to watch the battle, betting upon the outcome. The sun goddess, Shapash, was the only one to bet on Baal, and secretly warmed and dried him with her rays. Baal, who as you know was cunning, devised a plan to escape defeat. He waited until the sun goddess's kindly gaze was on him and then angled his mighty, bronze sword so that it reflected the sunlight right into Yamm's eyes. Yamm was dazzled and blinded, and Baal started to belabour him with the flat of his sword, raining blow after blow down upon the sea god, until he was beaten, and the sea became calm and still.

Now Baal had a wife who was also his sister. Do not ask me how this can be, but such things were possible with the gods of Canaan. Not only was Anath his sister and his wife, but she was forever a virgin. She was greatly loved by all the gods, and she took Baal by the hand and led him to see El, the creator, to whom all psalms were sung. There she told him that the reason Baal paced to and fro on Mount Zaphon was that he had no house to live in. If El would give permission for Baal to have a house built, then all Canaan would be a place of peace. El readily gave his permission.

Anath asked Kothar for help, calling to him sweetly, using the pet name she had for him. "O Hasis the Skilful, Hasis the Wise, make a house for my brother-husband Baal and me, in which we can live peacefully."

Kothar built a house for Baal on top of Mount Zaphon, and Baal was pleased. For a while all Canaan was at peace, the sun shone, and the gods dozed. Even Yamm forgot his quarrel with Baal, and visited him in his house. At such times the summit of Mount Zaphon was wreathed in mist.

One day Baal invited all the gods to a great feast. Yamm was there, and El the creator as the guest of honour. Shapash and Kothar sat together, and even Yutpan the deceitful had a place. The only god not to be invited was Mot, the god of death. When he heard about the feast, he strode up Mount Zaphon in a rage, and pounded so hard on the door of Baal's house that the food and drink was shaken off the tables.

Mot burst into the house and cursed and ranted at Baal for the insult of not inviting him. Baal was so enraged at this that he forgot he was supposed to be living a peaceful life. He sprang to his feet, seized the sword that he had used to defeat Yamm, and rushed at Mot.

Their duel was a terrible sight. Even the mighty gods fled from Mount Zaphon, as Baal and Mot reduced the lovely house to rubble in their raging. But even the mighty Baal could not defeat Death, and Mot eventually swallowed up Baal, and spat him out on the mountain top, dead and cold.

While the gods debated amongst themselves who could take Baal's place, Anath mourned for him. Not only did she mourn as a sister and a wife, but also as a mother and a daughter would, for she was all things to Baal. She wandered through Canaan looking for Baal's body, and when she found it, she buried it and wept over his grave. But her tears, at first cool and sorrowful, turned to drops of fire, and became a rage such as creation had never seen. She turned and ran and ran until she came to Mot, flinging herself upon him in a murderous frenzy. Struggle as he might, Mot found he was no match for Anath, because as she had mourned Baal as a sister, a wife, a mother, and a daughter, she had become four goddesses in one. In her wrath she killed Mot, ground his body to powder, and scattered it over land and sea.

Then she took the place of Baal on top of Mount Zaphon, where she ruled for many years, no longer as Anath the gentle and beloved of the gods, but as the goddess of slaughter, whom some called Ashtoreth, with a hideous aspect.

Many lives of men and women passed. One night El, the creator, dreamed a dream, in which Baal and Mot were alive and stood before him. What El dreams always comes to pass, and so when he awoke, there before him stood Baal and Mot, restored to life. He charged them solemnly each to keep to his own kingdom, and not to fight any more. They bowed low to him and gave him their promise.

When Anath saw Baal coming again to Mount

Zaphon, her heart was softened, and her face became beautiful once more. She painted herself with a dye made from her sacred plant, which she called Mehendi, making the beautiful patterns on her face and limbs, which brides do to this very day in India, and in Mesopotamia, and in all parts of Arabia.

And Baal and Anath lived in peace and happiness ever after. Some say that when the One God came they faded away. Others say they still live on top of Mount Zaphon, but now as an old man and an old woman, and have retired from being gods.

But one thing I know is this: Anath's sacred plant, Mehendi, which we call Henna, still grows.

*

I liked the story. I liked the way King Shaw winked at me when he said the bit about tides in the Mediterranean, because everyone knows there are no tides in the Mediterranean. Well, there are, but they are very small. When he stopped talking I looked up. Mrs Shaw had laid down her brushes. Becks gave a short bark.

"That dog knows a lot," she said. "Probably more than you do, King Shaw, you skylarker!"

She held up a little mirror, and I looked into it to see what my angel tattoo looked like. It was great! Beautiful! The archangel had a face which almost changed each time I looked at it – kind, stern, fearsome, forgiving – and his armour glinted and shone.

"Wow!" I said, and then, "Thank you."

"You want to know what I reckon?" said King Shaw. "I reckon you are now a lot more than one quarter Polish, Ashe Sobiecki. I reckon you are now half Romany. I shall have to be some kind of uncle of yours, just to seal the bargain."

I didn't know what to say to that, but Becks barked again, and as Mrs Shaw gathered her brushes and stuff together and took them to the other end of the caravan, she said, "Becks says it's time for you to go home."

"Well, there you are, then." Said King Shaw, standing. "You're going away with more than you had when you came."

I stood too, and went to the door and opened it, and Becks trotted after me. But I turned round and started to say something.

"Mr Shaw..."

"It's Uncle King now, I suppose," he interrupted.

"Uncle King, if you are sort of my uncle now, does that mean I can visit again, and... like... ask you things, and come to you for help and advice?"

He took my hand and shook it firmly. He had rather a stern look on his face.

"Advice is it? Let me give you one piece of advice before you do go. Never refuse what you are given, and never ask for more than you are offered. And that's the strangest piece of advice you'll ever get from the son of a horse-trader! Now, good bye Ashe Shaw Sobiecki, and kushti bak."

"Goodbye Uncle King, Aunt Kathleen, and kushti bak."

I stepped down from the caravan doorway, picked up Becks' lead, and headed back to the lane. When I got to the centre of the horseshoe of caravans, I turned and looked back. Uncle King and Aunt Kathleen were standing just outside the door; she had her arm linked through his. He gave me a wave and I waved back. When I looked again just before I got to the lane, they were gone, but the boy was leaning against the other caravan, and his dog was sitting beside him. He was too far away for me to see his face. But I didn't wave anyway.

I came away with more than I had when I arrived. I had an angel tattooed on my arm, a new middle name, and the idea that I was half-Gypsy. There was something else too. I don't think it was part of Uncle Shaw's gift to me, or if it was, he hadn't intended it to be. The edge of things, edge stuff... I carried it with me maybe... or maybe I started to notice that there were other, different edges, places where things merged, everywhere I went.

Chapter Three, in which I give you a history lesson and open a door.

My name had been Ashe Sobiecki up to that point. That's what was on the class register for class 2c at Chart Green Comprehensive. The fact that I was now Ashe Shaw Sobiecki would never get on there, because you need a letter from your parents when your name changes, like when Darla Kington's mum got married again, and she wanted Darla to be Darla Murray instead. If I told mum and dad about my new name there would be questions and worried looks, and I don't like to worry my parents.

There isn't actually anywhere between where I live and the school which you could say was on the edge – at least not really noticeably so – but there were things you could notice if you didn't hurry by. There were places where, if you sort of craned your neck and looked between houses and sheds, you could see that part of the countryside where the Chart Brook ran very lazily through the marshes to the estuary. But you would only really notice it if you waited for a day when the sun was low, and in the right direction, and then the estuary itself would reflect the sunlight, and it's be like one of those old films about a steelworks, where the molten metal runs down a channel. Well that was how the estuary looked, half-way to the horizon; and the Chart Brook, which ran through Chart Green (though often gurgling away through concrete pipes and culverts hidden behind walls and fences, at the back of supermarkets and the far end of the industrial estate) looks a bit like the trickle of new steel that escaped and ran away. So you might not be on what you think is an obvious edge, but the signs are there if you look for them – like when a couple of swans flew over, one day, on their way from the reservoir to the estuary. I saw them. I saw that they followed the line of the Chart Brook.

Here's something else. Bang in the middle of Chart Green is like a mall of shops, and it's pedestrianised, covered with slabs. It's called The Green. That's what it used to be – a green, a village green, maybe with a maypole. One of the streets leading away from it is called Marsh Lane, but it leads away from where the marshes are now. Then there is Quay Street, Causeway End, New Cut Lane, Ullesbeck Lane, and Ship Lane. All of these seem to be the like the spokes of a wheel, or the long bits of a spider's web, and in between them run all the streets with the newer names, like a net – Coronation Avenue, Elizabeth Drive, Elm Drive, Cherry Way, Beech Avenue, Beech Close, Bevan Crescent – right out to the three sides of Chart Green that mingle with the next suburb, where the main roads lead towards the heart of the city, and to the one side where the countryside started. The countryside, to me, seemed to fan out from there; the city is big, but the country just seemed bigger, older, more grown-up. Sometimes I would walk around Chart Green and find myself looking at a bit of an old building. Maybe a shed round the back of somewhere, something like that, only it was obvious it had been something to do with a farm once. There were little clues like that, which I always thought were much more important than things like the Windmill Inn, the pub in Chart Green, which had half-timbered walls. I was totally geeky about this, and found out stuff. Like Causeway End and Marsh lane had really been the last roads here, and they hadn't gone any further, when the Chart Brook had been a creek that small wooden ships could sail right up at high tide. Ullesbeck had been an old name for it, until the name it was known by further inland took over. The Chart Brook comes from those hills where the TV mast is. And the name of the village had once been Skippool. Down here there had been ships – back in the Middle Ages or even further back – and a quay of course, and a widened bit of the creek which was the Skip Pool itself. The estuary was closer, and the marsh almost surrounded the busy village which grew up round the quay, until a land-owner dug cuts to drain parts of the marsh to make his estate bigger. Two hundred years ago barges with sails still came here, and stuff was unloaded from the brand new canal, which ran straight inland through Chart Rise into cuttings, stepping up by lock after lock and linking with other canals. Then the railway came with its own cuttings and sidings and stuff. Then more houses where the marsh had been. And then here we were, part of the city. This sort of thing is really exciting to me. I used to sit for hours looking at Chart Green in the A to Z book, marking the old things with a highlighter. It drove my Dad mental.

My guess is that Chart Green Comprehensive was built right where it had been marshes once. It stands to reason. So much had been built like that. The place where there are edges between things changes over and over again. The town and the country, the country and the marsh, the marsh and the estuary.

The Monday after I had met King Shaw I went to school as normal. Mum dropped me off on her way to work, about two hundred metres from the back gate. She never liked to get closer than that, because it was difficult to turn the car round further along. I walked along by the high fence, looking through it at sunlight reflected from the school windows. It was like a strobe light, and made me feel dreamy. It may have been that, it may have been all the stuff that had been in my mind since getting my Archangel tattoo, it may have been my old thoughts about history, but it seemed to me that everything around me, everything in the whole world maybe, was rippling. It seemed to me that if I wanted to, I could take pieces of it and move them round. Everything was showing that it was edge stuff, like the edges of the countryside, the stuff that adventures were made of; or maybe I was edge stuff myself, because I had lived right on the edge and it had got into me, or I had become part of it all and could move in and out of it. It was calling to me in some funny way, in my mind, wanting me to do something.

I stood there, by the fence, and a memory came to me. I had been a little kid, and I was at Sunday School. The Sunday School teacher had asked us why Jesus could walk on water, and I had answered, "Because no one had told him he couldn't." Everyone had laughed, even the teacher though not unkindly. Well, the thing the edge stuff wanted me to do was like that. It wanted me to do something weird, and it was trying to convince me, like it was talking to me, that I could do it because no one had ever told me I couldn't.

It was telling me to open a door.

If everywhere is an edge, or edge stuff is everywhere, you could move from one side of the edge to the other. And if there wasn't any obvious way of moving – if there was something that seemed like a wall – then the only thing you could do was to open a door in that wall. I saw all this. It wasn't like anything you were taught about or talked about, so no one had told me I couldn't open a door.

So I opened a door, right there where the fence was.

It was like cutting a big oblong of jelly with a knife, about twenty centimetres thick and tall enough for me to step through. Only I didn't use a knife, or even my hand. I used my mind. No I didn't, because I did it almost without thinking. There was no magic word, no spell, no hand-waving, no decision-making. I just did it like a fish swims or a bird flies. I swung it back, stepped through, and closed it behind me.

Except... as well as stepping through, I went on towards the back gate, and had a normal day at school. There were two Ashe Sobieckis, but really there was only one of me. If you like, say that Ashe Sobiecki went to French and Maths, and Ashe Shaw went through the door in the edge stuff.

Ashe Shaw went in to the weird, quiet, school. It was empty, or so it seemed, except for the Guardian Angels. Ashe Shaw joined them, joined the eleven that had been waiting.

There was Reuben Flowers from 4b, the leader,

and Janet Mackie from 3a, his second-in-command. There were Ben Gillett, Charlie Seacole, and Kesha Patel from 3b. There were Sarah Leeming, Jessica and Joe Thomas, Mark Martinelli, and Kylie Marsh from 3c. There was Younis Iqbal from my own class, 2c. Then there was me, and I made twelve. We moved in and out of edge stuff, and we had such adventures. One day Kesha left us, then Reuben, and Janet became our leader; and a little after that Paul Lee and Kirsty Brownlaw from 2b came to join us. And the adventures went on, and on... and then Angela came!

CHAPTER FOUR, IN WHICH ANGELA IS WORRIED AND CHARLIE IS ANGRY.

I remember when I was little, mum and dad sent me to Sunday School. While I was there I learned about how God made the world in seven days, and put all the animals, and birds, and fishes in it that we know today; and then he put Adam and Eve here, and from them came all the human beings. And at the same time as I was learning that, I was at school learning how the earth took billions of years to make, and how there were all kinds of things like dinosaurs, archaeopteryx, woolly mammoths, and animals that died out thousands and thousands of years ago; and then there were cavemen, and last of all there were us. It didn't seem to matter. Grown-ups were teaching me two whole different histories, and it didn't really matter, because they were grown-ups and so it must all make sense.

Then later I went to mass and took my first ever communion. I knelt in front of the priest with a lot of other children, and the priest went along the line of us putting something on everyone's tongue, and muttering something each time he did it. I knew what he was supposed to say, because I had learned about it in Sunday School, but still I remember straining to hear, wondering if that's what he was really saying. And then it was my turn, and I stuck my tongue out, and he put this little, thin wafer on it, like a little piece of biscuit. It stuck to my tongue and I couldn't swallow it, and I missed him saying "The body of Christ". But I heard him say it to the next kid, so that was all right. Then when he had done that with all of us, he came back with a metal cup, and gave us a sip each from it. This time he said "The blood of Christ", and I remember thinking that it didn't taste like when I licked blood off my finger when I had cut it.

And I asked mum about it later, because she knew about all the Roman Catholic things better than any of us, because she had converted when she married dad. I can remember saying to her, "Mum, at the last supper, Jesus couldn't have turned the bread and wine into his own body and blood, because he was still alive and hadn't shed his blood yet; so how come the priest does it? The priest isn't more important than Jesus."

She said it was 'symbolical'. I can remember not being satisfied with that answer, but not knowing what else to say. It was only later that I realized how much people disagree with each other about big things like when and how the universe was made. But what they don't realise is that very often there's more than one thing going on at a time. That's a very important thing to remember.

Angela was beautiful. I don't just mean that she was hot. I mean that she shone, shimmered, I could see edge stuff round her like a halo. It was golden. The others pretended they couldn't see it, so I pretended that too. There were so many things that they pretended they couldn't do, so many rules they made up to say that they couldn't do things that I knew they could – because I could do them, and I was one of the youngest and still a bit of a newcomer. So I watched, and learned what a Guardian Angel was supposed to do, and what he was not supposed to do, and that's what I did. Or didn't. Except sometimes I mucked around a little, just to show I was in on the secret. I got the private joke.

Like when Angela came, and I could see that the room became just a tiny bit darker, despite her wonderful halo. That was Angela. She didn't know the rules, so she was bending them. The shadow that crept in with her was her pretending she didn't know what was going on, like she was testing the rest of us. So I played my secret little joke with her, and she laughed when she got it. I moved things, made it so that a thin shaft of light shone in on me, and I played with it, using the glass in my watch, and making a little reflection fly around the room, like a fairy in a kid's story, like Tinkerbell in Peter Pan. And that helped, because once Angela could see that I knew what she knew, she was okay. Anyhow, that's how I got the nickname 'Tinker'. I may have been Ashe Shaw Sobiecki, but amongst the Guardian Angels I was Tinker. I liked that. I changed my screen-name in our chat room to Tinker too. Before that I had been 'Poshrat', which is a Romany name and means 'half-a-gypsy'. I don't think Aunt Kathleen would have liked 'Tinker' though, because it has what people call 'negative associations' for the Romany people, but amongst the GAs it made me feel special, and I was able to join in even more with the secrets.

Secrets like this. Angela could get ahead of things. She could go out-of-phase with things, without really opening another door in the edge stuff. I saw her do this when she saved that woman from being run over by the bus – she moved to catch her before the woman had even begun to fall.

Afterwards I went to Angela and gave her what mum calls 'one of your looks', and told her she was awesome. I wanted to let her know I knew that secret. But it was like she was looking right past me, and I didn't know whether she understood what I was trying to say. And after that I stuck pretty close to her, because of the way the edge stuff rippled round her. She pretended not to notice, of course, but at other times she would sit and talk to me. It was more like she was talking to herself, though. Mum talks to herself sometimes, and I learned not to join in or say, "I beg your pardon?" or something like that, because she would look irritated, and rub her forehead, and say, "Look, I'm just sorting things out in my mind, I'm not really talking." So I guessed that's what Angela was doing. It made me feel a bit like I was a wall she was bouncing a ball off, but I didn't mind.

Once I sat with her while she was waiting for Charlie. It wasn't a school day, it was the weekend, and I guess they were going to go to Costa Coffee or something. Angela was leaning against a wall, and I was sitting on it, and she was sorting things out in her mind. She was talking to me, asking questions, but not like she expected answers. This was what she always seemed to do when there was no one but the two of us – that didn't happen often – and she would call me Ashe, not Tinker. I liked that, but it always seemed to be a signal that she was sorting things out in her mind.

"Okay, so we're the Guardian Angels, Ashe, but nobody seems to know why we're called that. Nobody will say who called us that. There's a war going on, and in a war there's supposed to be good guys and bad guys, but in all the wars you see on TV each side says they're the good guys and the other side is the bad guys; but that's just propaganda. Sometimes you can see that one side did something to the other side first, but that doesn't make them the bad guys just for doing that, because by the time the war is really going it's too late. Then you can't tell the good guys from the bad guys, because they are both doing bad things. Okay sometimes it's easy to say that the bad guys are the guys who are bigger and stronger, because that means they're picking on the others, but even that can be the wrong idea. But what about us? It's not like we even see the other side. We just assume they're there – unless, well, there was the kid Charlie ran after I suppose – and we assume that we're the good guys because we stop things happening. But no one has told us any of this. All the GAs say this is how things are, but no one has any idea how it all started...

"... And we have Risings, we see things, and we go out and stop stuff happening. But nobody ever explains where these Risings come from. Too much stuff just gets taken on trust, nothing is ever explained. It's like we're all caught up in something, and because it makes us feel special we just do it. And there's the whole tulpa thing, and how we split from it and merge with it, and split and merge again. It's not like there's a book of ancient lore, or any knowledge passed down from GA to GA, we just do it. No one knows how long it's been going on. I mean, do you know, Ashe? I expect not...

"... I'm sure there's someone who knows something, though, Ashe. Maybe not one of the GAs, but someone...

"... And I'm sure Charlie knows a lot more than he's saying. There's the Yellows, and the Avenging Angels – that means that there might be thirty-six kids at our school running around at any one time with a tulpa doing their lessons. I mean – duh! That's a big deal and nobody notices? And are we the only school where this is happening? Ashe, I have spent hours on the internet searching for anything like this and I have come up with a total blank...

"... Oh, I'm sorry to go on and on about this, Ashe, but it really weirds me out. I'll have to talk to Charlie about it all some time. Maybe I can persuade him to tell me more."

When Angela talked like this, well, at first I was puzzled, because I had been so sure she understood things. But then I began to realise that she didn't after all, and that maybe the GAs' secrets weren't secrets after all, and that they were things only I could see – and that puzzled me even more, because I wasn't special at all.

Anyhow, when Charlie came to meet Angela and take her off on their date he gave me a funny look, like a frown, like I wasn't welcome; and when they had gone I felt really, really alone for the first time since becoming a GA. Then after school the next Monday I was walking home when I heard footsteps behind me. Someone grabbed my shoulder and spun me round. It was Charlie. He had that frown on his face, like before. He looked at me really hard.

"We've got to talk, Tinker, right?" he said.

"Right, Charlie. Not a problem."

"Well yeah there is a problem, Tink. It's you. It's you hanging round Angela all the time. I don't like it. She doesn't like it."

"Did she say so, Charlie?" I said.

"Don't get clever, Tink. I'm being serious here. What you're doing is stalking her. Stalking. I mean we're Guardian Angels, and we've got to work together, but what you're doing is creepy. You understand? It's not acceptable. Zero tolerance, right? You understand me." He was right in my face, really angry. I didn't think he would hit me or anything, but he really was angry.

"I would never do anything to hurt Angela, Charlie, you know that."

"Okay, well, maybe you don't realise you're doing it," he said. "But that's not an excuse. You should realise. I mean is it so obvious you have a crush on her, Tink, but it's not like you stand a chance with her. And anyway she goes out with me. You got that?"

There were so many things I wanted to say in answer to all that.

"Charlie, who's it obvious to that I've got this crush on Angela you're talking about?" I didn't know how to put it any better. If I'd said something like "I haven't got a crush on Angela" he'd have taken that wrong. But even though I put it this way Charlie got really aggressive. He got hold of my jacket, and pushed me. I could see his knuckles were white.

"I told you not to get clever, Tink. You had to push it! You just had to push it, didn't you! Now I'm telling you, and I want you to get this. Outside of GA business, stay... away... from... Angela. Right?"

Four times Charlie pushed me with those white knuckles. It was the only time I had ever seen him like this. It was just ordinary, physical bullying – I'd had it a bit before from kids at school, and I had learned to ignore it, mostly. Now he was scaring me. It wasn't that I was afraid of him, more that I was afraid for him. I can't put it better than that. His anger was beginning to show in the edge stuff all around him, like there was a dull, red halo over him, but it was cutting out light, not shining. I don't think he knew what was happening. It was like he was burning up. Oh yes he could hurt someone, but he could hurt himself more easily.

I wanted to tell him, but I knew it would just make him madder at me.

"Right, Charlie," I said. "No problem. I'll stay away from Angela. I promise."

That seemed the best thing to say. Charlie's hand with its white knuckles was still gripping my jacket. I took hold of his wrist, and tried to pull his hand away. Charlie was still looking at me; his eyes were still hard, and he was breathing fast. Then he looked down at our hands, and his eyes lost their hardness. We both relaxed our hold on each other, then we let go. The waist of my jacket was half way up my sides, so I pulled it down and pulled it straight.

Charlie stood there for a moment or two, not saying anything. The dull glow around him had gone. It was like he was waking up, but still half-asleep. He turned to go.

"Okay, fair enough, Tink. Cheers, mate. It's all good. It'll be right."

"Yes, Charlie," I said, as he walked away. "It's all good. It'll be right. Everything'll be all right."

I didn't know if he was listening any more. He walked a bit hunched up. It was almost as if he was ashamed. Almost. Not quite.

Anyhow, after that I didn't follow Angela any more. I followed Charlie.

CHAPTER FIVE, IN WHICH I FOLLOW CHARLIE.

From time to time in my life, I have to stop and think. It's like I wake up one day and the world is completely different, and I'm supposed to know what I'm doing without being told what is actually different, and what I am supposed to do about it. It's what they call 'hitting the ground running'. That's another very important lesson, because everyone else acts like nothing has happened and everything is just how it was before.

Every day, at home, everything was normal. I would get up, and go across the landing in my pyjamas to the bathroom as usual. I would set the shower to '4' and count to twenty as I took off my pyjamas, so that the water temperature was just right. Every three days I would wash my hair under the shower too. When I had finished showering, I would dry myself while I was still standing in the bath, so I didn't drip on the floor so much – it always drove mum crackers when there was water on the bathroom floor, even though we had a bathmat – and I would dry each foot as I stepped out. Then, with the big bath-towel wrapped round me, I would clean my teeth, because I had seen on the TV that if you clean your teeth before meals, then there are fewer bacteria in your mouth to react with the food and build up on your teeth. When I was dry, I would put on my bathrobe, and carry my pyjamas back to my bedroom, making sure everything was switched off in the bathroom first. Back in my bedroom, I would fold my pyjamas and put them under my pillow, unless they were due for a wash, in which case I would just drop them on the floor. Then I would pick up my clothes one by one from the chair, where I put them in order the day before, and get dressed. Once I was dressed I would pick up my backpack, which I had organised the night before as well after doing my homework, and my pyjamas if they were on the floor, and I would go downstairs. I would leave the backpack by the door, and put the pyjamas in the laundry basket. Then I would get a bowl and a plate from the cupboard, a spoon and a knife from the cutlery drawer, fill the kettle with water and switch it on, and make my breakfast. I like a bowl of cereal – it doesn't matter what kind – with milk, two slices of toast with the crusts cut off so the slices are square, butter, and orange marmalade. I like to drink coffee like mum and dad. I have been doing this each morning before school since I was little.

Mum sometimes ruffles my hair and calls me her 'little obsessive compulsive', but it's not like that. I googled that, and it means that someone has the same thoughts over and over, and that makes them repeat things for no good reason, often finding other things to repeat to stop them having to repeat the first things. I have my routine because it makes sense, it makes sure everything gets done and nothing gets forgotten.

It's the same when I come home from school. Every day I would come in, leave my school shoes by the door, go upstairs and change out of my school clothes – that's when I would put them neatly on the chair, ready for the next day – and into jeans and a fleece or a hoodie. Then I would take Becks out for his walk. The length of Becks' walk depended on a lot of things – what time of year it was, what the weather was like, how much homework I had, and so on. Like I said, it all made sense, it got everything done.

All through the weeks since I got my henna tattoo from Aunt Kathleen I had kept up these routines at home. While I was with the Guardian Angels and all those things were happening to me which I couldn't predict, things at home went on exactly the same. But

I was different. Time and time again I hit the ground running, getting used to what was different and pretending nothing had changed.

Every day, in the shower, my archangel henna tattoo reminded me what things had changed. And it didn't fade.

The next time I was with the GAs too, everyone seemed to be exactly the same as they were before, all doing the same sort of things, all saying the same sort of things, but the world had changed. Before, it had been obvious to me that they had been pretending not to know things, and it was part of the game for me to pretend the same thing. Now that wasn't obvious at all. Probably when someone acted like they didn't know something, they really didn't know it. That meant that I knew things they didn't, and that worried me a bit, because before I had simply trusted Janet to make decisions because she was the leader. Now I felt like I knew more than she did, but I wasn't the leader and didn't want to be anyway. So for the most part I kept on doing what I had always done with the GAs – almost like tagging along. It was a bit like at primary school when I was always one of the last to get chosen when someone was picking sides for a game. That never made me feel bad, because I always knew what I could and couldn't do, anyway.

The only thing I could think of doing differently was watching, trying to make sense of it all. That's why I started following Charlie – not just so that I could still watch Angela.

Like I said, the edge stuff round Angela – and around Charlie – seemed different. That made them both special as far as I was concerned. But they didn't seem to know it, or if they did they reacted in different ways to being special. The glow around Angela seemed to be full of questions, always, "Why?"; Charlie's glow was alone, but the kind of alone that doesn't realise it is. Angela was black and gold, Charlie was black and red. That's the only way I can say it.

So when we went out doing what we did, I kept an eye on Charlie. Even at other times I made an effort to be places where I thought he would be. Twice I turned up at Costa when Charlie and Angela were there on a date, and he saw me. Angela didn't seem to pay any attention, but Charlie came over to me.

"You stalking us, Tink, or what?"

"No Charlie, I just happen to be here."

But I suppose I was. Sort of. I hadn't looked at it like that. Sort of not, though, because I was just trying to learn things. Stalking like someone would stalk a deer, but not to shoot it – to learn about how a deer moves, lives, and thinks. I was hitting the ground running that way.

Anyway I could follow Charlie without following him. There was no mistaking his black and red glow. The word 'aura' came into my mind one evening, and I googled that too: 'a field of subtle, luminous radiation surrounding a person or object'. It can be a spiritual thing, or something to do with migraine or a brain disorder, but for me it was how the edge stuff was around someone. How it looked, behaved, and felt. It was like gravity – we had done Einstein in physics, and had learned how mass bends space – and it was like I could feel from a long way off how Angela or Charlie bent edge stuff. I didn't have to see them. I could track each of them, or both of them together, like I was following the tracks of a deer, or I could hear it rustling through a forest or calling out to its mate. Charlie's red aura and often, just ahead, Angela's gold. That's how I knew that sometimes Charlie followed Angela. Stalked, even.

Mum says that people are most critical of faults in others which they are ashamed of in themselves.

When the Guardian Angels come into school by our own special doors, it's most often while the streets around the school are crowded with other kids coming to school. There are school buses, cars stopping by the kerbside to let people out, teachers' cars turning into the main driveway of the school and heading for the car park. People are chatting, arguing, sometimes fighting. The place is always bustling. And we each open our door and step through. Ashe Shaw goes through my door, and Ashe Sobiecki goes in to lessons, if you like; the other GAs call the part of them that goes in to lessons their "tulpa", and they ignore it. So I did too, until I realised they didn't just ignore it, they couldn't really see it. I hit the ground running again with that one. I was the only person who could feel each part of myself totally. If you like, Ashe Sobiecki was the part of me that kept all the normal things going.

One day, in the middle of all the noise and crowd outside school, I could see and feel Charlie opening his door. But he opened it in a different way. The door was in the same place, and it opened just as usual, but there was a whole different feel to it, like what was on the other side was different. So I counted to twenty to give him time, copied it with my own door, and stepped through.

As usual, I stepped through into the middle of the

school grounds, and everything was quiet. But it was a totally different kind of quiet to what was usual. I haven't told you before, but usually when I step through my door at the school, it is like being there during autumn half-term, or maybe early on a Sunday in November or March. Everywhere in and around the school is quiet – there is no one driving down the road outside, no one walking, no noise except from the crows in the trees, who seem to be part of the Guardian Angels' private world. The sky is usually full of broken clouds, and there is a wind. This time everything was different. Everywhere seemed dry, bright, and like things could break if you touched them, and there was a yellow sun which felt like it was in the wrong part of the sky. I knew Charlie was already inside the school building, and as I walked towards the main door I knew that there were eleven other people inside, and that they weren't the Guardian Angels.

The closer I got, the more I could feel the edge stuff ripple. Charlie disturbed it in his own way, and there was his black and red, angry aura. I could feel how he was always searching for something, but something else always blocked his way, and the edge stuff around him would quiver, like it was crying out for other people to notice it – that's the only way I can describe it.

I walked up to the main door of the school, opened it, and walked in. I didn't need to feel Charlie to know where he had gone. I turned and went down the corridor to where the classroom was where the GAs met. Only I knew they wouldn't be there, not in this bit of the edge stuff, not the way Charlie and I had used our doors. I stopped outside the classroom, out of sight. I suddenly realised I ought to be afraid, and the fact that I wasn't afraid made me nervous anyway. I leant against the wall and waited. Then I heard this... it was like a chant, but a bit like what cheerleaders do, and the kids in the classroom went through it two or three times... I could hear Charlie's voice above the rest, like he was encouraging them:

"We are the children of the yellow sun, the Golden Angels, the people who carry light – what has to happen has to happen!"

Then there were a few whoops and cheers, and the sound of slapping, like people were doing high-fives. Then it was silence, and the occasional bit of chat passed this way and that I think, and that went on for half-an-hour. I sat on a table in the corridor, though the top hurt the back of my knees a little, and kept on waiting. While I waited, I counted the number of drawing pins on the noticeboard on the opposite wall. I counted them again, and a third time just to make sure.

After some time, I began to feel a Rising happening. I knew what Risings were by then. They're when we are able to see round an edge, a group of us; and sometimes because not all of us can see as well, or can see exactly the same view – like we were looking at it from a different angle – what we see can seem dark and puzzling. I began to recognise the Rising, because it was almost exactly like one the GAs had had before. Everything became cold and dark, thick – I had the image of green molten glass, but cold like slowly-swirling water. It made thoughts slow, breathing slow, heartbeats slow, arms and legs numb, everything was heavy, like when you try to run in a dream and your legs won't work. I recognised this as the Rising about the man in the canal, and I made myself feel very calm, so I could see it and feel it but not let it press down on me. All the time, I knew that the Yellows were having this Rising. I could feel each one of them. In particular I could feel Charlie. He was dark, and cold, and green as a glass bottle; but he was hard, very hard like moss-covered stone, like the bottom of a cave. Cold and dark, but sharp and clear too, like he was spreading his arms over all the Yellows like wings. But he couldn't feel me, he didn't know I was there.

Suddenly it was like something had burst, like all

the weight of cold, dark water had pushed open a lock gate in the canal, flooded through, and left everyone high and dry. I was sitting there on the table in the corridor, gripping the edge of it tightly. The Yellows all gave a shriek, there were three or four seconds silence, and then they all started talking at once. Then Charlie's voice and someone else shouting for them to shut up.

When they were quiet, I heard a boy's voice saying "Does anyone have any idea what the hell that was all about?" I recognised the voice. I think it was a boy called Aidan Kavanaugh.

"I do!" That was Charlie. "It happened to the GAs just like this a bit back." But he didn't say any more, and there was another pause, longer.

"Well, are you going to let the rest of us in on this, or are you going to keep it to yourself? Come on Charlie, spill."

"No... look... I'll deal with this one. Let me deal with this one. I know just what to do." That was Charlie again.

Then the other boy said, "Sod that. I'm the leader. Sit back down again. Where the hell do you think you are going?"

"Look... trust me." That was Charlie again, and it was like there was a touch of panic in his voice, like there was something he didn't want the others to find out. "You all know me, right? There isn't time to explain. Look, you sent me to spy on the GAs, and this time there's something I could only know from being with them. I can't explain it, it'd take too long. If you all come with me, it will go wrong. Last time it took just one GA to cover it, and she wasn't the leader. This time I can do it alone, and yes I'm not the leader Aidan. But you've got to trust me. Let me deal with it on my own. Please!"

"It's not the way we do it." That was a girl's voice. I recognised Shireen Daniels. Then there was more arguing, and I could feel all Charlie's darkness swirling around him. Eventually I heard Aidan Kavanaugh shouting for everyone to be quiet again.

"OK, Charlie," he said, when things had settled down. "This time – just this time – we'll do it your way, okay?"

"Thanks, Ade," Charlie said. That was the moment I pushed myself off the table, and ran silently down the corridor, to hide somewhere, and to follow Charlie when he came out.

The Everywhen Angels

CHAPTER SIX, IN WHICH I SEE THE MAN AT THE CANAL DIE.

There is no good way of telling this.

I stood and watched at the top of the steps up to the canal bridge. I didn't shout out, I didn't run down, I didn't do anything except watch Charlie. I watched him walk slowly and deliberately up to the man who was sitting on the canal bank. The dark green edge stuff swirling around Charlie, with his own red aura at the heart of it, was merging with the dark green of the canal water. The man on the bank was surrounded by it. And I could see something I hadn't noticed before – a faint, grey rippling around the man. Somehow he knew about edge stuff, he could feel edges. I knew how he felt, how the things he knew about puzzled him and made him frantic because no one else could see them. I felt paranoia in him. And I saw and felt the grey, rippling edge stuff around him begin to darken, to swirl, and to join the dark green swirl around Charlie and the water.

I saw him raise himself up on his hands, slide over the stone lip of the canal, and go into the water. I saw Charlie kneel down at the edge of the towpath, and put his hand down into the water. I felt the man's edge stuff mix and merge totally with the dark green, and then disappear altogether. I saw Charlie kill the man that Angela had saved. I watched and did nothing.

I went home after a bit. I took Becks out for a walk, down to where Uncle King and Aunt Kathleen had camped. I looked at the fading marks on the ground which may or may not have been made by their caravan, and I stood and thought.

CHAPTER SEVEN, IN WHICH I SEE AN ANGEL WITH TWO FACES, AND A TRAITOR IS DENOUNCED.

Mum is part-Irish. She loves a song which goes:

The youth of the heart

and the dew of the morning,

You'll wake and they've left you,

   without any warning.

Hitting the ground running is another way of saying growing up.

I think that growing up means realizing that all the things you know don't mean that you are wise. That also means that some adults haven't really grown up. Others have grown up - even they don't know much - they're wise. Mum and Dad wouldn't call Uncle King wise, but maybe he is. Wisdom, I think, means that you have held on to something you had when you were a kid, and you know how little you actually know. It's not easy. It's all confusing. But it all has to be dealt with.

I had to deal with knowing Charlie had killed someone, but I didn't know how. I couldn't go to the Police, I couldn't tell the GAs – no one would believe me. I couldn't tell Mum and Dad because they wouldn't believe me either. I would have to tell someone who didn't know about edge stuff a story without edge stuff, and Charlie would just deny it. In any case, the man at the canal had left a suicide note. It said so in the local paper a few days later. So I did what I was used to doing – watching and learning, looking and listening.

A day came when most of the GAs were there in our classroom, but Angela and Charlie hadn't arrived. I began to get the feeling I always get when a Rising is about to happen – it's like a tingling, like knowing something is about to happen, like the stillness of the air just before thunder, or the smell of wet pavements from a street away before the rain reaches where you are. I was now certain that no one else felt this as soon as I did, but I didn't say anything. One by one the others became aware of it, and as the last one of us looked up and looked around, Charlie burst in, dragging Angela by the hand.

Then the Rising hit us. It was like a big hole had been torn in the edge stuff, and we were looking into a great darkness, darker than any darkness any of us had known. It was like the sky had been pulled away, and we were looking down into it. Then it was like the walls of this hole started to wriggle, and come alive, and things burst out, old bones tumbling over each other, forming into shapes like spiders and centipedes with eyes like grinning skulls. I could feel something like terror in everybody's mind, as these things spilled over the edge of the hole. This was totally unlike any rising we had ever had, and someone was sobbing. Then a bright light started to grow right in the centre of the hole, deep in it, and it got brighter until it grew into the figure of a shining angel with four wings. It hovered on one pair of wings, and covered its body with the other pair, and it held its hands outwards, down by its side, and I could see that there were wounds in the palms of those hands like the picture of Jesus at my old Sunday School. It's face was too bright to look at, and it shimmered and flickered. It was like its face was fighting itself for the right shape.

And while we were all looking at this angel, I felt and saw the edge stuff hard and black and red around Charlie, and hard and black and gold round Angela, and I realized that this was what was making the angel's face so bright and flickering.

Then the Rising stopped very suddenly; but before it did, I saw the angel's face flicker into something like Angela's face. Only it wasn't really. But it was close enough to make people gasp or shout or turn their heads towards Angela. She looked at everyone for a moment, then jumped up, knocking her chair over, and ran out of the room.

Other people jumped up. Janet started to follow her, but Charlie barred her way.

"Let her go, Janet," he said.

For a few moments Janet looked like she was going to push past him. Janet was our leader and, just like Aidan Kavanaugh with the Yellows, she wasn't just going to let Charlie take charge. I watched her hold Charlie's eyes with his.

"I'll let her go, Charlie," she said. "But you know more of this than you're letting on. You'd better spill, and quick, or I am going after her, right?"

"No worries, Jan," said Charlie. "I'll tell you all I need to know. Angela is a traitor – she's one of the Yellows."

There were more gasps. I got up.

"But Charlie..." I began.

"Yeah what, Tink... just what?" he snapped. "Just what, Tink? Just what, Tink? Nothing, that's what – you know nothing, right? You've just got a crush on Angela and you don't want to hear the truth. Just shut it, all right?"

He was sneering at me. Looking right at me. As far as he was concerned I didn't know anything anyway. I thought that for now it was better to let him talk, to see what he had to say.

"It's okay, Tink," said Janet. "Just chill for a bit, and let's hear Charlie. No one blames you for anything." I don't know why she said that. Blame didn't come into it.

Charlie went on: "I haven't felt right about there being thirteen of us since Angela arrived. It isn't right, the number doesn't feel right. I felt she was a wrong'un from the beginning."

"But Charlie," I said. "You were dating her."

"TINK!" Charlie turned towards me, balling his fists, clenching his teeth.

I felt a hand on my shoulder, and looked up to see Janet standing beside me. She was looking straight at Charlie. He was breathing heavily, like he was trying hard to keep his temper. Then he seemed to relax and went on.

"Twelve is the right number for us. It just feels right. Angela just kept on asking questions, right? No one has ever done that as long as I have been here. Why did she need to ask questions except if someone wanted to find out about us? She was a spy for the Yellows. I've been sure of that for a long time."

"Then why didn't you tell us, Charlie?" said Janet. "Why did you let her go on asking questions if you thought she wasn't right?"

"Well, it's not like I told her anything in my answers. I always said she should go and ask you, Jan. Most likely she didn't, because that would have been too obvious. Anyway, I wanted to wait until I got proof. But I don't need to now. We all saw the Rising, we all saw her face, right? We all saw her run out. We all saw her, right?"

"Okay Charlie," said Janet. "Things look the way you said. We'll see if she comes back and then see what she has to say. If not... well... she's out of line, and the AAs will do what they do. So we just wait. Got that everyone?"

Janet looked round, and people were nodding.

"Right, Charlie?"

"I could go and talk to her, Jan, if you want," said Charlie.

"No, Charlie, we wait, right? The AAs will know what to do"

"Okay."

"And you're not going round to her house tonight, Charlie, got that?"

"No, no, we split up anyway."

"Fine, whatever, but you're not going round. We wait, okay?"

"Okay."

So we sat around, not saying much, until it was time to go. At home I did everything as normal. I took Becks for his walk, ate my tea, did my homework, got my backpack and clothes ready and watched some TV. Then I went to bed and set my alarm clock half-an-hour early. I tried to sleep, but I didn't do much of that. In the morning, I surprised Mum by breaking my routine. Being half-an-hour early I said I wanted to walk to school instead of being dropped off. Mum was really surprised, but said it was okay. So I took my backpack and set off.

Of course I didn't go to school straight away, I went to Angela's house, or near enough to watch her come out of her gate and walk down the street. I didn't care what Charlie had said about stalking her. At the bottom of her street she turned right instead of left, and walked away from school, and into the local allotments. I followed her as far behind as I could. I knew where she was hiding, and I hid close by, between the next two sheds, until she stepped out in her street clothes. Then I followed her to the station, and made sure she was all right as she got on the train. I reckoned that was about all I could do under the circumstances. Then I ran all the way to school. Ashe Sobiecki was late and got a demerit; Ashe Shaw went and sat with the GAs as usual.

Nothing happened for the rest of the day. We sat there, we talked a bit, Janet had her iPod earphones in, and Charlie was reading. At least, he had a book open. Then, in the middle of the afternoon, he got up, saying he needed the toilet. I watched him go out of the door. He turned left, towards the front entrance of the school, not right towards the toilets. I didn't follow him.

CHAPTER EIGHT, IN WHICH I GET A CHESS SET AND HEAR A ROMANY WORD.

I remember that one day I heard Mum and Dad talking about hitting the ground running. Dad said, "The problem is, sometimes the ground hits you!" I think that was what happened to me, why I didn't follow Charlie that time, why I didn't do anything at all. Sometimes it is like you have carefully climbed up a steep bank, and then one of your feet slips just a little. For a moment or two you keep your balance, but then you sit down hard and slide all the way down to the bottom, and find you are covered in mud.

I told you I didn't follow Charlie. It was more than that. I didn't do anything. That morning I had got to school late because I had been seeing that

Angela was all right. For the rest of the day I tried to switch off; I was suddenly tired of everything. When a Rising happened suddenly, and we saw Angela and felt the explosion that ripped apart the train at Chart Rise station, I was numb. It was like I made my eyes go out of focus so that I couldn't see, tried to think about something else, so that I wouldn't have to understand.

We sat for an hour, maybe more, after the Rising, saying nothing. Then Janet got up and said she would be back soon. I didn't stay. I went home.

Next day none of us used our doors into the school. Janet was looking for each of us as we arrived, and we just went into school – normal school. There were all kinds of rumours. Charlie Seacole was in intensive care, or dying, or dead. Janet took me to one side at break and told me everything she had seen at the playground, and all about what Angela had said. I wanted to go and ask Angela about everything, but when I caught her eye later she just blanked me, and I was too nervous.

For the rest of the week we still didn't use our doors. Two days after our last Rising, we heard that Charlie was really dead. I had a dream about him that night. He seemed to be asking me for help, but I couldn't remember the dream properly when I woke up. All that time everyone else, everywhere else was talking about the suicide bomber on the train. Mum and Dad were very quiet. Mum cuddled me a lot. The TV was always on, always on the twenty-four-hour news programme, and Mum and Dad always turned their heads to watch and listen when there was anything about the bombing. If I wanted to say something, or if I made a noise, they would glare at me for a moment. Then they would look away, because they remembered that someone I knew at school was in intensive care. Or dying. Or dead.

All this time, I did what I always did – coming home, taking Becks for a walk, doing my homework, eating tea, getting my things ready for school, going to bed, getting up, showering, and all the rest. I spent a lot of time looking at the sky. I don't know why. I remembered one early evening the autumn before, when I had been looking at the planet Venus. It had been the only star in the sky, and it was so bright. Then a cloud had covered it, and I looked away for a few moments. When I looked back to exactly the same bit of the sky, a plane was just flying across. Its light was exactly as bright as Venus, and for a few seconds I thought that Venus itself was moving across the sky. Then I worked out what was really happening, but I watched the light as the plane flew on, and I pretended that it really was Venus. I recognized the feeling, the pretending, and I knew why Angela didn't want to come back. I felt like everything I had learned had gone away, and there was nothing left, but that was pretending, because it was all still there. I was just suddenly very afraid of it.

At the weekend we went to Charlie's funeral. I didn't want to, but it was one of those things that if I hadn't gone I would have wished I had. I thought his mum and dad were very brave. But his younger sister Dulice couldn't stop crying, and had her hands over her face for most of the time. Eventually her mum had to take her out of the church. It was the Baptist church because Charlie's dad went there sometimes; Charlie had never gone there since he was little, I think, but I had always noticed that people need churches when anyone died. The church was full of kids from our school. I saw Angela there, and I smiled at her but she blanked me again. All the GAs were there, and Aidan and Simon Kavanaugh were, and Shireen Daniels, along with others who must have been the rest of the Yellows. There was a bunch of kids who seemed to be very friendly with Dulice too, although most of them were a bit older than she was. There were sad faces, shocked faces, faces which were red like they were hot or had been crying, and there were faces like Angela's that I couldn't read.

Before the service, the Pastor had been speaking quietly to Charlie's mum and dad, and at one point Charlie's dad pointed over to Angela. Then the Pastor came over to her. He had a sad smile on his face, and he looked like he was a nice person.

"Mrs and Mrs Seacole wondered if you might like to say something about Charlie, during the service," he said.

Angela didn't say anything. She just shook her head very hard. Then he went over to Aidan Kavanaugh, and I think he asked him the same thing, but I couldn't see Aidan's reaction, because the Pastor was standing in the way.

Dulice cried for most of the service until she was taken outside, and some other people had handkerchiefs or tissues in their hands. Charlie's mum had one crushed into a tight little ball. I looked at her, looking for things in her that reminded me of Charlie. I looked at his dad too. I tried hard not to think of Charlie being angry with me, and when I couldn't help it and remembered, I tried to tell myself that he hadn't bullied me. I know what being bullied is like, because I have had a bit done to me; but it doesn't usually last because I don't react. That's what mum told me anyway. I know how easy it is to bully someone else too, because I have watched how its done. But I can't do it myself because I know what it feels like. So I tried really hard to make up excuses for Charlie – I knew now how hard it was for someone to understand anything about edge stuff and about what we can do with it, and what it can do to us, so I told myself it had made Charlie the way he was. But no matter how I tried to think good things about Charlie, I kept thinking about the man at the canal. I couldn't tell anyone about that. It would hurt his mum and dad so much, and no one would believe me anyway.

When the Pastor asked, in the middle of the service, if anyone wanted to say anything about Charlie, Janet got up and simply said.

"He was very special."

It's true. He was.

All the time this was going on, there were other people in and around Chart Green and Chart Rise, having to live with the bombing. It was still a news story, and it was still a new hurt for the people who had lost family members and friends. It hadn't been a big bomb, but the size hadn't mattered. It was a big hurt. It was the same for us – only one boy had died, but it was a big hurt.

When the service was over Charlie's mum and dad, and close family, and the Pastor, were all due to go off to the crematorium for the private bit of Charlie's funeral. The rest of us had to go home, or wherever we had to go. Before we left I went over to shake Charlie's mum and dad's hands. Charlie's dad smiled at me – I think it was because I looked so serious.

"I'm sorry Charlie died, Mr and Mrs Seacole," I said.

"You're Jan Sobiecki's boy, aren't you? Ashe, isn't it?" said Charlie's mum, and I nodded and said yes.

"Thank you, Ashe," said Charlie's dad as he shook my hand. I stood there for a moment.

"I know this is a funny thing to ask," I said. "But would you let me have Charlie's chess set? I mean the little travel set he kept in his locker at school. If there is anything of his you want me to bring from school for you, then I will do, and I don't mind if you want to keep the chess set."

I don't know why I said all that. They were surprised, but not angry with me.

"Thank you, Ashe," said Charlie's mum. "We hadn't even thought about Charlie's things at school. We'll ask the head teacher about them, and if he's okay about you bringing them I suppose he'll let you know." She looked at Charlie's dad, and spoke quietly. "Love, are you okay about the chess set?" He nodded.

"You're welcome to it, Ashe. If you're going to use it, take it. I didn't even know Charlie still had it."

I thanked them and walked back to mum and dad. As I went, I could hear Charlie's dad say, "That's a strange boy, but you can't be cross with him." I suddenly realized I hadn't said anything to Dulice, I hadn't even looked at her, and then it was too late anyway because Mum and Dad shepherded me out of the church.

On the next Monday I was allowed into Charlie's locker, and I took the chess set. I looked at his other things, and they seemed strange. The books didn't seem like books, the trainers didn't seem like trainers. I think it was because they didn't belong to anyone any more.

This is what happened over the next few weeks, as the end of term got nearer:

One. I went on the internet and learned how to play chess. I played against myself, and I played against an on-line chess computer, moving pieces on Charlie's board as they moved on the screen. And I found a website where you could watch old episodes of Primeval, added it to my favourites, and forgot to go back to it.

Two. Risings stopped happening. We wondered whether they had stopped altogether.

Three. People stopped coming to GAs. They didn't drop out altogether, but it was like we never had everybody there at the same time. Sometimes we had as few as five or six people. Angela wasn't there, and Charlie wasn't there of course, and the life seemed to have gone out of everyone else. The chat room was usually empty too.

Four. Edge stuff was still edge stuff, but it seemed only to ripple, like all it wanted to do was remind me it was there.

Five. My henna archangel started to fade.

A big part of me was glad. The part of me that had suddenly become tired and frightened of everything, the part of me that had been learning so much and suddenly had had enough and wanted to stop and be normal again. The part of me that knew how Angela felt, and knew that all she had said was true. Another part of me wanted everything to be put back together again. Another part – a small part like a little voice in my head – felt like something had hardly started, instead of just ended.

Then one night I had a dream about Uncle King and Aunt Kathleen. They seemed younger then they had been when I met them for the first time, and they were sitting round a camp fire. They waved to me, but it was a goodbye wave. I woke up with Romany words in my mind, lots of them. It was a Saturday, and I took Becks for a walk, and again I went to where their caravan had been. I got excited because I could see something white through the trees, and I hurried to get there. But it was only a transit van, and I could hear the sound of the chain saw belonging to the man who cut the dead trees. As I walked home again, one Romany word was still in my mind – drom, which means 'road'. It stayed in my mind all over that weekend, like a drumbeat or a tune that won't go away – drom, drom, drom. And it was still there on Monday, when I turned up for the last week of school.

Drom as I reached my door. Drom as I moved to go through it. Drom as I decided to open it a different way. Drom as I walked into the hot, dry world of the Yellows. Drom as I walked into the classroom, and saw that just like the GAs there was a small and frightened handful. Drom as I made another door and pushed it open. Drom as I stepped into the same classroom, but found it occupied by twelve other kids. Drom as I realized that I was among the Avenging Angels.

Unlike the GAs and the Yellows, there were a full twelve of them. They were sitting very close together, like they were keeping warm. It seemed to be night outside, rather than day. I recognised several kids from the next year up from mine; and I recognised Mohinder Singh Johar, Amrita Kaur Johar, and Dale Morris from my class. And I recognised Dulice Seacole. Charlie's sister was an Avenging Angel. So if it was true what Janet had told me after Angela had walked out on us, then Dulice must have been there at the playground. Dulice must have been with them when they came for Angela but took Charlie instead.

I didn't have long to think about this, because one of the older AAs stood up.

"Monday is our day," he said. He was angry, and his voice was shaky. "You shouldn't be here. You shouldn't be here at all. How did you get in? No one can get here except us!"

"You're wrong," I said. "If I'm here then I should be here. I have to be here. It's the drom."

"The what?" someone asked.

"The road. The road I have to be on." I know that was no explanation, but it's what came into my mind to say. But they weren't listening. More of them began to stand up, and they all started to build a wall of edge stuff around me – angry, blue edge stuff forming into four sides to hold me in. But each time they did this, I simply opened a door through it, pushing their wall further away. I wanted to talk to them, but they would neither talk to me nor listen. No matter how much I pushed their walls of edge stuff apart and stepped through, they kept building more and more walls. It was like they were desperate. I spoke to them, and I knew they could hear, but it was like their walls were screaming so as not to let them hear me.

And I heard "Drom" in my mind once more. I wasn't frightened of them, but I opened one more door, in a whole different way, a deeper, deeper door in edge stuff...

... it was like I stepped through that dream where Uncle King and Aunt Kathleen were, except I couldn't see them. When I stepped through, I stepped out of the room, out of the school, and found myself standing at the Knowle, the highest point in Charthill. It was night. I was looking down at the new suburb, and the horizon over the city was lit up with searchlights, and fires. There was the sound of aeroplane engines overhead, and bombs far away, and air-raid sirens. I knew it was 1941, and there was a clear thought in my head – 'Wars and rumours of wars' – and I knew it was from the Bible. I made another door and walked through it...

... my boots sank into mud and water, as I made my way between the banks of the slit trench. A soldier staggered into me.

"Pass auf, Junge!" he shouted. "Was machst du hier?" I could understand his words – "Watch out, lad! What are you doing here?" I was Private Sobiecki, a Kashubian from Danzig. I had lied about my age to join the Imperial German Army, and had been posted to the front. My mates and I had just been moved up from the support trenches – it was the 15th of September 1916 – to the front line at Flers Courcellette, and it was pandemonium.

"Immer Krieg," I thought, in German rather than in my Polish dialect. "Always war."

A soldier slid down from his observation step. His face was white with fear.

"Der Teufel kommt!" he gasped. "The devil is coming!"

I could hear the rattle of an engine, like a big motorcar or a tractor, I could hear the rattle and squeak of metal wheels. A large shadow suddenly hung in the air above us. I looked up and saw armour plating, tracks pawing at the air, the muzzle of the gun from the side turret. And in my mind was a word I remembered – not in German, nor Polish, nor Kashubian, but in the Zigeuner-Sprache of a Gypsy I had met. Drom. It meant road. I had to open another door...

Edge-stuff is wonderful and terrible. I now know

I am made of it – I don't just walk through it. It is me, and I am it – I don't just open doors in it. It is everything and everywhere. I feel the danger of it. Right at that moment I was feeling the danger of it, but it was so great. Every time I opened a door and stepped into another time and place, I became part of that time and place, letting myself slip into belonging there, recognising everything I saw, and heard, and smelled. Each time I opened a door, I went deeper and deeper. Right then I found myself in a press of men, all at least a head taller than I am. The stiff collar of my uniform was rubbing on my neck, my heavy hat kept slipping down over my eyes if I didn't keep my head up, and my drum swung on its baldric, banging against my right leg. My hands held two drumsticks and they were sweating.

I knew my name – Sobiecki – and I knew that I was a drummer boy in the Grande Armée of Emperor Napoleon Bonaparte.

My friends and comrades were milling, muttering, wondering what was going to happen next. Such a lot of the business of war is hurrying somewhere to wait. I wondered too; but mainly I wondered about going through doors, and why every door I went through only led to war. Then I stopped wondering - it didn't seem right.

A tall officer, looking even taller because of his cocked and cockaded hat, and the fact that he was astride a horse of at least sixteen hands, pointed along the road to the village of Waterloo – the one they had told me led to Brussels and to victory – with his sabre. He shouted something I could not hear above the noise, and our sergeants yelled at us, by way of a response. My friends, here in the centre of the regiment hurriedly fixed their bayonets and formed a broad column.

"That was Marshal Ney," said private Philippe Lejeune, bending down to me. "We're going to take La Haye Sainte at last!"

"A bad business too," said a voice behind me. "They're forming us into a regular column instead of letting us skirmish. Some officers know nothing."

"Knock it off," said Philippe to the other soldier, as we started to march. I beat my drum with a single stick to mark the fall of every left boot upon the road, and the soldiers' belts and cartridges and coat-tails began to slap and rattle in counter-rhythm. All I could see ahead of me were dark blue jackets, white cross-belts, and bobbing shakos, I had no idea where we were going. But I kept in step, and thumped my drum.

"Who are we?" I heard the shout from somewhere to the right – I thought I recognised the voice of Maurice de Carentan, youngest son of a landowner, who had joined as a private soldier and earned corporal's stripes – and a couple of dozen voices called back.

"La Treizième Légère!"

"Crap! We might be the Fighting Thirteenth, but we're not the Shouting Thirteenth," called the same voice from the right. "Riflemen – I said who are we?"

"La Treizième Légère!" came a much louder response, and the shout was taken up back along the column, before we fell into silence again. Our mood seemed to be grim. Then I heard the grumbler to my rear calling to me.

"Hey – General Poniatowski – give us a song to march by!"

I loved the nickname that the soldiers had given me. I puffed out my chest like a real Polish general, and began to rattle out a tattoo on my drum. I sucked in a lungful of air, and began to sing as bravely as I could.

"Brave drummer boy, returning from the battle,

Brave drummer boy, returning from the battle,

Ra-ta-plan Ra-ta-ta-plan,

Returning from the battle..."

My comrades began to join in. Those who knew the verses sang them with me. Most of the others yelled the refrain – "Ra-ta-plan Ra-ta-ta-plan" – and everyone stamped their feet as they marched.

"Sees Princess Joan, a-sitting at her window,

Sees Princess Joan, a-sitting at her window,

RA-TA-PLAN RA-TA-TA-PLAN,

A-sitting at her window...

Dear Princess Joan, come down and marry me-oh,

Dear Princess Joan, come down and marry me-oh,

RA-TA-PLAN RA-TA-TA-PLAN,

Come down and marry me-oh...

Brave drummer boy, you'd better ask my father,

Brave drummer boy, you'd better ask my father,

RA-TA-PLAN RA-TA-TA-PLAN,

You'd better ask my father..."

"We sing better than the bloody Fritzes anyhow!" shouted someone. I caught a glimpse, ahead of us, of a flag tied to a makeshift pole, sticking out at a silly angle from the roof of a farmhouse. It was the criss-crosses of the British flag, and I cursed a little as I always did, because they had stolen the colours of our tricolour. But I was puzzled too, because we were supposed to be attacking the Germans. A few rifle balls whistled overhead – ranging shots. Sergeant Lebrun's voice called back to us from the head of the column.

"Lads, it's the King's German Legion – Riflemen like us! Let's give them a good time!"

I marched on tip-toe so I could see better. It hurt my feet like hell, but I could see the walls of the farm buildings beginning to sprout green shakos like buds on a chestnut tree. A loud shout came for us to stop. I knew what was happening at the front – the first rank would have dropped to one knee, propping their left elbow on the other knee to steady their rifles... the second rank would be aiming at the enemy from a standing position... the third rank would be presenting over the shoulders of the second. They would be a target that enemy fire could not miss, but a volley from three ranks of the Thirteenth was reckoned to be something no enemy could stand against.

"Volley... Fire!"

Would I ever get used to the sound? A flat clap that shakes the air, like lightning striking a tree in the next field, dying into a rattle as the men who were late with their shots fired. An answering volley from the Germans' Baker rifles was ragged but murderous, as our front three ranks stood sideways on to let men from behind pour through. Rifle and musket balls began to make a wheatfield of us with their summer rain-squall. I kept marching, thumping my drum as hard, as fast, as heavily as I could, ra-ta-plan ra-ta-ta-plan, drowning out the rifle-fire, drowning out the heartbeat in my ears, drowning out what I could see, and hear, and feel as each of my comrades was hit.

I lost sight of Philippe, but I knew the pain of the ball that shattered his right shoulder and spun him round, so that the second one caught him squarely in his back and knocked him onto his face. I knew it hurt so much, but that the hurt faded fast as his life slipped away, and he scarcely felt the boot of a clumsy comrade treading on his neck. A face before his eyes... a name... Angelique...

As each stalk tumbled in the wheatfield, he became known to me, often six or seven at a time their thoughts were mine. As our first wave paused and volleyed and the volley was returned, Antoine and Auguste Bouteiller, brothers, were snuffed out as candles are, the younger falling to cover the elder's corpse. Sergeant Lebrun's overwhelming feeling was more surprise than pain, a kind of outrage that the ball that shattered his adam's apple, so that he gasped for air, had almost missed him... "No, no... let me go back and do it again... it would miss me... it would miss me..." and an absurd smell of green leaves was in his nostrils from God-knows-where.

Corporal Georges Babineaux, racked by such an intense pain that he thought himself on fire... screaming. My drumskin loosened and dented under the force of my blows, ra-ta-plan ra-ta-ta-plan. Some of my comrades had reached the farmhouse wall at a run, and were looking for a way in or up, wanting to get close enough to use their bayonets, desperate to get to the enemy before they reloaded. The German fire was peppery at best, but we were being hammered by it...

Big Pierre Pelletier falling, thinking of his mother holding him, making it all better. Names coming like a rapid roll-call of pain, fear, anger, and total bewilderment – Charpentier, Leveque, Bourque, Desmarais, Lambert, Grosmont, Arceneau, Laroche, Laurent – each one with a mother, or a wife, a duty left undone, a debt unpaid, a wrong unrighted. Some died cursing the enemy, and now as my comrades climbed the walls of La Haye Sainte, the enemy began to die too.

"The Fritzes' ammunition's done – come on lads!"

My drum seemed to blaze with its ra-ta-plan ra-ta-ta-plan, like flames were leaping from the skin, fanned by my drumsticks, now German and English names and feelings, pain and rage, and desperation joined all the French... Heinrich, Loewe, Ackermann, Yorke, Kastner, Allen, Schultheiss, Braun... Each name, each new set of feelings, each cry for a mum or a sweetheart set my hands thrashing my drumsticks faster and harder.

"The barn door... the barn door!"

The men of the Thirteenth left outside La Haye Sainte swirled around the farmhouse to where a wooden door was beginning to cave in under a rain of blows from rifle butts. As it gave way and they rushed in over the debris, the last volley from the King's German Legion took more of them... more names, more pains... Durand, Dubois, Lisle, Broussard... Hoch, MacKay, Schroeder... Then it was a dirty matter of bayonet against bayonet, grunt for groan, gasp for gasp, looking each other in the eye and trying not to think, "My God, but for the green jacket – or the blue – he looks just like a man I know back home". I stepped over body after body, marching closer to the breach with its few, jagged piece of timber hanging from broken hinges. All the time my ra-ta-plan ra-ta-ta plan became fiercer, almost insane.   Through the mayhem, as the Germans fell before my comrades, or ran for their lives, I was the only one marching. I was marching because I was marching for the doorway. I was marching because I had reached the doorway. I was marching through the doorway. It was what I did. Going through doors was what I always do.

CHAPTER TEN, IN WHICH AN OLD MAN AND A YOUNG BOY LEAVE A MOUNTAIN FORTRESS.

Once, my name had been Ashe Shaw Sobiecki – or so I remember. It is a long time since I used it. I tried to teach it to the people here, in the fortress of Alamut, but they could not get their tongues round it. Instead they have always called me Mirza, because I said I was half-Egyptian, and Egypt is known as al Misr in Arabic. Because I have not grown in height since the day I arrived, the men started to call me Mirza Buzurg, which means 'Mirza the Great'. They mean this as a joke, because I am no way great, but my name has been Mirza Buzurg ever since, and Ashe Shaw Sobiecki has been more of a shadow only seen behind Mirza Buzurg in the sunlight. Only vaguely, and only in my mind. Some of the men used to call me The Frank, because they said when I had stepped through the main gate of the fortress, blinking and dazed, I was singing a song in the language of the Franks – they called any Christian from Western Europe by their name for a Frenchman. But soon they left off using that name, and I have been Mirza, always Mirza, to them.

Here we perch, on this great rock, not far from the city of Basra. Here we learn from the eagles that wheel in the sky above us. We have always learned from the eagles, so much so that the very name of Alamut is said to mean 'learning from eagles'. It was built here, amongst bare, jagged peaks, and between dark passes with sheer sides, by a prince who – so the story goes – let a captured eagle fly free, and saw where it perched. On that spot he built this fortress which no army can approach, except one man at a time.

Our own leader, our prince, is the great Shaikh ai Jabal – the Old Man of the Mountain. There have been many Old Men of this Mountain. I have seen five. When I came here Hassan II was dying. His name had been auspicious, as the men he led were known as Assassiyun, 'The Believers', the followers of Hassan – the first Hassan, Hassan Sabbah who some say had built the fortress of Alamut, though to my eyes it seems much older. But this second Hassan commanded the men of Alamut for only a brief time, after which Muhammad II ruled us for forty-four years. Then Hassan III ruled for eleven years, Muhammad III for thirty-four, and then our new Shaikh, Ruknud-Din Khurshah, who has been here for what seems no more than a heartbeat. But to outsiders, to travellers on the caravan routes east, to the petty khans and chieftains of the deserts, and to the Franks of the Crusader Kingdoms, there is, and only ever has been, one Old Man of the Mountain.

The legends of the Old Man are many. Some are true – I have seen with my own eyes the origin of many of the tales. Others are no more than stories to frighten naughty children to sleep. It is said that the Old Man drugs his recruits, carries them dreaming to a scented garden full of beautiful women and, when they awake, convinces them that they have had a vision of Paradise. In this way he makes sure of their loyalty, when he commands them to go out and slay his enemies. Myself, I believe this story to be true of Hassan Sabbah, if of no one else.

There is another tale that the Old Man is himself a Christian, though his followers are Muslim. Indeed it is true that one Shaikh did send emissaries to the Crusader King in Jerusalem, proposing that they should form an alliance against a common enemy, and that amongst his hints and suggestions was the possibility that he would convert all the Assassiyun to the Crusaders' religion. But before negotiations could begin properly, one of the hated Templars murdered the emissaries.

Further, it is said that the Old Man did, in years gone by, send out his followers to kill Christian Kings, Jewish Patriarchs, and Muslim Caliphs. No one was safe from his wrath, or from the fanatical devotion of his followers, people said. Not the Children of the Book, nor the Fire-worshippers of Persia – his arm is long, and it carries a scimitar.

It is true that we Assassiyun are devoted to our King; this next tale I can swear to, having seen it with my own eyes. I was one of a number of us who were selected to escort a noble Crusader to Alamut, under safe conduct of our Shaikh. I had been sent because it was known I had been baptized as a 'Nazrin' – a Christian – in my infancy, and I spoke a little of the Frankish tongue, having learned it at a school on the other side of the world. We blindfolded the nobleman and led him up the secret, winding paths that lead to Alamut, right into the presence of the Shaikh. The Shaikh had arranged things so he stood with the morning sun at his back, and when the blindfold was taken off the visitor stood there blinking in the direct sunlight. The Shaikh was a terrible silhouette to him, standing hands on hips, speaking loudly in only Arabic or Persian, which I translated for him. Used to the treachery and double-dealing that went on amongst the ambitious barons and knights in Jerusalem, the Crusader asked the Shaikh whether he could count on the loyalty of his own men. In answer, the Shaikh commanded two Assassiyun to step forward. Now, it was his custom to present each of us with a special dagger for every new mission, with orders that it should be used only once – when it was plunged with deadly intent into the body of the chosen enemy. On this occasion the Shaikh handed such a dagger to the first man, and commanded him to thrust it into his own heart. The man obeyed instantly, and fell dying at the Shaikh's feet. The second man was ordered to leap from the battlements to his death. Again, the order was obeyed instantly, and the second man plunged onto the rocks below without uttering a sound. No more question about loyalty was raised.

If you are wondering, I hid the fact that I was shivering with fear. I had never taken a life in the service of the Shaikh, but I knew at once that if he had ordered me to die by my own hand I would have quit this existence without a moment's hesitation. It was our way, it was the way of the Assassiyun. But it was not my lot, that day.

Why not? I believe that it had something to do with the way I was, the way I have always been. On the day I arrived, to the surprise of the sentries who had not seen me pass, I was challenged to a wrestling duel by Rashid, a boy of thirteen, a little taller and heavier than I was, the son of an Assassiyun. I had never wrestled before, but I clung on to Rashid, hampering his arms and legs, until we were both exhausted. It was a draw, but Rashid proclaimed himself the victor, and myself his mortal but noble enemy for life. Of course, we became inseparable friends, and that was probably why I stayed. I had never had a friend like him. Rashid is now an old man, an Assassiyun still, as brave and reckless in his heart as he ever was when he rode out on the orders of the Shaikh; but now he is a fearless warrior of the chess-board. Every day he assaults me with his horsemen and foot-soldiers, as I try to close in on his king. His attacks are merciless, his feints are subtle and cunning, his defence is as solid as the walls of Alamut. He says he has taught me everything he knows, all the moves and counter-moves, but still, more often than not, he defeats me. I hear his sharp calls of "Shah!" when he puts my king into danger, and "Shah mat!" – which is Persian for 'The King is ambushed' – when I have lost all hope of escape. Sometimes I beat him, and it is then I who call out "Shah mat!" Under his teaching I have learned so much about chess that I could now beat... who? Some friend I knew in my lost childhood? I seem to have forgotten.

Yesterday, Rashid said to me, "Mizra, my beloved enemy-for-life, I am not so old nor my eyes so dim that I can't see the impossibility which is in front of them. I am more than one hundred years old, as you must be. I am bent, toothless, white-haired, one foot and four toes upon the Parsees' Tower of Silence in Tehran, where vultures pick clean the bones of the dead. You, on the other hand, look as you always have done, as you did when you first came here. Some of our comrades say you are one of the Djinn, or a sorcerer. Others that you are beloved of Allah the Merciful, or that you are an angel sent to protect us. Others simply look at you, shake their heads, and wonder how such things can be."

"And again others..." I said, "... think nothing of this, see only the fortress boy, the mascot. The new recruits know no better. Myself, I am at a loss to explain why the blessing of Allah – if a blessing it is, and not a curse – should rest upon me. A sorcerer knows he is a sorcerer, but a Djinn may be cursed not to know he is a Djinn. An angel too may not know his nature, but that would be a blessing. What do you say I am, Rashid?"

"I say you are my enemy for life, who cannot play decent chess no matter how well I teach him, and whom I showed his place by thrashing him soundly on the day he arrived." said Rashid, his voice lowering and becoming a whisper. "Also better than my brother, better than my best friend, the one Assassiyun for whom I would die... before I would die for the Shaikh!"

That was not such a terrible thing to say, for Ruknud-Din Khurshah was not the man that Muhammad III was, who had gone before him. Ruknud-Din was indecisive in the face of the greatest danger ever to face the Faithful. For two and a half years now the Mongol horsemen of Hulagu Khan had ridden unhindered over our desert. Assassiyun patrols and tax-collectors had been summarily slaughtered, or sent to Alamut tied backwards on their horses, naked and branded. Now the whole army of the Khan had encircled Alamut – if not directly, because we were still protected by gorges and cliffs, then at least at a few miles' distance. Their presence taunted us, and shamed our Shaikh. Double shame came when an ambassador from the Khan was allowed to stride insolently into Alamut, armed and without a blindfold. A mocking smile was on his lips as he told the Shaikh, in halting, vulgar Arabic, that the Khan would graciously allow all Assassiyun to live, if he surrendered Alamut the next day. Muhammad would have parted that coarse head from its body and kicked it all the way downhill to the Mongols' camp; Ruknud-Din bowed, and told the ambassador that the great Khan's generous offer would be seriously considered.

That was yesterday. In the night, the Mongol army moved much closer, guided by the ambassador, who had memorised the route. We all lay awake, listening to the strange lilt of the Mongols' songs – guttural notes with harmonics that buzzed like bees, or like desert wind amongst gnarled rocks, but in their own way hypnotizing and beautiful.

This morning the talk was that we were going to prepare for a siege, or maybe a last desperate, suicidal sortie, in which we would die with honour, charging for the enemy's throat. But Shaikh Ruknud-Din surprised us all, by ordering us to abandon our weapons, and to pack such few items as we would need on the road to Basra. The Assassiyun were to be no more, Alamut was to be surrendered on the guarantee of the Khan's mercy. All the men were too shocked to say anything but, accustomed to obeying the Shaikh without question, they did as they were told.

I had been looking out over the gatehouse wall, when Rashid came to me.

"Tell me what you see out there, Mirza Buzurg," he said. "Tell me if you see what I see."

With a sigh, I said, "I see the Mongol army, and its great Khan Hulagu mocking us. I see them preparing their spears and their arrows. I see them joking and wagering amongst themselves as to which one of them will cut down most of the once-feared Assassiyun. I can see war. I can always see war, and nothing but war."

"That is what I see, and it seems to me to be like the end of the world," said Rashid, spitting on the ground. "Mirza, my enemy for life, though I am old I will fight to save you with my bare hands if necessary. I will defy our so-called Shaikh and the great Khan and put myself in the way of any spear or arrow meant for you. If I can buy you even a minute more life, I shall do it."

Rashid, for the first time in his life, was weeping. I took his right hand in mine.

"No you shall not, Rashid," I said. "Look, our comrades are forming up to leave, and the gates are opening. Join them bravely, Rashid. Farewell... masalaama... peace be with you."

"Masalaama, Mirza Buzurg. Are you not coming with us?"

"Maybe. Maybe not. Rashid, we will not meet again outside of Paradise – that much I know. Now go."

Rashid turned and walked away, straightening his back as much as an old man could, determined to walk as proudly as only an Assassiyun can. I watched him and all our comrades, with the last Shaikh ai Jabal at their head, ride out of the open gates of Alamut, and into the mercy of Hulagu Khan.

For a while I just stood there, almost wanting to run after Rashid, the true Old Man of the Mountain. Because after all, I was only a boy. Maybe I was a boy who, for some reason, had lived one hundred and thirteen years without growing old, but I was still a boy, for all that. Without Rashid, without the Shaikh, without the other of the garrison of Alamut, I could be nothing more. Without them, Mirza Buzurg began to fade, and Ashe Shaw Sobiecki, his shadow for a century, to become stronger. Then, as if I was tired of standing, tired of being between two realities, I did something I had almost forgotten I could do. I opened a door.

I stepped through it, out of the dry air of the Mountain, and into cold, swirling water.

The Everywhen Angels

Chapter Eleven, in which the water tries to take a little girl away from me.

I was drowning.

Just like no one tells you how to walk on water, no one tells you how to drown. It's very easy. There's a story of how, when the world was very young, a great flood came and washed everything away, except for a pair of every living creature and one family of people. Then, when the flood went down, they all went out and inhabited a cleanly-washed world. A lot of people laugh at this story, but I reckon it's something like a tsunami that wiped out the dinosaurs. Something else I reckon is that people do not really know how close the world they know is to the world of stories. Really it is the same world – everything is the same world – but there are edges, edge-stuff, and people don't want to see beyond the edges.

Like right now, I was in the water, and I was very close to a moment where you give up, stop breathing, and everything becomes calm and gentle. I was floating in the edge-stuff between life and death, or between one story and the next; I knew this because I had lived the last moments of the man who drowned in the canal, feeling what he felt, deep, sad, gone... And as well as that I lived Angela's moments saving him, and Charlie's moments killing him – that's all there in a Rising. It was almost like a game, all this, almost a dance, like pieces fitting together, like a picture getting clearer and clearer.

The water was flowing and rushing round me, dragging at my clothes, pulling me down into it's darkness. It was so cold. My heart was beating more and more slowly. Bit by bit, my body was forgetting how to feel. But there was something in my head telling me that there was more to the world than freezing, pulling water. There was edge-stuff too. There is always edge stuff. And suddenly, there in the water and the edge-stuff, my fingers touched... found... gripped... and held on to a metal pole. It was swaying and bucking in the torrent, vibrating like a ruler when you hit it against the top of a desk, but I pulled myself up, out of the water, held on to it, and gulped in long, hard, desperate breaths of air.

If anything, the air was even colder, like the swirling water was causing a wind to rush over it. And the rain was coming down, stinging hard, like sharp pebbles. Hard things floated in the water, or if they didn't float, the water pushed them along under its surface. The things that didn't float looked like darker shapes in the darker water. The things that did float looked wrong, upside down, out-of-place. They were sharp and heavy, and banged into me, trying to make me let go. The water was already neck-deep on me and getting deeper. At first, when I had grabbed the pole, my feet seemed to have found the pavement beneath it. Now I was clinging on higher up the pole, and sometimes my legs were whipped away, so that I had to kick and kick like I was swimming, and wrap them round the pole again, until the next hard thing bashed into them.

The water was rushing up Marsh Lane into The Green, all the way to Chart Rise and beyond. It was washing all the way back to the hills, and then it was going to sweep back again. Right now it was being sucked down the station steps here. It was grey and filthy, becoming filthier and more full of wrong things by the minute. As I clung on to the pole, I could hear its angry roaring going on and on. The whole of Chart Green was edge, like it was drowning on behalf of the whole world. Although my mouth was filling up with rainwater and I had to spit every time I breathed, because I was gulping in rain with each breath, I started to recite facts I remembered from geography and environmental studies lessons, and to shout them against the roaring... all about how if a spring tide and a severe storm happen together, the tide is high and Yamm walks on the land... and when that happens at the same time as rainstorms in the hills where the TV masts are, and all the water rushes down to the flood plain... and all the storm-drains and culverts back up, and I have lost the sword and shield that Kothar made me... then there is no edge between land and sea, only a battle raging, only anger.

And it's like murdering to clean up murder, and it's a story and real at the same time, and deliberate and accidental at the same time, and it's justice and wrong at the same time... and I knew that as I fought against Yamm, and was losing, the people of Chart Green were so very frightened. They were frightened like they were carrying the fear of the whole world!

They were frightened like the little girl was, who was being swept along by the water, her arms wrapped tightly round a piece of wooden fence, spinning, screaming with every breath even though she had no strength to scream as she was being rushed towards the station steps, which were nothing but a filthy, black whirlpool. She was screaming for the whole of Chart Green as she was dragged past me, but I wrapped my legs and my right arm hard round the pole, and reached out my left hand, stretching and stretching as things banged into me, hurting me badly. And even though they were so cold, so tired, so numb, my fingers caught hold of her sleeve, and I pulled. She kept on screaming, not letting go of the piece of fence, and her sleeve was being dragged out of my fingers. My arm was being pulled back, the pole was bending, everything really hurt! But I would not let go. Yamm was not going to take the little girl away from me!

The piece of fence must have shattered, because suddenly there was only her weight dragging my arm down into the water. Her clothes must have been full of water, and now there was nothing holding her up. I pulled with every bit of strength I had. More strength seemed to flow into me from the edge-stuff, flowing into me as the water flowed and raged round me... the strength I had held on to Kathor's sword and shield with. I gave the biggest heave I could, and the girl came up out of the water and towards me. Her head came out of the water, she grabbed hold of me, and I wrapped my left arm tightly round her. Here eyes were tight shut. It was only because I could feel her shivering and clinging on that I could tell she was alive.

Then I knew what I had to do.

Adults talk about making "moral decisions". Being right or wrong is easy – anyone can be right or wrong – what's really hard, what you really need courage for, is making the decision. Because you can't see everything that is going to happen after that. But just think what it would be like if, with every step you took, you began to see more, not just what was going to happen next, but other things after that, like branches on a tree spreading out, thousands of rights and wrongs, and things that were right and wrong at the same time. But you still have to make a decision. That's what a Rising is like, that's what a Rising is – it's when you see more and more, when you look over and past edges. And bit by bit you begin to realize that you are not just doing what you are told, what you are supposed to do, and you begin to make decisions. You begin to make things happen.

When we all saw the man drowning in the canal, and when I saw Angela save him, and Charlie kill him, I didn't really realize that. Now I did, as I saw past edge after edge after edge.

And so I opened one door, and through that I

sent all the water and the destruction, or I let it go. And I opened another door opposite it, and I stepped through that one, holding onto the little girl, and pulling along behind us the whole of Chart Green that had been drowning on behalf of the whole world... or I let it follow me... and we all went into a place beyond the door where it was still Chart Green, but there was no spring tide, no storm surging up the estuary and up Chart Brook, no rain pouring down from the hills, no angry sea-god walking on the land. And where I was not Baal in a story... and everything was where it should be, except I was clinging to a pole, and a puzzled little girl was clinging on to me. She let go, looked down like she was surprised to be dry. Then she looked at me, still puzzled, but after a while she decided to smile, and then ran off. I felt like something that was owed had been paid back.

Then I opened two more doors and stepped through them both - simultaneously!

CHAPTER TWELVE, IN WHICH THERE ARE A LOT OF DOORS.

I remember hearing the Child Psychologist tell Mum and Dad that I don't learn things by finding out for myself. That's a problem for me. It's not a problem because it's true, it's a problem because it's the other side of not telling me I can't. That means that I don't try, and so I don't find out that it's wrong. I used to think that things the Child Psychologist and other people said to Mum and Dad must be true, because even though I was there, they were talking about me like I wasn't, and so it must be true otherwise they would be hiding it from me.

The more I had been with the Guardian Angels, the more I realized that they weren't pretending not to be able to do some things, they really couldn't do them. Because they believed they couldn't. Once I realized that, that meant I had learned something for myself, and that even though the Guardian Angels would say things and mean them – Just like Mum and Dad and the Child Psychologist – they could still be wrong. So I went on and on learning things for myself. Like the whole tulpa thing. There's so much more to it than having a kind of dummy-me doing the schoolwork while I have the adventures. Edge-stuff isn't like that at all.

It's like this...

...It's like I can open doors anywhere, to anywhere, any time... I can go through those doors, I can bring things or people with me, I can send things to places. It's like opening two doors and walking through them both at the same time. I learned this from having to open two doors, just where and when I wanted or needed them. It's like opening two doors, just like I was doing now, and then two more doors beyond each of them, and stepping through all of them. Then beyond each of those doors, opening another two, and on and on and on. And all the time it's me who goes through all the doors.

So I went through all the doors. I went through all the doors that could be gone through, until I could see everything, everything there is or ever could be, and hear everything. And everything was sound and light and colour and talking... and knowing everything, and feeling everything, and being round every edge that was or could be. And that was like Hell!

So I went back through all the doors, closing them behind me. For every two I closed behind me, I went through one, and on and on until there were no doors left. And then I went through the last door, the one that wasn't there at all. And through that door was nothing at all, and it was so peaceful. And that was like Heaven.

And somewhere between the two I saw, or felt, or heard these things:

I saw Angela near the station, saving a single life. It was the only thing she could do then and there. The person wasn't special, he wasn't a great surgeon or anything, he wasn't going to save the world. He was just one man.

I saw Charlie watching Angela, making pictures in his mind to suit the way he saw things.

I heard the thoughts of the martyr in the train, and I felt the edge stuff shimmer around him. "There is no door. There are no doors. Prophecy is sealed for ever. Our war is holy. Our war is just." And what I felt as I heard this was such terrible sorrow, because I knew he was like us, like me, but that he hated what he was, wanted to destroy what he was, and that he had needed a cause to do it for.

I saw Charlie, and Angela, and the Avenging Angels at the playground. I saw how the edge stuff swirled round each of them, but no one's touched anyone else's, no one's had any effect on anything. And I saw Janet lead Angela away, and Charlie die.

I saw things I could change, and things I couldn't, and I started to understand the difference.

I don't know how long I went through doors, or how long I stayed in the place that was like Hell, or in the place that was like Heaven. I had been places where time didn't matter. I had been a hundred years in Alamut. And I was still Ashe Shaw Sobiecki, after all, stepping back through the last door, the door that wasn't there at all, back to where I had started from.

Chapter Thirteen, in which we probably lose everything.

I remember very clearly the day that the Child Psychologist spelt things out for Mum and Dad. He said:

"I'm going to Spell Things Out for you."

When he said it, I could almost see the words written down, with capital letters, just like that. Again, like always, I was listening as the Child Psychologist, and Mum, and Dad talked about me. The Psychologist did most of the talking, and I can remember every word that he said.

"I think we have all been reluctant to put a name to Ashe's condition, mainly because he is such a well-behaved boy, and does so well at school, and never seems to get into trouble. But you've always realised something made him special – I'll put it that way, because I would hate to classify him as having something 'wrong' with him, or say he is 'not normal' – Ashe is, in fact, a very special boy. In my opinion he has a form of what we call Asperger's Syndrome – you've heard of it? It's a condition within the autism spectrum disorder, but no, no – of course he's not what you'd recognise as autistic, he has had no problem with language or cognitive development. But the things you have described to me in the way he behaves and interacts, seem to me to be examples of... of difficulties in social interaction, stereotyped patterns of behaviour, and in some cases atypical use of language. You told me that his English teacher, for example, praises his way of expressing himself – what was it she said? – 'very straightforward, but with an occasional, startling metaphor'. His interests are very... very focussed, almost obsessive. His friendships are awkward..."

I had stopped listening just then, because it had been time for Becks' walk. But as I walked him out towards where the suburb and the countryside became a blurred edge, on the day I was going to meet King Shaw, I was thinking about what the Child Psychologist had said about me learning things by copying. He had been sure about that, and he had had examples to give Mum and Dad, and they had nodded and given more examples from when I was growing up.

But since that time, since I had started to have what I suppose you could call adventures, it seemed to me that I had found out that I was not learning by copying at all. I was learning by feeling. I was learning by knowing. I was learning because things were being shown to me that weren't being shown to the others. Or maybe these things had been inside me all along, and were being pulled out. Mr Callister once told me that's what 'education' meant; it comes from an old word meaning 'led out from'. Perhaps inside me there had always been Ashe Sobiecki, before mum and dad had ever called me Ashe, and Shaw was inside me too, and Mirza Buzurg was inside me too, and all the things I have seen and been when I opened door after door – maybe all that has always been inside me. What does 'always' mean anyway? 'Always' seems to me to be another name for the edge stuff, because it isn't just everywhere, it's everywhen. And that doesn't do it either, because it's everything too. I'm edge stuff myself. I'm in it, I'm part of it, it's part of me... and somehow, me and it, we're all of it. I'm still Ashe Sobiecki, but I have taken on so much more, and I am really, really sad, because it feels like I've left so much behind.

I know that if I reach out right now, there is nothing I can't touch. And I'm longing to do that, but I'm afraid to do it, or maybe cautious is a better word, because it's a responsibility. It's a power, a bigger power than I would ever imagine anyone having, and that means – I know this – that it's almost too big to use. That's the responsibility. Adults are always saying that teenagers have no sense of responsibility. Maybe I have grown up, then, and I'm being sad because I already miss being a kid. Part of me is still a kid, though, and it seems important to hold on tight to that.

The last door I walked through was back to our empty classroom, the empty classroom set apart, just for this, while the school went about its business somewhere else. Very carefully I reached out, touching my friends in the Guardian Angels who were sitting in another room just like this one. I made my touch say, "Come here," very gently. I reached out and touched all the other Guardian Angels with the same call, and I made the edge stuff tug gently at their ankles. I made it so that wherever they were, they would come in here, where I was, through the actual door to the classroom. I knew I could have forced them, I could have dragged and pushed them, using edge stuff like chains or magnets, or like gravity. But instead I drew them like a friend asking a favour; and they came.

I reached out further, feeling my way through the edge stuff bit by bit around Chart Green, just

Chart Green. It's amazing. I knew who I was looking for, or feeling for. It's totally amazing, because there was Becks pricking up his ears as I touched him – remember I told you he listened, remember I told you he was a responsible dog? And there were the others, so I began to pull, gently, and they began to go with the flow. I wasn't forcing them, they were all coming because they wanted to.

The Guardian Angels waited. They didn't seem impatient. They all knew something was happening, and it's like they were happy enough to wait and cool about it. The classroom door opened again and other kids walked in now, some with something yellow on them – a badge, an Alice-band, a watch-strap. Some of the Guardian Angels looked at each other, and then at me. I couldn't help smiling, and thinking, "There's more!" as the Yellows filed in. They looked at me, sitting up on the table at the front of the classroom, swinging my legs a bit, and then took some of the empty seats; a couple of them leaning against the far wall.

Then twelve other kids began to come into the room. They had no need for badges or anything else, because everyone knew who they were. Someone gasped. One of the Yellows got up as if to back away, still not getting it, still stuck in our old ways.

"It's all right," I said. "It's okay, honest."

They were the Avenging Angels of course. Everyone could see who they were, and recognised that they were kids from our school; but there was still something hanging over them like a mystery, a darkness. They had never been in the same room with GAs or Yellows, at least not through the same door, though I knew they had been in this very room at the same time as us but through their own door. That's what edge stuff is like (and I know you're beginning to see it that way too, which is good). And then the Avenging Angels' darkness began to lift, because the darkness and the mystery is part of edge stuff too and everyone began to realise it.

I could feel more people coming, letting themselves be pulled along, lots of people I knew, and one I didn't. A handful of older kids started to file in, looking around – Angela was there now, and Kesha Patel both looking really surprised, and Reuben Flowers in amongst them too – and then came Mr Callister, and his eyes were bright like he was really excited.

"I knew it! I knew it!" he said. "I knew it wasn't just my imagination, I knew it wasn't a dream. I knew I had been in this room when I was in my teens, and it wasn't like an ordinary classroom. I have been certain of this ever since I came back here to teach!"

And he smiled at me, like I'd given him a birthday present, as the last few kids came in.

There was another arrival, a man in a suit. He looked like he would have been smart if he hadn't been caught by surprise. He had a dark tie which was pulled to one side a bit untidily, and he had one of those bags airline pilots use and a name-badge on his lapel. He was sweating a bit, and looking round, catching sight of Angela and... whoa... his eyes went wide. She looked back at him, and she was so gobsmacked.

"This is why I became a preacher... this feels like the day I first knew I wanted to be a preacher!" he said, kind of to Angela, but kind of so the rest of us can hear him. His voice was American, and this made me feel warm. I mean of course I know edge stuff is everywhere, but it's still good to see it.

There were no more to come – no more from round Chart Green anyway, although the preacher was proof, which I didn't need, that there were other groups like us in other parts of the world. Then everyone was looking at me. All around us, all around the room and the school, the edge stuff was shifting, flowing, like we were in the eye of a great hurricane like you see on satellite pictures. I could feel it – we could feel it – spreading out, stretching out, far, far out. Like it's not just outwards but upwards, and downwards, and every angle in between.

I took a deep breath, and spoke.

"I suppose you're wondering why I brought you all here..." I said, and then I began to tell them everything I have just told you, from the moment I found Uncle King right up to my journeys through all the doors. I told them about all the things they had been through, and how they looked to me. And they really listened.

When I had finished, they were stunned. I don't think they could take it all in. A few of them asked me questions, or raised objections, but half-heartedly.

"Tink... I mean Ashe," said Janet. "Do you mean that we can move through time and space?"

"No," I said. "I mean we are time and space."

"Is this really the last war, the End Times?" someone else asked.

"There is always a war going on," I said. "First or last it doesn't really matter. It's like the only war that matters is the one you have to fight inside yourself. Lots of people don't fight, or they fight and lose or give up. It isn't easy. You have all believed that you are in a sort of war against each other. But that isn't true. You just felt that way because you couldn't deal with the edge stuff like it really should be dealt with."

"But people died!" said Angela.

"No one died, no one who wasn't going to die anyway." I said. I didn't tell them what I knew about Charlie and the man at the canal. I didn't tell them what we all know, deep down inside – that people die every day, every minute. Everyone who lives dies, and so many of them before their time, not just because they have grown too old and worn out. I didn't tell them all that. They had enough to deal with.

Dulice Seacole was crying. "Charlie died. We killed Charlie. I killed my own brother!"

I shook my head. "Dulice, you didn't. Honest. Charlie really died of a juvenile heart complaint." Janet, who always was very kind, went and put her arm round Dulice's shoulder. That was the first time that anyone from the GAs, the Yellows, or the Avenging Angels had done anything like that to someone from another group, and it was like a dam had burst; I could feel that everyone was so relieved.

"What about our angel things?" someone asked.

I rolled up my sleeve and showed them my bare arm. My henna tattoo had faded to nothing.

"You don't need them," I said. "The AAs never had anything, and some of you are here right now without your yellow things, or your angel things, aren't you."

"That's right," said Angela. "My prayer-book is at home in my room."

Kesha felt round her neck, and couldn't find her Indian cloud fairy.

"The thing is this," I said. "Everything has changed for you, from this moment on. The world has changed. It's like everything has been made new. You can do things you never realised; but you'll find there are things you can't do too, and probably you'll learn them for yourselves, like I'm learning. When I got up this morning I was Ashe Shaw Sobiecki. I knew it was possible to be completely Polish, completely English, and yet half Romany too. That was this morning. I'm not sure, but I think after all the things I have seen and done since then, there is no such word as 'impossible' any more. I have opened doors and been though doors. I have lived for more than a hundred years on a mountain top, and I have turned back a flood. I have been in a dead friend's dream, I have been completely at peace, I have had adventure after adventure and I don't have time to tell you all of them because they would fill a million books. What has come to an end for me today, is my childhood. I have stopped being a human child. You could say I went through one door too many; but at the same time I was supposed to go through it, and I couldn't help but go through it. What has come out the other side of that door is so much more than Ashe Shaw Sobiecki. When you go through that door, each one of you, what will come out the other side will be so much more than you. Everything will be different; it already is. All of us, we will no longer be human – it will be like we have lost that just like someone loses childhood – but we will bring everything that is human with us, everything that makes up ourselves. We will be what is going to come after being human, we will be people who can open doors, people who will know everywhen, and I don't know how easy we will find that. I don't know how we will fit in the world, because that is the next door I have to open. On the other side of it there are many things, like how the human people we are leaving behind will react when they know what is happening, and that it really is their End Times – for all I know that will be another battle, another war, but I'm not afraid to push the door open. But I do know this: it's a beginning. It's the beginning of everywhen."

I felt very sorry for them. Like Mr Callister for instance - he was a scientist, and yet I told him that I had watched God create the world and he knew I wasn't lying. And the preacher, Elder Phillips – he was a Christian, and I told him I had seen the Big Bang and he knew I wasn't lying. They were both trying to come to terms with the truth that there can be more than one thing happening, and that's the best way I can put it. And everything comes to an end sooner or later. It used to be, for some reason, that if you became an Angel, like we all became, you get to a point like the top of a hill. Being an Angel happened to us so suddenly, and then it seemed to go away again. But people like Mr Callister and Elder Phillips, and now people like Angela and Kesha and Reuben, well they know that it never really goes away at all. That's because it's... everywhere... everywhen. But before now there was never anyone who could actually see that, or allow themselves to see it. But there's 'coming to an end', and then there's 'becoming something new'. It's like the day you realise you aren't a child any more. Ashe Shaw Sobiecki is a child, a teenager, a kid diagnosed with Asperger Syndrome, someone on the fringe of everyone else's adventure. But also I'm at the centre of everything.

Elder Phillips said, "And a little child shall lead them!" But he was wrong. I'm not a prophet, and I'm not Jesus. I'm just Ashe Shaw Sobiecki. And I am not really leading, even though I may be about to step through the door first. I am just as much being led, and it's the same thing. Leading and being led are the same. I know you feel this too. You feel the next door opening...

EPILOGUE

A whole lot of dazed kids and a couple of dazed adults filed out of the room that day. I stayed behind, just lagged a little, that's all. Tinker was leaning against a desk, two hands pressing down on it as if he was taking some of his weight on his arms. He was looking up, not at me. There was a bit of a smile on his face, but he seemed to be thinking.

I went over to him, put my hands on his shoulders, and kissed him. There wasn't anything in that. I just wanted to thank him. So I said, "Thank you, Ashe," as well, and I used his real name for the first time in I-don't-know-how-long. I found it difficult to believe this was the same kid who had come up to me and told me I was awesome after the thing with the woman and the bus. The boy who had played a trick with the face of his watch, making a tinkerbell fairy fly round the walls of the classroom.

"You're welcome, Angela," he said, like someone

rehearsing being polite. He was grinning, but his eyes looked sad.

"Quite a burden you have been given to carry, eh?" I said.

"Yes," he said. We left it at that.

"You know I still don't want to be any part of this, don't you?" I said. "I don't think I have much choice, though. But there are still so many questions, and the answers to them are only going to lead to more problems – you know what I mean?"

"I do Angela. But nobody asked those ones. I suppose they just haven't thought about them yet. Or maybe they have and they're too scared to ask."

"Yeah – like why is it only people of our age? And why does it go away? And why doesn't it go away for a few people – like Mr Callister, and Elder Phillips, and I guess like me and Kesha, and probably you too – why do they keep going and not lose it? Why are some people even more special? Even Charlie was special, in his own way. And what will happen when the rest of the world really gets to know about us? Will they call us Angels or Demons, superheroes or freaks? Will they welcome us or fight us? And when we become adults, will we try to run things? Adults always do. And what's going to happen when two people disagree about what to do? I mean, Mr Callister and Elder Phillips, they're both really nice blokes, but they're bound to look at the world in different ways. Mr C is a rationalist, and Elder Phillips is an Evangelical Christian. Each one of them is bound to see things differently, and even to look for things that suit their point of view."

"Confirmation bias," said Tinker. "That's what they call it. The tendency to search for and interpret new information that confirms your own preconceptions, and avoid anything which contradicts your beliefs." It was as though he was reading it from a page. He still staggered me. Part of me still looked at him as a kid with mild Asperger Syndrome who had a crush on me; but that's not how it was at all. If anyone was awesome, he was.

"God, this is going to be bloody hard work!" I said.

"Yes."

"There is just so much we don't know!"

"I suppose we'll pick it up as we go along."

And with that, we walked through the door.

The Everywhen Angels

www.ingramcontent.com/pod-product-compliance
Lightning Source LLC
Chambersburg PA
CBHW072320280626
47159CB00027B/101